THE ONE EXILED

GAME OF PARADISE

BOOK 2

JENNIFER LEWY

ALSO BY JENNIFER LEWY_

The Game of Paradise Series

When the Light Came (*A Prequel Story*)
The One Game (*Book One*)
The One Exiled (*Book Two*)
The One Reborn (*Book Three*)

JOIN THE READERS CLUB_

Want to dive deeper into the Game of Paradise?

- Download *When the Light Came* (the prequel story) for free
- Enjoy exclusive character art and behind-the-scenes extras
- Be the first to hear about new releases—and join early reader teams

Sign up at:
JenniferLewy.com

"In order to rise from its own ashes, a phoenix first must burn."
  —Octavia E. Butler, *Parable of the Sower*

"For the first time in our species' history, we have built something wiser than our worst impulses. The NEWRRTH will not forget what we have forgotten. It will not repeat what we have chosen to ignore. The age of human error ends here."
  —Address to the Consortium, 2138

BANG_

Rayne

"Where the hell are we going?"

"Get over here. It's this way." Rayne's boots crunched over crushed stones. She was running out of Games to search. Running out of reasons to hope.

The others hurried behind her. "Welcome to the Bastille," she said, her voice low. "Took you long enough."

"You didn't exactly wait for us." Rook hesitated, tugging at his officer's uniform, blond hair tumbling over his eyes.

"Stow it, Rook." Cha jabbed her finger into Rook's chest and he stumbled back, startled. "Time to focus."

Rook recomposed himself, his face hardening as he jogged to keep up.

Rayne's breath came in labored gasps as the four of them ran through the night-shrouded alley. The humidity closed around her like a wet blanket. Her silk-embroidered jacket was a dead weight. She shrugged it off in mid-stride, hearing it fall to the ground with a thump. The night was stifling. Even in her light shirt and breeches, she could scarcely draw breath.

The small group of Game Designers reached the end of the wall. Peering around the corner, Rayne held her fist high. *Stop.*

Briz, their hair hanging in a dark sheet over their white shirt, inched forward to where Rayne stood. In the dim light, Rayne noticed the sweat glistening on Briz's temples and dampening their chest.

"Is it too late?" Briz asked in their silvery voice.

Rayne shook her head. It was perfect. The soldiers at the gate wouldn't be expecting a visit at this hour. The early morning darkness gave Rayne and her friends good cover. Plus, the soldiers were foreigners and weren't familiar with the prison's layout. No doubt they'd be exhausted and slow to respond once they realized something was amiss.

Straining, Rayne listened for sounds that would give away the guards' locations.

"What do you want us to do?" Cha cupped her hands around her mouth to muffle her half-whisper. Her brown hair fizzed out in the humidity, framing her face. "The Parisians arrive at first light. That's in... thirteen minutes."

Rook shucked his coat onto the ground and loosened the drawstrings of his shirt. Briz and Cha tipped their faces to Rayne, waiting for her instructions.

Rayne silently thanked the three of them. They didn't know that finding proof of Freya's Path was the only thing she had left. The Seers could take away her Thread. Her mother was in a coma and under arrest. Cas was dead. And Avalon and the rest of the coders she'd trusted with her life had simply vanished.

If she couldn't find answers here, she didn't know where else to look.

"We can't stay here," Rayne said. "We'll get caught up in the battle as soon as the mob arrives. I want to get inside the gates before then. I'll only need a few minutes to search."

Cha gave a single nod. "No problem. We'll create a distraction. You can slip in." At twenty-one, four years older than Rayne, Cha held a wisdom beyond her years.

"I don't know what you think is in there." Rook slumped against the stone wall, picking at his shirt. "It's too hot for this. Can't we just ask them?"

Briz shot him a look. "Rayne has a plan. This is her Game. I say we play through."

"And what would we ask the guards, Rook?" Rayne forced herself to whisper. Damp circles spread under her armpits and sweat trickled down her back. She smelled gross, but she stepped close to Rook's face, nearly matching his height. "Should we ask if they've seen anything suspicious? Something that didn't fit with their reality? Maybe they had a tea party with a group of coders called Freya's Path. That would sure be helpful."

Rook rolled his eyes. "I didn't mean that, I just—"

"I know what you meant." Rayne turned back around. "But they're aspects I programmed. The guards don't know anything I haven't coded. What I'm looking for is outside their awareness."

The ancient walls of the French prison complex stretched up into the sky like a mountain of stone. Criss-crossed with shadows, its turrets and chimneys disappeared into the darkness. Rayne's friends fell silent.

"This is what we're going to do." Rayne placed her palm against the rough stone. "The three of you are going to run at the guards in this courtyard. Run in opposite directions and keep swerving so they won't be able to fire at you. Keep them engaged as long as you can. This might be my last chance to find something."

Rook huffed and glanced away.

"And afterward," Rayne continued, "You can come over to my house and eat all the food in my refrigerator."

Rook swiveled, his eyes bright. "Fine. That's a deal."

"What else can we do here?" Cha asked. "Can't we help you search?"

I wish.

Her friends couldn't help her search because Rayne didn't know what she was looking for. Not exactly.

All she wanted was confirmation that Freya's Path existed. Just a scrap of proof that losing Cas had meant something.

Finding Freya's Path wouldn't change the past, but maybe it could give her some answers. Yet the more time passed, the more fruitless her search seemed. Was she truly alone in this?

Briz yanked their hair off their neck and fanned their face. "Let's go already. No more talking. It's too hot."

Rayne paused for a moment, her gaze drifting up to a small window at the top of a door across the courtyard. There was something strange about it, something almost familiar. But it was too far away for her to make out.

"Stop whining," Cha said. "I'll count to three, and we'll run." She glanced at Rook and Briz. "You gonna play? Or are you too hot?"

Rook managed a crooked smile. He pushed off from the wall and crouched into a runner's stance. "This is gonna be way too easy. Then I'm having snacks."

"Wait for my count," Cha instructed, and moved a short distance away.

Briz shot Cha a challenging glare before stepping into place next to Rook. "Bossing us around because she thinks she's the best," they muttered, raising their arms in readiness to sprint.

Cha's mouth twitched in response.

Rayne glanced from one face to the other, taking in the determination of her three Game Designer friends. She knew they were all up to the challenge. Even if they didn't know what the real reward was.

"One..." Cha began. The Designers adjusted their spacing so they faced different directions.

"Two... THREE!"

They took off. Rook let out a whoop. Rayne waited for the guards to shout.

"Qui est là? Arrêt! Aller!"

Right on cue.

An angry voice barked orders to ready weapons and capture the intruders. The guards moved in a frenzy after her friends. French curses echoed in the courtyard. A musket blast startled her, but it was too dark to see if anyone fell.

Rayne didn't waste another second. Running as fast as she could, the warmth of the air grazing her skin, she traversed the courtyard in long strides and fell against the heavy door. Patting the pitted boards, steadying her breath, she searched for anything out of the ordinary. A stray piece of code, a hidden message, a portal she hadn't planted, or... she didn't know what.

Her fingertips scraped against the old door, feeling for any indentations or hidden compartments. She pushed her face close, inhaling the warm scent of ancient wood, inspecting every inch she could make out in the darkness.

But there was nothing to find. Just an old, nicked, splintering door. She jangled the iron rings in frustration.

Another musket shot rang out, closer this time. Rayne flinched.

She craned her neck, searching for the window at the top of the door. That could be it. A place no one would think to look. She had to get closer. Taking a few steps back, her eyes scanned the walls for anything that could be of use. Then she stopped, her gaze landing on a large, rusty pipe snaking up the wall.

With a running leap, she grabbed the pipe, dangling for a

heart-stopping moment, then found purchase. Hand over hand, she hauled herself up. She had to be right about this. She had to be.

It was a treacherous climb, and more than once, she nearly lost her grip. But eventually, she made it to the window.

Peering inside, her eyes widened. It was dark and she couldn't make out much, but she saw a few figures, their faces cloaked in shadow.

There was a clang. The door swung open on groaning hinges.

Her right foot slipped on the slick pipe. Her arms reached out wide, pinwheeling, trying to catch hold of anything that could stop her fall. It was no use. She tumbled backward, the smooth cobbles hurtling up toward her. She hit the ground with a thud. Her lungs crumpled and she gasped, trying to drag air into them.

A musket appeared in front of her face. Its wooden stock was well worn, the brass on the end of it freshly polished. The cool metal barrel touched her forehead. A guard leered at her from underneath a black hat. He closed one eye, a thin mustache curling above his lip. His other eye closed down to a slit, as if trying to see into the depths of her heart.

"Wait," she rasped. "I just want to know—"

THEY'RE HERE_

Rayne

RAYNE'S FINGERS curled around the chipped ceramic mug. The tea had gone cold hours ago, but she had yet to move from the kitchen stool. She'd been sitting there since she woke up in the night, unable to sleep.

I should move around, stretch a little. Get something to eat.

The dappling light outside held her gaze. In the distance, windmills churned. Their thin blades cut through the air, slicing lines like a stopwatch, pulsing the day forward. Bringing her closer to the event she had been dreading for weeks.

The skidder would arrive any minute. She'd close her cottage door, climb into the cab, and go straight to the Center for Future Guidance. There, the Seers would read the verdict, deciding her fate in the Atlantic Ark.

Not just deciding her fate, but hers *and* Vic's.

Rayne pushed the tea away, liquid sloshing over the rim. A gentle whirring came from the corner.

"Filthy." Luci the housecleaning bot appeared at Rayne's

side. Before Rayne could tell Luci to go away, it swiped the spill with its cleaning pad.

"Thanks, Luci," Rayne said to the retreating bot.

Breathing out, she told her Thread to calm her frayed nerves. Nothing too strong. She needed to be alert for what was to come.

While the Thread rebalanced her system, she silently repeated the incantation she had been saying to herself for weeks: *I trust the NEWRRTH. It knows everything about us and the Atlantic Ark. It will offer the Seers all the guidance they need to make the right decision about my future. Our collective future.*

Reaching across the counter, Rayne picked up her gamescreen and thumbed its slim eye covering. It had been reckless, she realized, summoning the Game Designers to her Bastille Game last night without prepping them. Her friends had shown up, though. They knew she was in a dark place and wanted to help. But what if that Game was her last hope of finding Freya's Path—and she had already failed?

She slid the gamescreen away from her.

She needed to stay positive, to have faith in her Thread and the Seers. She'd done nothing wrong. Whatever their decision, she'd deal with it. She always did.

Besides, what could the Seers actually prove? She and Vic hadn't violated the Principle, and they'd been working so hard to restore the Games these past few weeks.

A low rumble pierced her thoughts. The floor vibrated faintly under her bare feet. Turning, she glimpsed yellow through the front window. The skidder.

She had played this moment in her mind a thousand times, had anticipated feeling terrified or angry or sorrowful. But when she heard the vehicle gradually ease to a stop outside her door, pebbles popping under its giant wheels, she was struck by an odd sense of detachment.

Rayne rose from the counter, giving her legs a shake to clear the pins and needles. "Luci. Go to your dock." Without glancing back to see if the bot followed her instructions, she made her way to the front door. She slipped her feet into her lined boots, grabbed her long coat, and stepped outside to meet the skidder.

A metal panel on the skidder's flank swung open with a rasping clang. Two Peace Officers climbed out, their faces solemn. Rayne's mouth dropped open. *An escort to the Center.* Nausea stabbed her in the gut.

Inside the dim cab, Vic's form hunched on the far end of the bench. Under the watchful gaze of the Officers, Rayne clambered in and settled herself next to Vic. The Officers perched behind them, alert.

"I'm sorry," she whispered.

"Shh." Vic kept his voice low. His warm palm slid over hers, and he gave a light squeeze. "We'll get out of this. I'll get us out. I promise."

Guilt stung her. She'd been so sure that nothing would come of the Seers' investigation. That she and Vic would be free to work on their Games, move forward with their lives after what had happened. But here they were, facing a verdict serious enough to warrant the presence of Peace Officers.

She untangled her hand from Vic's. This was all her fault. If she hadn't dragged their friends into that volcano Game last winter, Cas would still be alive. Maybe Jesla, too. Rayne pressed the cool fabric of her jumpsuit against her roiling belly.

THE SKIDDER LURCHED to a stop in front of the Center for Future Guidance. The Peace Officers pulled the metal panels aside and gestured for her and Vic to get out.

Rayne jumped down first, with Vic right behind her. Unable to resist, she turned and wrapped her arms around him. Vic stiffened at first, then gradually relaxed his body against hers. Rayne's fingertips brushed his upper back, sensing the tension there, and she held him tighter.

"Come on," she whispered into his neck. "We got this."

She took his hand and led him straight through the arched doors of the Center. The Peace Officers trailed close behind. The air inside the Center was warm, fragrant. Rayne's eyes swept upward, taking in the balconies curling around the interior walls like a spiral staircase. A dizzying array of foliage hung from each of the seven levels, creating a lush wall of green tendrils and flowering plants that resembled a thousand tiny, verdant waterfalls.

A crowd of people moved through the atrium. Their chatter filled the air.

"Forward." A Peace Officer nudged Rayne and Vic toward a set of double doors where everyone seemed to be heading.

Rayne pulled her hand back from Vic as they entered the hearing room. The sound of the Peace Officers' boots echoed off the curving walls. Spectators parted in front of them, whispering to each other, their conversations like a river rushing over Rayne's ears.

She and Vic shuffled through the watching crowd and took seats at a table in the front. Chairs squeaked as they pulled them forward. The tang of sweat reached Rayne's nose, mixing with the scent of wood from the table under her palms.

Her stomach twisted as she scanned the room. Most people appeared in their holographic form, since there was no way for them all to travel overland to the Center. People's virtual aspects perched on ladders or stood on chairs in order to get a better view. Even more people would tune in to the broadcast from their homes.

Present in person, Scrubbers hovered near large screens displaying diagrams and data. They were ready to translate data into visual form, make rapid calculations, or anything else the Seers required in real time. Several members of the Center's staff sat in neat rows, along with representatives from other organizations across the Ark.

There were so many faces staring intently at her. Some she recognized—from the Orchard, where her mother lived and worked, and from the Haven, where Rayne spent time over the winter. Some she knew from school. Many people she didn't know. But even as she met their gazes, Rayne couldn't help but wonder if anyone here truly understood what the Seers were about to do.

No other Game Designers were in sight. *Good.* They had listened to her. They'd be gathering at her cottage about now. Ready to go into action when the time came.

The crowd fell into a hush as Nilo and the other Seers entered through a side door and made their way up onto a raised platform at the front of the room. Enayat settled his large frame on a seat in the center, his face solemn. Next to him was a small woman with red hair, her gaze swiveling nervously over the crowd. White letters flickered into holographic form behind their heads. It was the official slogan of the Center for Future Guidance: *Progress through Unity.*

Enayat caught Rayne's eye. His frown deepened. Vic reached over and nudged Rayne's leg under the table.

Nilo spoke then, her voice ringing out clear and strong as she addressed the crowd. "Citizens of the Atlantic Ark. We are here to determine the fate of two Game Designers, as we decide whether we should ban them from further participation in the Games."

The spectators in the room reacted with murmurs and whispers. Rayne sensed a thousand eyes boring into her, but she forced herself to stay calm and keep her focus on Nilo.

"Quiet, please," Nilo said, silencing the crowd with a raised hand. Her neck tattoo emitted trails of light, which Rayne knew were translating the sounds in the room directly into her brain. "Many of us suffered the events of this past winter. The anomaly plagued our Games and threatened the integrity of our Threads' guidance. A series of unprecedented events caused some of our Seers"—Nilo glanced at Enayat, who shifted in his seat—"some of our Seers to lose their way. One of our beloved Seers, and several of our beloved citizens, lost their lives. They will never see the dawn of a new day. We are still reeling from the trauma of those events. But we must not let that trauma cloud our judgment in this matter."

A chill ran up Rayne's spine. They couldn't blame her for Cas's death. That had been his choice. Still, she was uncertain about why the Seers' investigation had gone on for so long. They should have ended it weeks ago. Should have cleared Rayne and Vic of all wrong-doing.

Nilo's blue sleeves billowed as she brought her arms out and together again. "We sit here today in our grief and in our mourning, but also in our unwavering dedication to our collective mission to restore civil order after the events of this winter's tragic events."

Rayne swallowed hard, her throat suddenly dry. This was it. There was no turning back now.

"As your Seers of the Atlantic Ark, guided by the wisdom of the NEWRRTH, we've focused our analysis on the extraordinary Game executed by these two Designers. A Game that took place during the last eruption of the Krakatoa volcano in the nineteenth century."

More murmurs and gasps from the crowd. Many people didn't know about the Game at the center of the Seers' inquiry. Vic's Game reenacted a dangerous and violent time on Earth. It was the kind of Game that was usually prohibited, or least strictly limited to specific learning objectives.

"Game Designer Rayne and Game Designer Vic stand accused of interfering with our community's principles of peace on three counts." Nilo lifted a finger. "One, they exposed dozens of aspects in a Game to extreme and unwarranted violence."

Rayne closed her eyes briefly, picturing the choking clouds of volcanic ash, cinders dropping around the players, trees bursting into flame. What people didn't realize was that the purpose of this Game wasn't to hurt anyone, but to stop the dubious upgrade Vennor had planted inside of Rayne.

Nilo's second finger came up. "Two, these Designers supported an untested experiment directly affecting and manipulating NEWRRTH data streams."

The NEWRRTH, or the Networked Ecosystem for Wisdom and Resources Relative to Humans, operated through a grid of nodes placed around the world. Although only a few people could understand and modify the NEWRRTH itself, everyone else tapped into its knowledge through their Threads.

Seers were special. They interacted with the NEWRRTH directly, acting as its managers, making changes so that it stayed in line with what was best for humankind.

Rayne remembered her mother's hands during the volcano Game, pushed deep into the moss and other plants on the floor of that cave, the green things pulsing with data. Connecting her own Thread to the living plants. Creating a new Earth Thread.

"And three." Nilo held three fingers up high. "Vic and

Rayne each personally and relentlessly blocked a sanctioned and essential upgrade to the NEWRRTH."

"That wasn't an upgrade." Vic shot out of his seat. "It was a mind-virus, and if you had released it—"

"Silence!" Enayat's voice boomed over their heads. Vic's mouth clamped shut, and he lowered himself.

Nilo continued. "If we find them guilty on one or more counts, they will be banned from the Games and their records in the Archives will be deleted."

More gasps and whispers swept through the room.

"Further," Nilo said.

There's more? Rayne instructed her Thread to reset her adrenaline. Her nerves were on fire, threatening to consume her.

"These Designers are accused of conspiring against the NEWRRTH with entities hostile to the Principle of One. This offense is punishable by permanent Thread termination."

All around her, people started talking and pointing. Rayne sensed Vic tense up next to her, his knuckles going white on the tabletop. She wanted to reach out to him, to say something, but was unable to utter a sound.

"They can't do this," he snapped. "Freya's Path reached out to us, and if we hadn't worked with them, they would have found someone else."

"Please be assured that we investigated thoroughly." Enayat raised his voice to be heard above the din. The chatter died away. "Our research and conclusions are available for all on the Archives."

The silence hovered over them like a storm about to break.

Enayat put one hand into his pocket and glanced at the floor, then over the crowd. "The Seers have concluded that these Designers have violated the sacred principle of unity that we founded our society upon. There is enough evidence to support all charges against both Designers."

The air left Rayne's body. The spectators in the room erupted into a chorus of exclamations and shouts. Some people started to get up out of their seats, as if they couldn't believe what they were hearing.

"As such," Enayat continued, holding his hands up for quiet, "the Seers of the Atlantic Ark ban Vic and Rayne from all future participation in the Games and permanently revoke their Threads. Effective immediately."

Rayne could barely make out Nilo's next words over the ringing in her ears.

"We do this out of love for our community and for our collective future." Nilo stepped forward. "There is no future without the Games, and without the intelligence that guides us all. These Designers have gone beyond the confines of their duties to interfere directly with that intelligence, with the NEWRRTH." Her last words were swallowed by the noise of the crowd, but landed on Rayne's ears like blows. "Officers, bring them to my chambers."

Numb, Rayne got to her feet. Out of the corner of her eye, she saw several Peace Officers approach.

Is this really happening? Just a few weeks ago, she had been protecting the Games with her life—ready to sacrifice herself to keep the mind-virus from infiltrating the NEWRRTH—with Vic by her side. They lost Cas and Jesla to Vennor's deadly crystal code.

They should celebrate us as heroes.

Instead, they were being accused of crimes against the NEWRRTH, stripped of their Threads, and banned from the Games forever. It didn't seem real.

As the Peace Officers escorted them from the room and

down the hall to the room where their Threads would be terminated, Rayne knew she was firmly rooted in reality. And there was nothing she could do to stop what was coming.

WAKE UP_

Vennor

THE COLD SHIMMIED up her ankles and burrowed deep into her bones. Wisps of clouds glowed purple with the first rays of brightness. The rising sun did nothing to temper the iciness in the air.

Vennor bent double and reached for another piece of wood from the pile. She dragged it toward herself, lifting with two hands. Her left elbow flared with pain. She shifted the wood to the crook of her right arm. Bending again, she picked up a piece of kindling, smaller than the piece she cradled. She winced as her left hand closed around it.

The calls of others on the wood pile rang in her ears as she straightened. They were quicker than she was, more nimble on the pile. Most had the same number of years as she did, if Vennor had to guess. Some were well past that, pushing into their eighth decade or beyond. All assigned to the old person's task of gathering wood for the Settlement's fires.

After a handful of months here, Vennor was getting faster, stronger. She was learning her place. But she still wasn't used to the hard ways of the people here. The rotten food, the cold rooms, the hard bed she slept in—it all made her feel twice her sixty years. Every time she remembered her old life, her throat tightened. Her determination had once been tempered with optimism, but now it blazed like a fever within her. She remembered how she had fled, running away without so much as a goodbye, covering her tracks to make sure no one knew which way she had gone. Every time the memories resurfaced, so did an agonizing reminder of all that she had lost.

Her bitterness extended to her fellow Seers, who had allowed the Peace Officers to target her for arrest. Vennor, arrested for violating the Principle of One. As if she were to blame for the failure of the upgrade. They didn't understand. No one did. It was all the fault of Freya's Path, the elusive group she never guessed was real, that had interfered with her plan and caused it to fail.

She would find them. When she did, her first impulse was to make them pay for everything they had taken from her. To make them regret every shred of code they had used against her.

Then her higher wisdom kicked in, and she realized that revenge wouldn't solve anything. It wouldn't bring Trueno back, and it wouldn't pave the way for her to return to the Atlantic Ark. So she would seek Freya's Path to learn from them. After all, their skill with manipulating the NEWR-RTH's code exceeded even her own ability. Vennor was hungry for their knowledge.

She hefted the cut wood onto her shoulder and turned toward the waiting wagon. Cobbled together from scraps of more elegant modes of transport, the wagon was an awkward vehicle, but served its purpose. Once it filled, Vennor and the other workers of the woodpile would push its bald rubber wheels over the bricked pathways to the Commons. There, children waited to collect the wood their families needed to heat and cook that day.

As Vennor moved toward the wagon, she lifted her gaze to the spires of the Settlement. Standing about a quarter mile away, the tallest Settlement buildings bounced light from their steel and glass, sparkling against the gray-blue dawn. It was almost pretty.

If you didn't know about the rot and decay hidden under all that gleaming metal.

The wood pile sat in a small clearing at the end of a warren of alleys. A few others like her moved around, gathering their own pieces. Vennor passed a stout middle-aged woman and they nodded at each other.

"Sleeping better?" the woman asked.

"The same." Vennor tried to smile.

"Fates bless." The woman's face was friendly, but her tone was not.

"And you." Vennor dipped her head in what she hoped was a deferential gesture, both arms weighed down with wood. She didn't slow her pace, leaving the woman behind.

The sweat that had pooled on the base of her neck cooled her skin. Her shoulders and arms ached. The small pile of wood she carried was heavy, but not so heavy that she couldn't manage the load. With determination, she made her way to the wagon.

"Morning, Vennor." The wagon driver stood watch over the pile of wood accumulating on the wagon's bed. He had several missing teeth, salt and pepper hair that receded from his temples, and an odor of unwashed skin. His gaze traveled over her arms.

"Morning," she replied.

"You're getting stronger."

"I am." The work was becoming easier each day.

If only she could work her mind as hard as her body and expel the blame that circled in endless loops there.

"You're not so slow anymore." He ran his tongue over chapped lips.

"Thank you."

With her left arm, she reached for the first log on her shoulder. The weight of it threatened to topple her, and she rocked on her feet to try to keep her balance.

"I'll take that for you." Another male voice, this time not one she recognized.

"Go on," she called back. "I have it."

"Nonsense." He appeared at her shoulder. "Let me help you."

A young man reached for the bundle of logs that was about to slip from her grasp. His movements were smooth and practiced, much quicker than hers. Vennor shifted to help him lift the wood, then stood and watched as the man tossed the logs onto the stack on the bed.

He was strong and nimble. Dark hair framed his face, and his skin was russet and smooth. The tips of his ears were pierced. A silver ring hung from the middle of his nose.

"Hey," the driver said. "Get moving. You'll earn your breakfast today, like always."

"Take it easy, *pacha*. We all help each other out." Turning to Vennor, he tipped an imaginary hat. "The name's Mas. Apprentice to the wood supplier. Here to inspect the goods." He rocked back on his heels, smirking at his own comment.

"I'm just saying," the wagon driver said. "You don't need to help her. They look old, but they like the work." The driver waved a hand at Vennor, as if her appearance explained everything.

"Thank you," Vennor said to Mas. "But I'd better get back to it."

"Don't worry about it." He grinned, the rings in the tips of his ears moving. "I like to help."

Vennor turned, about to retrace her steps to the pile for another load.

"You know, you're still pretty slow," the driver called after her. Under his breath, he added, "She's an old one."

"She's special," Vennor heard Mas say.

"Is she?" The driver made a throat-clearing sound. "I didn't think she was anything in particular."

"She is."

The man with the piercings, Mas, caught up with her. "I don't think you deserved that," he said. "Kam runs his mouth sometimes, being the wagon driver and all."

Vennor pulled her woven coat closer. She was grateful for this man's help but wanted to end their conversation. Best if she kept to herself, did her own work. That was her mantra here in the Legacy Settlement.

"I have a confession to make." With a little jog, he turned to face her, walking backward. "You're Vennor."

Her foot caught, and she nearly tripped. Recovering, she offered a tight-lipped smile. Her black hair, bunched in a heap on top of her head, moved under her woolen wrap.

"That's not a confession."

Mas chuckled. He walked with her to the woodpile. Not getting the hint. Vennor bent to pick up a medium-sized log. Its splinters were the size of paring knives. Her thick leather gloves protected the flesh of her palms as she wrapped her hand around it. She squeezed it, dragged it closer.

"Hey. I said, I know who you are." Mas squatted next to her, his face close to hers.

Vennor resisted the urge to recoil from this man, to put distance between them.

She managed another nod. "It's a pleasure to meet you, Mas. Fates bless."

Mas snorted. "You hearing me? Or you getting confused in your old age like the driver thinks?"

Vennor nestled the splintery log into her elbow and reached for another. Her lower back screamed with pain. "Oh —" she said, freezing her expression in place as best she could.

"Here, let me." Mas reached for the log she had been trying to get, put it into his own arms, and stood up.

With difficulty, she rose. She couldn't return to the wagon with a single piece of wood. She took a moment to breathe through her back pain before bending again to the pile. "Thank you again for your help. But I really should—"

"There's a few more." He winked. "I'll get 'em."

She couldn't do it. Become friendly with him. Friends and allies were too dangerous here. There was the temptation to relax one's guard. The opportunities for betrayal. She knew that. She would be strong now.

"Mas, I—"

"Don't worry about it."

He lifted the wood from the pile and brought it to where she stood. The muscles in his calves bunched as he hefted the wood from the ground. He placed several logs gently in her arms.

"Thank you," she said again, with a nod.

"No problem."

She had to move now. She didn't want to hear what this young man had to say, or what he thought he knew about her. She started toward the wagon, her eyes on the ground, her boots shuffling over the brick path. Her teeth gritted with the shooting pain.

"You know," Mas said, "I could show you some things that might help."

Vennor bowed her head. "I'm sure you could."

"And I'm sure there are things... you could teach me."

She paused. Took a deep breath, then continued straight ahead without acknowledging him.

Kam the driver was arranging wood on the wagon bed, his back turned. Vennor reached the wagon and tossed her logs onto the pile. "That's a good girl," Kam said without looking at her. "Almost got enough for your breakfast."

Vennor paused, her hand on the bed, girding herself before returning to the pile. *Just when she thought she couldn't be in any more pain.* With effort, she brushed her thoughts away. Arranged her face into a mask.

"What're you waiting for?" Kam said. "Go on."

She turned. And that's when she saw him.

A man she recognized. The man who had brought her to the Settlement.

He led a group of men striding toward them. There were about ten of them moving in a pack like wolves over the cracked pavement. Their black flapping coats brushed the crumbling brick wall of the nearest alley. Their faces were stony. His eyes fixed on her.

She stopped and stared.

As they entered the clearing, she saw his cloud of hair was combed back, and his face was clean-shaven. He wore a black wool coat like the others. A red scarf wound around his neck, a color that displayed his high status in the Settlement. The color reflected onto his bronze cheeks with a rosy glow.

He moved with a lithe grace to cover the distance to where she stood.

"Vennor?" Mas called from behind. He drew level with the wagon, arms full of logs. "I got another load for..." He trailed off as he saw the men. The logs clattered to the ground.

The men surrounded the wagon. They looked nonchalant,

bored even. One of them, a lumbering fellow with a mean face, pulled aside his coat. A green patch stood out from under the filthy shirt. Peering at it, Vennor thought it looked like an outline of an eye.

Kam backed away from the wagon, showing his palms. "We don't want trouble. I wasn't harassing anyone, I just wanted to keep—"

"Quiet." The man didn't even look at Kam. Or Mas, who had frozen to the spot, arms at his sides.

The man moved next to Vennor, so close she could smell his sweat.

She glared at him. "What are you doing? I thought I told you not to associate with me."

"It's time." The man's eyes softened. "Come with me." He reached to grasp Vennor's elbow.

Vennor tried to jerk away, but his grip was strong.

"What are you doing?" she asked again, trying to keep the tremor out of her voice. "Let go."

"Sister." The man gave her a small, sad smile. "Your work here is done." He jerked his chin at the wagon, and the two men standing a few paces behind her.

"She can't leave. We don't have a full load yet," Mas said.

Without another word, the man led her away from the wagon. His followers ambled behind them.

"What's going on?" she asked, trying to ignore the thrumming in her belly. "Where are you taking me?"

"You'll see," her brother said. "It's time to put your talents to better use."

TERMINATED_

Rayne

As they walked along the Center's corridors, Rayne stared ahead. No matter what people thought, she knew that she and Vic—and all the Game Designers—had done the right thing. She would never regret her decision to help Freya's Path and prevent the Seers' mind-virus from releasing. But it was hard not to feel defeated as she saw people staring at her with shock and anger, as if she were the traitor.

We don't deserve this. She blinked to clear the moisture from her eyes. For as long as she could remember, Rayne felt like she was born to do something special. She had dedicated her life to the NEWRRTH and the Games, wanting nothing more than to immerse people in thrilling adventures of the past to reveal the special essence of humanity.

Without her Thread, that dream was over. Her life was over. Yet no matter what was going to happen in the room ahead of them, Rayne was determined to keep her integrity intact.

But what if the Seers were right? What if she and Vic had

damaged the NEWRRTH, enough to justify Thread termination?

Rayne pushed the doubts away. It was done now. Her friends would help her cope, like they always did.

But her friends couldn't fix everything. Rayne reached out to her Thread, wanting to feel its reassuring presence one last time. She sent a silent plea for dopamine, oxytocin, anything to steel her for the procedure to come.

As the Thread recalibrated her system, she remembered the last time the Seers had threatened to take her Thread away. It was two years ago, when she was fifteen. Her Teachers discovered violence coded into one of her Games at school. Rayne only dodged the punishing consequences due to her mother's assistance. Kai was tied up with her work at the Orchard as usual, yet managed to come through for Rayne that time.

The Seers let her off with a warning against getting too involved in the virtual worlds, as they could lead to self-absorption and a lack of empathy. Rayne understood their point, but knew it didn't apply to her. She was only trying to make a difference, even if it meant risking her own safety.

Now here she was at the Center again. This time, her mother was unconscious and in holding. Her father and best friend were dead. Rayne was all alone.

Well, not alone, exactly.

Vic strode beside her, fists clenched. Agitation rolled off him like a fog. She tried to catch his eye, wanting to reassure him they were ready to face whatever was coming. That they would get through it together.

He glanced at her, pupils black with fury, and gave her a grudging nod.

. . .

THE OFFICERS PAUSED in front of a door. One took Rayne by the arm as he turned the handle and pushed it open. The room was spare, with only a couple workstations against a bank of windows that framed the Center's gardens. Light spilled across the stone floor, tinged green from the reflection of fresh growth outside. A single chair had been placed in the middle of the room. The door clicked shut behind them.

Rayne's heart froze as she realized what was about to happen. This was the room—just an ordinary office by the looks of it—where the Seers would take her Thread offline. Cut her access to the Games. To the NEWRRTH's guidance. Her mind seized up as she tried to process what would happen after that.

One of the Peace Officers gestured for Vic to sit in the chair.

Vic shook his head. "I'm not going to just sit there and let you end my life."

The other Peace Officer stepped forward and grabbed Vic by the arm, forcing him into the chair. Vic struggled against him, but it was no use. The Officers stood on either side of him with a firm grip on both of his broad shoulders.

Rayne could see the terror in Vic's eyes as he realized what was happening. He turned to her, reaching out a hand. "Rayne, I—"

The door banged open.

"—don't see why it has to be this way," a young Seer was saying. It was Ana, her red hair in rough spikes as if she'd been twisting it, hurrying behind Nilo. "You just don't decide like this without consulting the totality of the models."

Nilo ignored her Seer colleague and strode across her office to where Vic sat in a single chair pulled into the middle of the room. Her blue robes fell in graceful layers around her feet as she approached.

Vic lunged at her, teeth bared. He looked like one of those feral beasts that roamed the unprotected lands outside of the Ark. The Officers on either side of him pushed him down, strengthening their grip on his shoulders.

"Be still," Nilo said. "You may not appreciate the methods we used to restore order." Her tattoo twinkled as it sent messages up and down her neck. "In time, you'll see this is the only way back to peace in the Ark."

"Coward," Vic spat.

Rayne twisted toward him. "Don't."

Nilo's robes stilled, brushing the floor. Her network of filaments glittered from her ear to her shoulder.

"I beg your pardon." Nilo brought up a holographic display at the edge of the closest workstation. The sleek image activated with a soft clicking sound, like tiny stones thrown into a still pond. "I don't believe I heard you."

Vic glared at her. "I said you're a *coward.*"

"I see." Nilo's voice grated, sharp and cold. "Is that your accusation?"

Vic met her gaze without faltering. "You're too spineless to do the right thing and bring the real killer to justice. Instead of doing your job, you're going to pin this on two of the best Designers this Ark has ever seen. You'll regret this."

Nilo faced the windows and her jaw worked, as if holding herself back from saying something.

"The actual killer's one of your own," Vic continued. "But you let her get away. Was that intentional or was it—"

Nilo withdrew her hand from the display. A cool spark lit her blue eyes with a brilliance that held for an instant before fading. Vic fell silent.

An unexpected wave of pity washed over Rayne. This Seer had lost someone close to her, too—someone who probably meant a lot to her—and she still struggled to come to terms with it. Who knew where Vennor went, and whether the Seers let her escape or not. But she wasn't here today, and likely wouldn't return.

Nilo straightened and reached her hand toward Vic, palm open. Ana stepped in front of her.

"Wait," Ana said. "I want to make sure you understand the danger you're creating here. We've seen how the Designers work together, how they've contacted and engaged with Freya's Path. We haven't even determined if... this entity... can return to us. If the Designers don't trust the verdict came from a vetted bank of data, they could band together to form a sort of uprising. The models are showing us that faith in the data is paramount. Without faith, there is dissent."

She took a shaky breath. "We could be putting the conditions into place that would start... a revolution."

Rayne felt a surge of hope at the Seer's words. *Yes, that's exactly right. My friends are ready to fight. Our plans are already in motion.*

Ana must have seen a glimmer of that potential outcome in the NEWRRTH's data. The outcome where Rayne and Vic took their friends to the Guild of Seers, who could override the Atlantic Ark Seers, to appeal the verdict and re-activate their Threads.

Nilo scoffed. "What do you think they're going to do? Take control of the Center? Threaten the Seers? The Designers know what's at stake here. They know that we're doing what's necessary to ensure the survival of all. And if they refuse to cooperate, well..." She trailed off, a menacing glint in her eye.

She turned back to Vic. "Now, let's get started."

ALL THAT'S LEFT_

Rayne

RAYNE DIDN'T REMEMBER STANDING up from the chair, walking out of the room, or retracing her steps through the Center. She didn't recall what anyone said to her. She didn't even know how she and Vic had gotten back into the skidder, whose engine rattled beneath her seat.

What she did remember was Vic's face, just after Nilo finished terminating his Thread. Seeing it—the look in his eyes —was like a physical pain.

The skidder bounced along, headed for home. Rayne turned away from Vic, who slouched beside her. It was useless to think about what had just happened.

It was done.

Nilo had taken it upon herself in the name of peace to silence their Threads forever. She had severed their only connection to the Games, to the wisdom of the NEWRRTH. To the Thread's life-giving support of their nervous systems, easing grief and anxiety and all manner of emotions.

Rayne was numb, empty. As though she'd lost something of herself.

She had. They both had.

Vic reached over and touched her shoulder, but she shrugged away from him. She didn't trust herself to speak.

"Hey," he said. His voice sounded strange, broken. "I'm sorry about this."

She thought she might scream. Sorry? Sorry for what? The Seers' disastrous verdict, their friends' deaths, working with Freya's Path in the first place? His apology—as if he believed he alone was responsible for this whole mess—made her lip tremble.

But then his face hardened, and she saw he was just sinking into bitterness. "I hate this. I hate this is happening to us."

Rayne wanted to reach out to him, to touch his leg that rested close to hers, and offer some sort of comfort. But she couldn't find the right words. So she said nothing at all.

The skidder shuddered as it turned. She leaned against the side of the vehicle, letting the vibration wrap around her. Rested her left hand gently on her right wrist. Over the spot where her Thread should have been pulsing blue.

She closed her eyes, tired and worn.

If Cas were here, he'd know what to say to me right now. Something to distract her, to make her smile, to keep her spirits up. That was his talent: he could see the best in things and make everyone feel like they were part of it, too.

Rayne clenched and unclenched her fingers around her wrist, trying to steady herself. She thought of Cas's gentle eyes, his hair as brown as bark, and his half-smile when he joked with her. She imagined him performing in one of his Games on stage, his favorite place in the world. She saw him in a sequined pink gown behind a Game-piano, belting out lyrics into a microphone in front of an entire stadium full of cheering fans.

The image in her mind shifted, and his face became steely, frenzied. His wet hair plastered to his cheeks, scattering droplets all over her face. It was how he looked when she had last seen him alive. When he removed his own living code from his chest, clear of the mind-virus, and offered it to her. He had saved her life. But ended his own.

Gods, she missed him. Her one best friend.

She blinked to clear the moisture from her eyes, shifted in her seat, straightened her back. If she didn't get it together, she'd start bawling and wouldn't stop. Cas was gone now. Buried next to Jesla in the meadows. The only thing left of him was his living code, passed into her own body. She had to believe that he lived on inside of her. Somehow.

SHE WAS STILL CURLED against the window when the skidder pulled to a stop in the middle of a sandy stretch of road.

"What's going on?" Rayne asked, rousing herself.

The driver didn't answer. He opened his cab door, jumped out, then came around to the back where they were sitting.

Rayne did a double take when the driver approached their side. It wasn't the same driver who had brought them to the Center that morning. The right side of this man's face was misshapen. Rayne noticed a red, puckering scar on his temple that traveled across his cheek, ending somewhere under his collar.

The driver reached up to unhitch their door.

"Bit windy out here." A gust blew his scraggy hair on end. "But it's the best place." He offered his hand.

"Best place? For what?" Rayne turned to Vic, who slumped against the opposite window. He shrugged, just as clueless as she was.

"For what I'm gonna discuss with you." The driver extended his hand further toward her.

She took it. Stepping out of the skidder, the wind whipped through her long coat, carrying sand and debris in swirling gusts. It was too early in the spring for any real warmth. The sharpness of the air, and the driver's intriguing words, did nothing to dislodge the hollowness in her chest.

They were on a hill, a slather of bald rock beneath their feet. Far from any signs of civilization.

Vic dropped to the ground behind her. Slipped his hand around hers.

"What's going on?" she asked, as they followed the driver. "Why are we out here, away from everything?"

He led them a few paces away from the vehicle, then turned to her with a grim expression on his scarred face.

"Just some news," he called over the wind. He gestured for them to continue following him, toward a copse of trees down a little slope.

Tensing, Rayne hurried to keep up with him. After a few more paces, the driver paused at the curved edge of the hill and faced them.

"So the Seers made their decision," he said.

Rayne shivered. Vic dropped her hand, took a few steps toward the driver. "If this is some kind of joke, it's not funny. Tell us who you are, and what we're doing here, or we're walking home ourselves."

"Heard about your temper." The driver chuckled. "The name's Flay. Like I said, your Threads are done." He spat on the ground beside them. "Say what you want about the verdict, doesn't matter if you thought it was justified."

Vic took another step forward, his eyes narrowing.

Flay raised his hands, palms out. "But I know what it's like to be without one. To be... unconnected." He tipped his head to the side. His lumpy scar caught the sunlight.

With a huff, Vic crossed his arms.

Flay continued. "I brought you here because there's hope for you yet. I'd like to make you both an offer." The wind caught the bare branches above him, making a clattering sound.

Rayne drew her coat tighter. The coat had been Cas's. It still carried the sweet-sharp scent of pine embedded in its soft olive fabric. It was all she had left of him. She hugged it close, knowing she could never part with the only physical reminder that he had existed.

"You see that rise over there?" Flay leaned over, pointing. A long, flat valley stretched below them, and beyond, a cluster of hills. The fading light gave them a bluish hue. If she squinted, she could just make out the shadow of a building. A tall one.

"Yeah?" Vic's brow furrowed.

"Down there, over those hills, is a whole city of people who live without Threads." Flay turned back to them, his misshapen face set in a serious expression. "They're like you are now. And they've found a way to make do."

Something stirred in Rayne. "What are you saying?"

"I'm saying I can take you there." Flay held out his hand again, like he was weighing something. "If you want to join them. They could always use extra help, and I think you two might set yourselves up nicely there."

Was he asking them to throw everything away and let him lead them away from the Ark? Forge a new life in the wilds of the Legacy Settlements?

Flay's words came quicker. "It could be your chance to start over. You'd have a whole bunch of people who understand what you've been through. A place where you'd fit in."

Rayne considered the hills before them. The single tower loomed like an old-style painting at the far edge of her vision.

Could she really leave this all behind—the Ark, her family and friends—and make a leap into the unknown? Or would she just be trading one kind of emptiness for another?

"So thoughtful of you," Vic said with a sneer. "But we're not interested in throwing away our lives here. We're not leaving the Ark."

Flay sighed and shook his head. "You don't understand what you'd be giving up. They're nice people, the Settlers. They have traditions. They take care of each other."

Vic touched Rayne's elbow, getting ready to leave. "I don't care. They're not our people."

"Think about it," Flay said. "There's more than one way to make your path from here."

Flay turned, and they heard his footsteps on the sandy rock as he trudged back up the slope. Rayne pulled her arm from Vic's grasp. She let her gaze rest on those blue hills, that distant building poking into the sky.

"I don't know," she whispered. She let herself believe, for a moment, she could leave this pain behind.

Then Vic was by her side again. "That's not our plan," he murmured into her ear. "We have other options, and that"—he thrust his chin toward the valley—"is not one of them." He gently turned her around, running his fingers through her short hair, smoothing it, and holding her head so she looked into his eyes. "Remember?"

His sharp features, his ocean-green eyes, softened into a smile. She gave a small nod. Yes, their plan. She must remember their plan.

The hollowness came back, an ache that sucked the oxygen from her lungs.

"Let's go home," she said. With a last glance at the blue hills, she took Vic's hand. Together, they shuffled up the hill toward the skidder.

. . .

THEY STOOD beside the yellow vehicle, waiting for Flay to catch up. Rayne let herself sink back into the emptiness, shrouding herself with it. She almost didn't hear Flay approach until he was right behind them.

The driver put his palm on the side of the skidder. He angled himself in between them and the door handle. The three of them were silent for a moment before Vic spoke up. "We're going to have to pass on your offer."

Flay nodded slowly, looking disappointed. "I'm not surprised," he said. "But I understand. If you ever change your mind, you know where to find me." He removed his hand from the door of the skidder and gave it a couple of raps with his knuckles. Then his wrist lit up.

"Incoming," Flay's Thread announced. "Incoming."

Rayne reflexively touched her own wrist. It was blank and silent.

Frowning, Flay glanced at them before taking a few steps away and tapping the glowing blue dot to accept the call. "Yes?"

A figure came into virtual form beside Flay. It was the person calling him, taking holographic form.

Rayne gasped when she saw who it was.

Vic blanched. "Gods. That's—"

"I know. It's Ana." Rayne swallowed.

"What does she want with us?" Vic said. "Haven't the Seers done enough?"

"Quiet." Rayne moved closer to where Flay spoke with Ana's image.

"They're right here." Flay turned.

Ana's red hair glowed under an artificial light, her face a shade of green, before becoming lost in a shadow.

"Rayne," Ana said. The Seer's face turned green again, then went dark. Her hair turned different shades of blue. She was walking. Passing under colored lights. Doorways. "I'm glad I caught you."

Rayne remembered then. Ana was the Seer who brought the crystal to Vic's volcano Game. Vic explained it afterward, since Rayne had spent most of that Game immobilized in a cave. It was Ana who programmed the clear quartz, the piece of code the Seers used as a failsafe. The quartz crystal would delete anyone who blocked the Seers' upgrade. But the crystal code worked too well and killed people in real life, too.

It wasn't Ana who used the crystal, though. It was Vennor. But Cas grabbed it and used it on himself...

"What do you want?" Vic grumbled. He planted himself in front of Ana's image.

"Vic. Rayne." Ana's image kept moving, her face and hair changing colors under the lights. "You need to hear this. Please."

"Whatever you have to say, you've already said it. You're done. We're not interested in your damn platitudes."

"Let me finish." Ana's mouth was set. "I know what it is you're about to do. Your plan. With your friends. The other Designers. Setting out for justice, for vengeance, whatever it is you think you're going to get." She jogged a bit, hurrying. "And I'm sorry to tell you this, more sorry than you'll know, but..."

Rayne's brow furrowed. "But what?"

"It's not going to work."

THE REBELLION_

Vennor

VENNOR FELT the weight of people's stares as her brother guided her away from the wagon, away from the people working at the woodpile. The people she had labored with to collect firewood these past months all stopped now to watch her retreat with the procession of men.

She didn't need the NEWRRTH to tell her what the hostility of their stances and the heat of their glares meant.

After a few moments, Kam the wagon driver found his voice again. Vennor heard him unleash a litany of abuses entreating the elders to return to the morning's collection. To work faster, harder, or risk being late to their delivery at the Commons.

Vennor blocked out his voice and marched on.

They advanced through the disintegrating alleys, walking with purpose. Vennor asked her brother several times where they were heading, but he remained silent. Gedeon had never been one for small talk, and she could tell that he was preoccupied with something.

The group wove through the edge of the city. She tried to keep up with their brisk pace past barns where bleating animals poked wet noses through wooden slats. At a hardened mud patch, dirty geese honked and darted away from their approaching feet. The air became thick with a mix of wood smoke and animal dung. Vennor's nostrils stung from the stench, but she kept her eyes forward, determined to see where this was leading.

There was nowhere to run, no place to escape to. Best to stay with the group.

The sun rose higher, warming their backs as they neared the tallest buildings. After winding past several low brick structures with missing windows, they turned into a rambling square. The air filled with the laughter and shouting of people who were starting their day, boots thudding on uneven paving stones, wooden wagon wheels creaking and metal tools clanging.

A pair of seabirds screeched overhead, their calls ringing out over the bustle of the city. Everywhere she looked, she saw signs of a place that had been worn and weathered by centuries. Vennor locked her gaze on the chipped monument at the center of the square, silently remembering the engraving at its base.

In celebration of our founding 500 years ago
1630 - 2130

Gedeon steered her through the flow of people, avoiding piles of debris and patches of overgrown weeds. The once-elegant, bricked buildings, decorated with crumbling archways, were a testament to the long-forgotten history of this place.

The group of men slowed in front of a grand hall, pausing when they reached its cracked flagstone landing. When Vennor was young, this building had been the headquarters of the Settlement's Council. By then, the city had already been relegated to the fringes of civilization. Now, the Council's gathering place was little more than a ruin, its roof caved in and its walls cracked. But the men didn't seem to notice, or care.

As they drew closer, Vennor could hear raucous shouts and cries coming from inside.

Her stomach lurched. "What are we doing here?"

A proud smile spread over her brother's face. He took her elbow and guided her up the steps to the entrance.

Inside, it was chaos. Vennor blinked into the noise and brightness. Hundreds of people—men, women, and children alike—shouted and cheered. Electric lights reflected off sweaty, animated faces. The air was thick with excitement and anticipation. The men who had accompanied them from the wood pile melted away into the crowd.

Her brother propelled her forward into the hall, into a sea of people. Everyone was so engrossed in the speaker at the back of the great hall that nobody acknowledged their presence as they passed by. All eyes were on the woman at the podium, everyone captivated by her words. Out of the corner of her eye, Vennor caught flashes of green from what appeared to be cloth banners as people waved them in support.

The roar was deafening, a cacophony of voices rising in defiance. Amid the shouting and cheering, Vennor heard the speaker's voice, a rhythmic cadence marked by sharp commands and stinging insults.

"Who is that?" Vennor shouted to be heard above the din. "Gedeon! Who is that speaking?"

Her brother gave her a sidelong glance, but didn't slow his pace. "Keep up."

They shoved past a group of women with green painted on their cheeks, all yelling something together. It sounded like

"Fates will decide! Fates will provide!" The group moved aside when they saw her brother.

Vennor took note of a girl waving a small piece of cloth with an emerald eye painted in the center. For an instant, Vennor felt as though she were looking at her own reflection. The girl's hair was meticulously pulled back in the same stern way Vennor's mother used to do for her, the girl's face set in the same defiant expression Vennor knew so well.

The speaker at the back of the hall was a stout woman with rounded cheeks and a space between her front teeth, her hair an intricate mix of loose, imperfect braids that hung down her back. She wore a simple dress of brown wool, but it did nothing to detract from her commanding presence. She paced back and forth as she spoke, her voice carrying easily over the noise of the crowd.

"My dear friends," the woman said, flipping her braids with a twist of her head. "The time has come for us to recognize our collective responsibility. We cannot stand by as the machine god seeks to consume our lives, stripping away our autonomy and turning us into pawns of the false light. We must rise, united in purpose, to save our fellow humans from this perilous path. We must rise together to reclaim our destiny!"

The crowd erupted in cheers. Vennor wanted to press her hands against her ears, blocking the noise. Where had all these people come from? And why weren't they tending to their own fires and families? There was precious time for leisure in the Settlements.

The woman waited for the noise to die down before continuing. "In the realm of ancient myths, we remember the Fates— the Moirai and the Norns—who teach us profound lessons about our existence. They remind us that all of our destinies are intertwined. That we are bound by a shared responsibility to preserve the human spirit.

"Allow me to share a story that illustrates the power of believing in the Fates and the peril of relying too heavily on technology for comfort and entertainment.

"In a time not too long ago, in a world much like our own, there lived a young man named Ethan. A seeker of truth, Ethan held faith in the wisdom of the Fates and the profound beauty of life's arbitrary nature.

"One day, as he walked through a park, he chanced upon an elderly woman weaving an intricate tapestry. She spoke of the threads of destiny, each strand representing a life, and every pattern recounting tales of human existence. Ethan, enraptured by her words, spent hours at her side, absorbing the teachings of the Fates.

"Yet, as the years unfurled, technology surged forward at a relentless pace. The people of his world became ensnared by the lure of AI-driven comforts and simulated pleasures. Virtual reality emerged, offering an illusory escape from the hardships of life.

"Ethan, too, succumbed to this seductive world, gradually forsaking the lessons of the Fates and life's inherent unpredictability. Human events and behaviors became cultivated and predictable. Humanity grew distant from its essence.

"Then, a day of reckoning arrived. A catastrophic event plunged the realm into darkness, disrupting the virtual reality that had ensnared them. People awakened to a harsh reality, their bodies weak, their minds disoriented, having long neglected the toils of the physical world.

"Ethan, too, was thrust back into the tangible realm. As he struggled to adapt, he recalled the teachings of the old woman and the wisdom of the Fates. He realized that genuine contentment and fulfillment could not be found in artificial pleasures, but in embracing life's uncertainty—its trials and tribulations, its fleeting moments of joy.

"With time, people began the arduous process of rekindling the human spirit. They rebuilt connections to one another, and they found redemption in the rediscovery of their shared humanity. Technology persisted, but it no longer held dominion over their lives.

"After his transformative journey, Ethan's heart and voice were forever changed. He longed to share his newfound understanding with others, to guide them toward a life of purpose and meaning. And so, he set out on a journey across the land, speaking to those he met and spreading the teachings of the Fates."

The audience began a clapping frenzy as Magna went on with the story. This was not the first time they had heard it.

"My grandfather's story is a testament to our resilience. It's a testament to the power of the human spirit. Our faith in the path the Fates make for us is the only way forward.

"Let us not be swayed by the false promises of convenience and entertainment. Instead, let us rally together, united in our commitment to shape a future where the power and beauty of our shared human experience reigns supreme. Let us embrace our responsibility to ensure that future generations experience the full spectrum of what it means to be human."

The crowd went wild, and Vennor felt a surge of energy coursing through her body. A trickle of sweat made its way down her back. She wanted to remove her warm coat, but didn't dare lose her brother in the crowd. They pushed forward.

"We have waited long enough," the woman shouted. "We reject the notion that algorithms and data govern our lives. We are more than lines of code. We are beings capable of love, compassion, and free will."

The crowd responded with equal fervor. Vennor felt like she was being swept up in a riptide of excitement.

"What's going on?" she asked again breathlessly. "Who is that?"

"That," her brother said with a grin, "is our new leader."

The speaker paused for a moment, and the crowd stilled with her. In the sudden quiet, Vennor heard her own heart pounding in her chest. Black spots danced in front of her eyes, and she realized she hadn't eaten since the day before.

"Fates will decide! Fates will provide!" A woman shouted, her fist raised in the air.

The crowd erupted again, even louder than before, as they picked up the chant. Vennor's brother turned to her with a wild look in his eyes. "This is what we've been waiting for. This is our chance to make things right."

He grabbed her hand and pulled her along. Vennor took several breaths to steady the levels of adrenaline rushing into her system. It wasn't as effective as asking her Thread to do it for her, but that wasn't an option now.

They drew closer to the woman in the brown dress. With a start, Vennor realized her brother was taking her there. To the podium.

"I'm not sure what you're doing," Vennor said, "but I don't want any part of this."

The leader saw them coming. Her eyes registered Gedeon's presence with a flicker of irritation before she broke into a warm smile.

Vennor's breath caught. Those eyes. She had seen them before.

"My friends," the woman said, turning from the crowd and opening her arms to Gedeon. "The fates have provided yet again. You see before you today the humble servants who would take you to freedom."

The people in front of Vennor and Gedeon parted, clearing

a path to the stage. Her brother tightened his grip on her arm and dragged her up the steps.

"We are together again for a reason," the woman said. "I know this because I have seen the future, and in that future, we are victorious. We are free!"

The crowd roared its approval. Gedeon stepped forward, and the woman engulfed him in a hug. Vennor stood frozen, her mind racing.

She remembered it now. The last time she had seen this woman. It had been a dark, chilly night, lit by a full moon and the distant lights of the Settlement. Vennor had deactivated her own Thread, and watched Hax steer the Ark's skidder back into the woods.

That night, the woman had charged out of nowhere, wearing black wrappings over her face and body in the manner of the soldiers here. Her companions drew their crossbows and took aim at Vennor.

She was sure the woman would have given the order to shoot had Gedeon not arrived when he did.

"And we are blessed, blessed indeed, with a very special guest," the woman said. "Someone who has traveled here from deep inside the land of the Arks, and who will give our people a magnificent gift. The gift of *freedom!*"

More cheers. Vennor felt her mouth go dry as the woman held her arms out to Vennor. In that instant, her careful attempts at blending in, at being invisible in this place, vanished. What did this woman want with her?

She shook off her surprise and managed a weak smile. She would not be deceived. She would not allow her brother to trick her into stepping into the middle of some unhinged movement.

But she had nowhere to go. The crowd closed ranks and surged around the stage, blocking any hope of getting away.

Her brother pulled her into a side embrace and grabbed her free hand. He raised their hands together into the air. The crowd roared its approval.

A flush of heat engulfed her head and neck. Her cheeks flamed. Pressure built behind her brow, a bead of sweat running into the corner of her eye.

She needed cool air.

"Free!" the woman thundered. "Free!"

The crowd took up the chant. They shook their pieces of cloth, green eyes shaking at them all around. Vennor bit her lip, trying to summon an ounce of calm. But she was up against a current that was too strong.

"Free!" Gedeon shouted beside her. "Free!"

The woman threw her arms to the sky.

"Free!" the woman cried.

Vennor's head swam.

"We are blessed," the woman said. "Fates bless each and every one of you for being here today, for showing your faith in freedom. Let us break free from the chains of technological servitude and forge a path where we remain the masters of our own fate. Together, we create a world where the human spirit thrives, untouched by the dominion of machines."

With that, the woman raised her hands again, and the crowd exploded into frenzied cheers.

Her brother released Vennor's hand. He waved to the people, driving them into a pitched furor. Vennor scrabbled at the fastening of her wool coat, but couldn't get it open.

"Gedeon, help me—" Vennor breathed. He turned.

The woman placed herself right behind Gedeon, her dark eyes shining.

"Vennor," her brother said. "Meet Magna. The leader of the Settler's rebellion."

The last thing Vennor saw was the floor rushing up to meet her.

Rayne

"WHAT ARE YOU TALKING ABOUT?" Vic sniffed.

Ana took a breath. The colors suddenly stopped changing over her head. With a glance over her shoulder, she closed a door and leaned against it. "I thought you might want to know that your mission is bound to fail."

"Fail?" Rayne asked. "What do you mean?"

"How do you know what we're planning to do?" Vic said.

"Because they run probability models." Rayne turned to Vic. "The Seers. They're practically merged with the NEWRRTH's code. They can predict human behavior in their sleep."

Vic blinked several times, calculating. He put his hand on his temple before whisking it away, the realization coming again that his Thread was silent.

"If you ran all these prediction models, what were we planning, then?"

Ana's expression stayed grim. "You were going to take a trip. To our neighboring Ark, the Pine Barrens. Although traveling overland this time of year presents challenges, you would have found a way."

Ana turned to Flay, who made a sound of surprise, and raked his fingers through his hair.

"Once at the Pine Barrens," Ana continued, "You would have sought an audience with their Seers. Appealed our verdict. Maybe even tried to secure a ruling from the Guild of Seers, who have the last word among all the Arks. A ruling from the Guild would make sure the Atlantic Ark honored a request, if the Guild ruled in your favor, to reinstate your Threads."

Vic nodded, not taking his eyes away from Ana.

Flay muttered something under his breath.

"And?" Rayne tried to ignore the knot in her stomach. Ana and her models landed uncomfortably close to the truth. Her friends had planned to help her leave the Atlantic Ark to appeal the verdict at the Pine Barrens Ark, several hundred miles to the southeast. The Designers ran their own probability models and found nothing problematic. Or anything they couldn't overcome. "What did you see in the models that would predict the plan's failure?"

Ana shook her head. "I'm not sure I can go into all the details."

"Just tell us." Rayne tried to stay calm. Was Ana trying to prevent them from lodging an appeal with the Guild of Seers? Why did she even care? Was this about keeping harmony in the Arks—and preventing an uprising? "Tell us what you mean when you say it's not going to work."

Ana looked up and to her left. "Flay knows..."

Flay's face contorted, his mouth twisting into a grimace as he tried to hold back whatever emotion was storming through his body.

"You're going to fail." Ana took a step back from the door,

gazing directly at Rayne. "Because the Pine Barrens no longer exists. It's been wiped out. They're all—" She hiccupped once, then collected herself. "They're all gone. There is no more Pine Barrens Ark."

Rayne stared in stunned silence. She wasn't sure how much more appalling news she could handle.

Vic barked out a laugh, startling her.

"The fuck is this?" Vic looked at Ana and Flay. "First, we get handed our asses from the Seers, for no good reason, get our Threads fully deactivated. Then this wacko says he can bring us to the promised land of Unconnecteds. Now this." He narrowed his eyes at Ana. "You tell us we can't appeal your fucked-up decision because the Pine Barrens is gone. Just gone!" He threw his arms wide.

Rayne watched as Vic continued to rant, his voice croaking. She knew he was just as frustrated and frightened as she was, and she couldn't blame him. She took a deep breath and stepped forward, placing a hand on his arm.

"Vic, I think we need to listen to what Ana is saying."

It was the lunacy of the day that made him hysterical, Rayne thought, as Vic burst into a fit of giggles.

"This beats it all. This is just cracked." Vic doubled over, hands on his thighs.

They watched him for a minute. He struggled for breath through a wave of uncontrollable laughter. Then he gathered himself. Wiped at the tears leaking out of his eyes.

The knot in Rayne's stomach grew as she stared at Ana. "Are you... are you trying to help us? Or what?"

Ana glanced over her shoulder. "Oh, I wouldn't say I'm helping anyone. I'm not taking sides here. I just want what's best for everyone."

A rasping sound made Rayne startle. Ana's image flickered.

She cried out as the door behind her slammed open, nearly knocking her over.

Enayat's shadow loomed in the doorframe.

"I have to go."

The call ended.

Flay ran his hand over the back of his neck. "It's true, you know. About the Pine Barrens Ark."

Rayne's breath caught. "It's gone? Why? Why didn't you— or the Seers—say anything? To anyone?"

"They said it was better this way. So no one panicked." Flay kept his eyes averted. "When I got back, they told me to keep it to myself. All the... things I saw."

Rayne didn't like the sound of that.

"Flay. Flay, isn't it?" The ghost of a smile lingered on Vic's face. "I don't care what you say anymore. Or the Seers. I'm done here. We've got our own business to take care of." He grabbed the skidder's door handle. "Let's go. Get this thing fired up and bring us home."

"Stop it," Rayne said. "Stop being so... so..." She shoved Vic's hand away and took hold of the handle herself. "Stop being so single-minded. Can't you see this changes everything?"

She yanked the door open and climbed into the back seat. To Flay, she muttered, "We need to get going."

Vic stood outside the skidder, arms at his side, his face set like marble. His eyes flashed at her, their icy green giving her a chill. Then he straightened and swung himself into the cab without a word. He scooted as far away from her as he could on the narrow bench.

Flay settled into the driver's seat, checked the dashboard, then started the skidder and pulled away.

.   .   .

Rayne gazed out the window as they jolted over the rocky terrain. They descended the hill and crossed a bridge over a creek. After a long while, they rounded a familiar curve. Rayne recognized Outlook Park on her right, an imposing stone structure atop a hill. The skidder made a sluggish turn, skirting the incline. Rayne tilted her head to catch sight of the lookout at the top.

The hill was more overgrown than she'd remembered. Her father used to bring her up there to show her the view. One spring, when she was about ten, he brought her to the park to celebrate some new discovery in his lab. He said it was groundbreaking, it would change the way people lived. Rayne never understood all the details of her father's work, but she remembered the smell of grass that day. The lanes and cottages of the Ark spread out below them.

He'd been so proud of her. She excelled in her lessons and had just started tinkering with the Games they gave her at school. Playing Games allowed students to experience real historical events in an interactive virtual world. It was the best way to instill curiosity and compassion, and to teach the reasons their ancestors had built the Arks and created the Thread all those years ago. Games reminded them why the NEWRRTH was necessary: to keep humanity on the correct path so they would avoid repeating past mistakes.

That day on the hill, her father told her what she couldn't possibly understand at the time—that she was going to be the best Game Designer in all the Atlantic Ark. She'd laughed, thinking he was being silly, though part of her thrilled at the idea of being a Game Designer, and a talented one at that. She decided she would create the best Games, and set them during the most pivotal moments in all of history.

As the skidder rumbled away from the Center, and the

verdict on hers and Vic's future, she'd never know if he'd been right.

Rayne dug her palms into her thighs. *Stop it.* She would not make it through the rest of the day if she started thinking about her father, or the hole he'd left in her life after he died.

Instead, she scooted forward and spoke to the back of Flay's head. "What do you think happened? To the Pine Barrens?"

From behind, Rayne saw him stiffen and his fingers tighten around the steering wheel.

"I don't know," he said. "I've never seen anything like it." His shoulders moved up and down, as if he were about to say more but thought better of it.

"You ever see something like that in the Games?" Rayne asked. "Did you ever play a Game that took you to a..." She didn't know the reference she was supposed to make. A battle-field? A war zone? Those were strictly limited in Game design, and when they were permitted, it was for specific instructional purposes only.

She settled for something more neutral. "Did you ever play a migration Game?"

The Seers closely monitored migration Games, since they often involved violence. But they also taught essential lessons. Teachers assigned migration Games so students could learn about the failure of land policies that relied on domination and control.

Rayne wondered if what happened in the Pine Barrens resulted from a collective decision—whose, she didn't want to imagine—to leave that particular Ark behind. It was the best scenario she could think of out of a collection of horrifying possibilities.

"I've seen enough in this life," Flay answered. "I don't need to play Games."

Rayne bit back her surprise. "But Games teach us how to

improve our lives," she said. "So many of them are beautiful, uplifting, fun—"

Vic made a noise at her, blowing his cheeks out.

Rayne heard herself. *Uplifting. Fun.* Yeah, just like the Game that had taken two of their friends' lives, and nearly ruined the NEWRRTH forever.

She sighed and faced the window again. And didn't speak for the rest of the ride.

THE CRUNCH of gravel and the whine of the skidder's engine signaled they'd arrived at their destination. *Home.* Rayne's cottage came into view, framing a rolling woodland beyond. The wind turbines rose in the distance. Their blades were still.

Flay shut the engine off and hopped out of the cab. He busied himself with something under the hood.

Rayne had barely touched the ground when her feet lifted again and arms came around her in a crushing hug.

"Hey!" Rook spun her, his long hair whipping around them both. Rayne allowed herself to rest her cheek on his thick shoulder.

Rook set her down and she quickly wiped the tear that rolled down her face. The other Game Designers rushed out of her cottage.

"Rayne!" Mo was nineteen, but had the round features of a little kid. Rayne could tell he had been crying. "We saw everything on the broadcast. It's horrible what they did."

"Not now, eh?" Rook gave Rayne's shoulder a squeeze and nudged her toward the cottage. "Let's get them inside first."

The aroma of loamy soil permeated the air, mingling with hints of wood smoke from nearby chimneys. Rayne was grateful for the peacefulness of her cottage, its windows catching the reflection of the lowering sun. Her Oak tree spread its gnarled branches in a protective embrace over her roof.

Rayne tried to catch Flay's eye, to thank him for his well-meaning offer, but his head was buried inside the skidder's engine. Rook hustled her away from the hulking machine.

There were footsteps behind them as Vic approached. "Okay if I join this party?"

"Come on." Rook pulled Vic into a half hug with Rayne on the other side.

Rayne's heart stuttered with relief. She held out her hand, and Vic reached for it. He hitched his mouth up at one corner. Rayne's toes tingled.

She and Vic would make it through this together.

As the three of them half-stumbled into Rayne's cottage, with Mo and her other friends surrounding her, Rayne could almost believe that everything would be okay.

Rayne

"ARE YOU SAYING YOU BELIEVE THEM?" Vic stared at the Designers assembled in Rayne's kitchen, a piece of apple cake clinging to his lip. He swiped at his mouth, and the crumb disappeared. "The Seers? They've lost it. I mean utterly lost it. I don't trust anything they do anymore. Or say." He glanced around at the Designers assembled around Rayne's kitchen counter before pushing the last bite of cake into his mouth.

Luci positioned itself in front of Vic and lifted its arm, wiping cloth ready. Vic reached over the bot's head to put another slice of cake on his plate. "Not now, Luci." Luci didn't budge.

Rayne sank onto the stool at the counter, letting her head fall into her hands. She angled away from where her packed bag sat by the front door. Their plan to leave, for her and Vic to travel to the Pine Barrens to appeal the Seers' verdict, was a distant memory. Any hope of reinstating their Threads had vanished like a puff of smoke in the wind. What were they supposed to do now?

Mo and Briz lowered themselves onto the stools on either side of her. Briz put a tentative hand on Rayne's back, patting in circles. "I never thought they'd have the *cojones* to do it. Not in a million years."

Rayne accepted their attempt at comfort.

To her left, Mo tapped his fingers on the counter. Rayne sensed his helplessness. He didn't know what to say.

Cha, her frizzy hair pushed back with a black headband, made soft *tsking* sounds as she pulled dishes out of the refrigerator.

"What's in this one?" She held a covered oval container up to the light. Rayne didn't look up. Rayne's neighbors still brought over food, even though the funerals of Cas and Jesla were months ago. Her neighbors meant well, especially Cynthia, but it was too much food for Rayne. The Designers had gone through piles of snacks while they waited for Rayne and Vic to return, but there were still untouched containers tucked into the refrigerator's cool shelves.

Cha cracked the dish open, sniffed it, and put it on the counter. Turned back to the fridge to see what else could be excavated.

Mo pulled the platter toward him. With two fingers, he lifted out a round brown lump. Taking a bite, he said, "Mm. Acorn mushroom ball."

Vic gestured with a piece of apple cake as he spoke. "I'm telling you, I've never seen the Seers so rattled. They've always had disagreements, but they've never gotten so upset about something like that. Ana was genuinely afraid of being caught. Usually they're so calm, right?"

"Unified." Rayne uttered softly. "They always act as one. All in strict agreement with the NEWRRTH's guidance." She raised her eyes to meet Vic's.

What's our guidance now? she silently asked.

"Yeah, and why would they lie about the Barrens?" Mo asked, reaching for another mushroom ball.

"Come on. It's obvious." Vic broke Rayne's gaze and toyed with his apple cake, pushing it around on the plate with his finger. "They want to stop us. They can't allow whatever scenarios the NEWRRTH came up with to materialize."

"What do you mean?" Rayne wasn't sure she wanted to know the answer.

Cha pulled another bowl out of the refrigerator and slid it in front of Rayne. "Here," she said. "I know you like this."

Rayne glanced down. It was pinto bean casserole with a blackened spice crust. Trust Cha to find that in her fridge. "Thanks, Cha." She tried to give her a smile.

"Want me to heat you up a bowl?"

Rayne shook her head. She wasn't hungry.

If it had been an ordinary day, she would have eaten half of the casserole straight out of the fridge. Gulped it down with some spring cider and a piece of that apple cake.

If this day had been anything close to normal, her friends would all be working together on their Threads, pinging each other on the D-boards or in virtual huddles. One of them would snap Thread into visibility to show the others a snag or a triumph of code. They'd be chatting nonstop about the virtual worlds they created.

Now, after their visit to the Center for Future Guidance, this day was one disaster after another. All of her joy evaporated, leaving her with an emptiness that couldn't be filled with food. Or Game designing.

Briz gave Rayne's back a last pat. "What Vic means is that the Seers saw something in their data models. They must have turned up a possibility that you, Vic, and maybe some group of us Designers would lead an effort to... I don't know, overturn the verdict? But that doesn't explain why they lied to us about the Pine Barrens. And why Ana would suddenly decide to say something about it. To you."

"The Seers know what we're capable of." Vic gazed into the distance, his eyes becoming unfocused, seeing something beyond her cottage walls. His volcano Game, perhaps. Or members of Freya's Path, the genius programmers who designed that Game with him. "And they don't like it. They want us to retreat gracefully, go gentle, disappear into the night, or however it goes. You know. Not make a scene. Just go away forever."

Rayne's heart squeezed. Vic mangled the reference, but it was one of her father's favorites—that Dylan Thomas poem. Cas knew it, too. It popped up all the time from her random poem generator she used in her Games.

She corrected herself. Cas *had* known the famous poem.

Why was she still thinking of her best friend as if he were still alive? Rayne flexed her fingers, and the image of her living code came to her. In her mind's eye, it lifted from her chest and withered into blackness as Vennor watched. It was part of the sacrifice Cas made to save her life.

The other part of the sacrifice was his own living code pouring into her. Blooming into every cell of her body, but taking life away from Cas.

She clenched her jaw to make the image go away.

"But why?" Briz asked. "What does it matter if you two leave the Ark to appeal their decision? Or even if you try to start something here, some sort of rebellion? You don't even have access to your..." They trailed off.

"Because they're Seers," Vic said. "That's what they do. They want to keep everything the way it is. The way they want it to be." He tossed his empty plate on the counter, where Luci promptly scooped it up.

Rook shouted something from the living room. They couldn't hear what he said.

Briz stood suddenly, their mouth hanging open.

Rook rushed into the kitchen, ropes of hair flopping in his face, eyes bright. "It's true. It's true! Gods, you're not going to believe this. I saw it."

Cha let the refrigerator door close. "What's true?"

Rayne's neck prickled. She slid from her stool. Leaned her weight against the cool countertop.

Rook cleared his hair from his face. Stood in the middle of the kitchen, gamescreen dangling from one hand. "This. Is. Cracked." He punctuated each word with a chop of his hand. "It's a Pine Barrens Ark Game."

"A Game? What are you talking about?" Vic's black eyebrows crunched together.

"You made a Game?" Mo finished chewing and spun to face Rook. "To see what happened to them?"

Rook's cheeks shined. "I didn't make it. The NEWRRTH did. Put on your screens." He slipped his gamescreen over his eyes.

Before anyone could stop her, Cha flew around the counter and punched him in the arm.

"Ow! Hey!" Rook whipped off his screen and gripped his shoulder. "That really—"

"Idiot," Cha hissed. "You forget what happened today?"

Rook's face fell. He glanced at Rayne, then at Vic, his cheeks growing bright spots of color. "Gods. I'm sorry."

Vic crossed the kitchen. "You'll have to show it to us. What did you see?"

The bloodless feeling crept back into Rayne's body, her hands ice at her sides. Her gamescreen sat in her bag by the door. A useless piece of junk without her Thread. Her vision blurred, tears pressing against her eyelids.

"You okay?" Briz guided Rayne back to her stool. "Sit."

Rook dropped his gamescreen on the counter and pushed it away a little. "It's just... well, if the Pine Barrens really was gone... the Thread would have recorded it, whatever happened, and then we could design a Game for it." He got quiet. "Like any other event we design around."

Beside her, Briz sucked in a breath. "Good. That's good."

Cha started nodding. "Yes, yes. Not bad at all." She punched his arm again, lightly this time. He pretended to flinch, though Rayne wasn't sure how much.

"So what is it?" Vic stood next to Rook. "What's the Game?"

Rook blew out a lungful of air. "That's the thing. It's wild. Let me pull it up so everyone can see it." He touched his temple and made a motion with his hand. Rook's Thread became a visible holograph in the middle of the kitchen.

Mo pushed some dishes out of the way to give them all a clear view.

Rayne pressed a finger under each eye to keep the wetness from escaping. She wouldn't fall apart now. She ached to see the image in front of them. As her friends slipped easily into design mode, despair closed a fist around her heart.

No time for that now, she admonished herself. They needed to figure out if the Pine Barrens Ark was still standing, whether it was worth a trip there. If there was anyone left who could hear her appeal and reinstate her Thread. Rook's new Game was the best option for figuring out if that was a good idea or not. She focused on the colors taking shape.

The Thread showed them a river of blurry green. Then the image came into focus, and Rayne realized what they were looking at.

The Pine Barrens woodlands. Part wetlands and part pine forest, the area around the Barrens formed a barrier of silt and sandy soil that had never been developed into a city. With its meandering rivers and rolling green hills, the Pine Barrens was an ecologically perfect place to situate a self-sustaining Ark.

The image paused, hovering over a heavily wooded spot, then zoomed closer.

"It's getting the lay of the land," Rook explained, but they all knew that. It was the baseline for any Game. The NEWRRTH called up the texture of an event, the season, the details of the historical setting, the shape of the land in a given moment. The Thread created the foundation, then the Designers added players and a strategy.

They wouldn't be designing the Pine Barrens Ark Game. They just wanted to see how the Thread set it up. What it put into the setting.

As the Thread took them soaring over the forest, Rayne's head filled with questions. Was the Pine Barrens still a thriving Ark, full of houses and long Orchard greenhouses and their own Haven? Or were Ana and Flay telling the truth—was it reduced to a wasteland?

Cha moved away from Rook, squinting at the Thread. Rook shifted from foot to foot, tapping his fingers to his thumbs.

The Thread would show them the truth. Were they prepared for that?

Rayne didn't want to see death. Or sickness. Or worse. The options for what happened to the Ark made Rayne's stomach churn. She tried to concentrate on the pine trees getting closer, closer.

The scene began to fill in as the Thread built its Game. The Ark came into focus. Pine trees stretched tall, their needles a dark green, almost black. The sky was a bright blue, with a few fluffy white clouds. The forest was so thick that very little sunlight made it through the thick covering of branches.

And then, like a butterfly on a current of air, they followed a ray of sunlight as it broke through to the forest floor. The trees parted, and a small dirt road appeared. Straight and narrow, it wove back and forth through the dense forest, disappearing into the woods.

The Thread took them along the road. They came into a cluster of low buildings, their circular levels enclosed in glass, green plants hanging over their roofs, small piles of—what was that?—all over the ground.

It was part of an Orchard, a food growing facility.

Rook's hand shook as he guided the Thread closer. They surfed over the strange piles, moving past buildings with arching doorways. The buildings were arranged in a circle, with a larger structure in the center.

Rayne's breath caught in her throat.

It was clear that whatever happened, it had happened quickly.

Rayne stared at the images, her heart racing as she took in the devastation around the clearing. Shattered glass was everywhere and entire walls had caved in, leaving gaping holes in the round buildings. Twisted branches stuck up from the ground in places where there had once been trellises for vines. The plants that grew under the glass had died, their leaves brown and brittle.

"What's that?" Rook asked, zooming in to one broken window. They leaned close. A bright green design splashed under the window frame, with dried drips underneath.

"Is it a fish?" Mo asked.

"It's not a fish. It's an eye." Rook pointed out the pupil in the center, the lashes thick lines above the arch of the lid. "It's a green eye."

Further along, they saw rows of smashed smoke racks over long-dead fires. Silvery fish that had once graced the racks decayed in the mud.

They skirted past the piles until the Thread locked onto another path. This one led away from the buildings of the Orchard. The Thread took them through the trees on a wide, well-worn road.

Rook became still. As they wove through the forest, painted green eyes stared back at them from the tree trunks. Someone had drawn dozens of green eyes on the trunks.

Just before they came out of the woods, the huts appeared. A network of waterways came into view. All along the tufted banks were more homes made of what looked like bark. As they passed by, they saw one hut after the other had a smeared green eye on its door. An overturned skiff floated by. They rounded a corner, and one of the dwellings revealed a gaping hole in its side.

"Stop," Cha said. "We've seen enough." She took a step back.

"This doesn't prove the whole Ark was destroyed." Vic was glued to the images unfolding before them. "We need to keep going. See their Haven at least."

Mo closed his eyes and put his hand over his face. "I can't. I can't look at this."

"We have to," Rayne said. "We have to know. Why would this happen?"

Vic nodded along as she spoke. "She's right. Ana wanted us to know about this for a reason. The NEWRRTH wanted us to know."

Rook cleared his throat. The images kept unspooling in front of them as the Thread took them through the winding waterways. A neighborhood of thatched houses, one by one revealing their doors hanging open and the contents of people's homes strewn over the soggy ground. All the devastation. All the loss. But...

Something nagged at Rayne. She couldn't put her finger on it, but something pulled at the edge of her brain.

"This is straight-up awful." Cha backed all the way against the fridge, hands on her heart. "I've never seen anything like this."

Then it clicked. The people. There were no bodies. No signs of anyone having died there.

"Where is everyone?" Rayne asked.

They didn't hear her. They all talked at once, over one another's heads, Briz beside her saying "It's true, though" and Vic instructing Cha to work with her Thread.

Rayne repeated herself, raising her voice. "I said, where is everyone? There's no one there!"

Her friends turned to her, quieting. Vic's expression hardened. Rook paused the Thread, and shut it down with a flick of his wrist.

"Yeah." Mo rocked back and forth, his wiry arms wrapped around his knees. "Shouldn't there be people? Where'd they go?"

"Or... where were they taken?" Rook said.

For the first time that day, a measure of heat began to seep into Rayne's limbs. She raised her chin and scanned the faces of the other Game Designers—her friends who had saved her more than once, and were willing to lay everything on the line for her and Vic.

"We need to find out what happened there." Rayne willed the wobble from her voice. "We can't let the Seers cover this up. It's too huge. We need to find out where they all went, the people of the Barrens, because we need them. Their Seers are the only ones who can help us get our Threads back."

The muscles in her shoulders tightened, and she forced herself to exhale before she continued. "So that's why I'm going there. To the Pine Barrens Ark."

FRESH MEAT_

Vennor

THE COOLNESS SOOTHED the burning in her chest. Vennor
rolled her head to the side and opened her eyes. She was lying
on the floor in an unfamiliar room, wetness on her neck.

Her ears rung in the silence. The crowd was gone, the air
still.

The blurry brown of the woman's dress stood some
distance away. Vennor took a deep breath, then raised her head.

She blinked, her head pounding.

Gedeon loomed into view, grinning. "You're awake."

"Yes, and I'm fine." Her voice sounded small.

"You sure?" her brother asked. "You dropped like a stone."

Vennor sat up, reaching for her Thread. But her mind was
empty. She couldn't feel the NEWRRTH, couldn't even sense
where it was. She struggled to remember what it felt like when
her Thread took care of her nervous system in pulses of
soothing enzymes and hormones.

As she rose, the damp cloth slipped from her neck, landing
in her lap.

A clump of people gathered in the center of the room. Their faces turned to her. The woman in the brown dress stood in the middle, her hands clasped in front of her. She leaned in as she spoke to them.

"Get me out of here," Vennor snarled at her brother.

Gedeon grabbed her arm and helped her to her feet. The room swam out of focus. He pressed something into her hand. Vennor looked down. It was a water flask.

Vennor took a deep drink. The cool water eased the pounding in her head.

"You did well," Gedeon whispered to her. "I didn't think you had it in you."

Vennor turned to him. "What have you dragged me into?"

"That's no way to thank me." Gedeon let go of her arm and she swayed, looking for a table or chair to steady herself with.

"Vennor." Magna broke away from the circle of people. "We were beginning to worry about you."

Finding nothing to lean on, Vennor thrust the water flask into Gedeon's hands and staggered to the nearest window. Pressed her palm against the cool glass. She gasped when she saw through it.

"Gods," she whispered, and jerked her hand from the window. They were high off the ground. People were black dots below, scurrying around the red brick square. Trees were tiny bare twigs.

What was she doing here? And how would she get away?

Magna slitted her eyes like a cat's and came to where Vennor stood. "It's been a while since you've been in a high-rise."

Vertigo gripped Vennor. She felt she might fall. Her hand shot out to the glass to steady herself again, this time averting her gaze from the scene below. She looked out over the tops of nearby towers, into the air above.

"I don't know what you want from me." Vennor kept her eyes on the pale blue sky. "But I'm afraid I have nothing to offer you. Any of you."

"That's what you think?" Magna cocked her head, appraising. Her eyes were a light brown, holding a hint of purple. She had refreshed herself after her performance in the hall, washed her face and tidied her dress. Her hair was re-braided into a single thick plait, a lump of metal woven into the end that glinted when she moved. "Don't you want to belong?"

"Belong?" Vennor glanced at Magna, unexpected venom in her throat. "I don't belong anywhere."

"Your brother told me your story," Magna said. "About what your fellow Seers of the Atlantic Ark did to you."

The coolness of Vennor's sweat turned clammy on her skin.

"We've all been hurt," Magna said. "We've all been angry. We've all been cast aside."

"You and I have nothing in common." Vennor kept her breathing steady.

"Maybe." Magna took a step closer. "But when you're hungry, even a small piece of bread is better than nothing at all."

"I'm not in the habit of accepting scraps from strangers. Or their pity."

After a moment, Magna threw her head back and gave a throaty laugh. Vennor frowned. The other people in the room drew closer, looking alert. Some slipped hands inside their coats. Vennor noted her brother stood in front of them, facing her, arms at his sides.

"Stand down," Magna said, recovering herself. "All of you. Relax." The men in front eased their shoulders, glancing at each other. Her brother nodded, and they dropped their hands. One lifted his lips at Vennor, without a hint of mirth in his eyes.

"Don't you see?" Magna continued. "She's perfect. Absolutely, one hundred percent perfect for us. Come."

Magna gave the window a friendly tap and began walking, gesturing for Vennor to follow. The other people made space for her to pass through. Vennor didn't see that she had much choice in the matter. She straightened and trailed behind Magna. Magna's people encircled them.

Two men pressed through a set of double doors at the end of the room. As they passed through the doors, Vennor saw a table in the middle laid out with food. The smell of roasted meat and baked cornbread made her stomach growl. Magna turned to her with a smile.

"See? I can tell when someone's hungry. Livia!"

A small woman with dark hair and thick eyebrows approached. A patch covered her right eye.

"Yes." Livia's high cheekbones shone as she glanced at Vennor with curiosity. Vennor stared at Livia's features. There was something familiar about her.

"Seat our guest at the table, and make sure she has a good meal," Magna said. "We'll eat, then we'll work."

Livia bowed her head.

Magna and her entourage found their own places while Livia took Vennor to the other end of the table.

"You can sit here." Livia pulled out a battered chair.

Vennor lifted her eyes to the walls, which were decorated with tattered flags and old weapons. She wondered what kind of work Magna had in mind.

Vennor sat down and Livia placed a plate of food in front of her.

"I'm Livia." She offered her hand to shake. Vennor paused, then reached out and touched Livia's long, tapered fingers. Livia's hand was dry and cold, her grip delicate.

"I'm glad you're here." Livia's left eye, the uncovered one, squinted in pleasure as she took the seat next to Vennor.

Turning to her plate, Vennor saw it was full of gray meat. She restrained a gag. The meat gave off a burnt smell that turned her stomach. The Thread always guided them to fresh plant-based food, making sure their bodies had all the nutrients they needed for optimum health. This pile of rotting gristle made her bile rise, even as hungry as she was.

Livia noticed Vennor's reaction, and the corners of her mouth turned down.

"Of course you haven't acclimated to the Settlers' cuisine." She found another dish and watched Vennor's face as she slid a spoonful of tightly curled ferns onto Vennor's plate.

"Ramps," Vennor said, welcoming the sight of the brightly colored greens. "Thank you."

Livia smiled. "You're welcome. Give me a moment, and I'll find you more to eat."

Vennor's fork hovered over her plate. She watched Livia out of the corner of her eye. Why did she look so familiar?

"It's important you feel comfortable with us." Livia pulled a dish of wilted greens toward them. "So we can help each other."

Vennor put her fork down. "What do you think I'm going to help you with?"

But Livia had already gotten up in search of more food. Vennor turned to her plate. The ramps smelled delicious. She took a small bite. The sautéed fiddleheads had a light crunch, their bitterness balanced by a sweet cooking oil.

"It's not like home, is it? Not like the food we used to eat." Her brother slid into the seat on the other side of her. His plate clattered to the table. It was covered with blackened meat on a bone.

Vennor looked away in disgust. She swallowed her small bite.

"We didn't have so much," Gedeon said. "Remember? We used to dig those old potatoes from the weeds along the rails. Nasty things." He grabbed the bone with his fingers and drew it to his mouth. He gnawed the reddened flesh hanging from it with smacking noises.

Vennor pushed her plate away. She wasn't hungry anymore.

"You should eat," Gedeon said through a full mouth. Grease trickled down his chin. "My daughter won't be happy to find you've wasted food. She likes to see we put our food to good use. Feeding the army, she calls it."

"Your what?" Vennor's breath caught. "You have a daughter?"

"There's a lot you don't know about us." Gedeon's eyes twinkled. "Oh, here she is."

Vennor's palms grew moist.

Livia returned to her seat, placing two large plates in front of them. "I found these," she said. "This one is a mushroom we harvest from the forest, I don't know what it's called, and this one's—"

Vennor's chair scraped loudly as she stood. "You're—you're—"

Gedeon smirked. He ripped another piece of red flesh from the bone and chewed it. "The great Seer. The famous leader of the Atlantic Ark. She's finally lost her power of speech." He chuckled, bits of meat spitting out of his mouth.

Livia furrowed her brow. "What's this about?"

The searing heat returned to Vennor's upper body. Her underarms prickled with sweat.

I won't pass out this time. I will stay alert.

Her brother observed them.

Vennor faced Livia, appraising the woman's features with fresh eyes. There it was. The resemblance to her own father. The firm jaw. The tawny skin stretched tight on high cheekbones. The knowingness around the eyes. Or single eye, in Livia's case.

"It seems we haven't been properly introduced," Vennor said.

"I know who you are." Livia sat, tilting her head so that Vennor would return to her seat in between the two of them. "You're my Auntie."

Vennor pulled her chair underneath her, her legs like melted wax, and inched back to her place. "Yes," she managed. "Yes, I'm your... Auntie."

Gedeon chuckled again. "Now you know." Pieces of meat stuck in his teeth. "Give me that plate there."

He held out his hand, and Livia pushed the dish into it. Gedeon's eyes fixed on Vennor's. "So much you've missed."

"What do you want from me?" Vennor asked.

"I think you already know," Livia said. "We need you to help us."

Vennor's jaw clenched. "No."

"Come now. You're a *Seer*." Gedeon made the word sound like a curse. "You knew what you were doing when you left us. Abandoned me here, with not much to survive on. Even knowing your gifts, your talents, and what you could do to help us—"

Magna raised a hand. Conversations died and forks stopped in mid-air.

Gedeon closed his mouth.

"Friends." Magna waved her hand, and a person stepped forward to take her plate away. Several others materialized to clear the dishes around the table.

"We find ourselves at a crossroads." Magna pulled a cup to

her chest and out of the way of the clearers. "This is the moment we have been working toward. With our sweat, and our tears, and our blood."

One man banged a fist on the table, startling Vennor. He slapped a palm over his heart and hung his head low. On either side of him, Settlers clapped his back.

After a pause, Magna continued. "We have assembled a significant movement. An army of liberation. Our journey has already begun. We have seen how powerful collective action can be when people unite under a common cause. Look at what we've already accomplished."

Murmurs rippled around the table.

"We have made progress, but there is more to be done. More minds to set free from the false gods that rule them. And we now find ourselves with more than faith on our side."

Magna's dark eyes glimmered. Vennor heard Livia's breathing speed up beside her.

"Our strength has grown exponentially with Vennor's return. Vennor, former leader of the Atlantic Ark Seers and master of the machine gods. She brings a powerful alliance to us, and will prove invaluable to the future of our cause. Fates will decide."

The room erupted into cheers, voices chanting, *Fates! Freedom!* and raising their cups in solidarity.

Vennor rose from her seat before she knew what her legs were doing. The cheering subsided, and all faces turned to her.

"No." Vennor placed her palms on the table to steady herself. "I won't help you."

Livia's voice was gentle as she put a hand on Vennor's wrist. "You will. You just don't understand yet."

"The Fates know all, of course." Magna pushed her chair back and stood. Her tone was cool. "We know the circumstances of your birth in the Settlement, what you had to do to survive. What you've achieved since then. We know the talent you developed in learning the ways of the implanted. And we know the ache you have to see peace in the hearts of people everywhere. All people. Even us *Unconnecteds.*"

Vennor's thoughts churned. They were right. She wanted peace. And she knew exactly what they wanted from her. How they believed she would help them.

Dread pooled in her gut. The quiet life she had tried to make for herself in the Legacy Settlements, her old homeland, slipped out of her grasp forever.

"We need your help," Magna continued, "because you're the only one among us who knows, truly, what they're capable of. And how to stop them."

Magna's eyes glowed as she looked straight at Vennor. "I want you to help me take down the Atlantic Ark."

A HARD PLACE_

Rayne

THE ONLY LIGHT came from a single Thread lit up in the middle of the table in Rayne's living room. Outside, the night echoed with the spring peepers' chirping.

Mo curled up on a pile of pillows in one corner of the room, while Rayne and Vic perched on the couch across from Cha and Rook. Rayne had her feet tucked beneath her, her chin resting on her knees. Cha was on the floor, leaning against the base of an armchair.

Luci charged in its port, powered down.

Briz paced the length of the room while they talked. "Traveling all the way there, even though there might be no one left? Even though whoever did this is maybe still there? Ready for someone to come after any survivors? It's not a good plan."

"We all saw the same thing," Rook said. "There could be no one there. But it's the closest Ark and the best chance they have right now."

"I wish we could do this in a Game." Cha picked at the rug under her knees. "Not actually go anywhere."

"We've been through that." Rook's hair danced across his back. "If Rayne and Vic want their Threads reinstated, they'll have to ask the Seers in person. Not in a Game or on a call."

"But do they have to go to the Pine Barrens?" Mo asked from his nest in the corner. "There are Seers in the other Arks. What about them?"

The Designers began arguing again.

Rayne scooted closer to Vic on the couch and reached for his hand. He leaned back, tucked his palms under his thigh. Out of her reach.

"What's going on?" Rayne whispered. "You've been quiet all night."

Vic stared at his lap. "I don't want to do this." His dark curls had just grown in again, one escaping over his ear. Rayne wanted to reach out and tuck it back.

"Why not?" she asked. "It's not like it was before. We have each other. We're a team."

"I know. But that doesn't make it any easier."

Rayne was silent for a moment, letting Vic gather his thoughts. "It's just"—he finally said—"where is Freya's Path? Why are they letting us do this alone? I thought they'd be here for us. Especially after everything that happened. But it's like they've written us off. I don't know what the hell is going to be waiting there for us in the Pine Barrens. And I don't know if I can face it alone."

"You won't be alone," Rayne said softly. "I'll be there with you."

"You know what I mean." Vic sighed and rubbed his face with his hands. "I'm just tired. I'm tired of all of this."

"I am too." Rayne reached out again and tugged his hand into hers, interlacing their fingers. "But we have to go. It's the only way we're getting our Threads back. And people in the

Arks need to know what happened to the Barrens. The Seers aren't investigating this. We need to."

"I don't think it is."

"What?" Rayne squeezed his hand.

"Going there. I don't think it's our only option." He squeezed her hand back, then let it go. "See, that's the difference between us. I don't think there's anything left in the Pine Barrens that can help us. I'm not hopeful like that. I think it's time to consider other... ways to deal with our situation."

Rayne blinked. His words hurt more than she thought they would. So Vic didn't want to come with her to find the Seers and appeal their case. Didn't share her *hopefulness*. She tried to tell herself that it didn't matter, that she didn't care what he thought, but deep down she knew that wasn't true. She cared what he thought. Very much.

"Our best bet is to find that code," Vic said. "The one Vennor used before she—"

"All right, listen up!" Rook roared above the chatter. He clapped once, loudly, and everyone stopped to listen. "Cha has a new idea. About how to get to the Pine Barrens. And beyond."

Rayne glanced at the small table in front of the couch, where Cha's Thread still glowed.

Cha held her hands over it. She spoke a few words to her Thread, and the image changed. It became something large, silver, moving. Metal bubbles, one after the other, on wheels. Slanted red script on the side whizzed by over and over again.

Rayne tried to read it, but the tube moved too fast. *Oh, this is a—*

"It's a train," Cha said. "Maglev. Built about a hundred years ago when people tried to connect the last remaining cities. It was abandoned during the last wars. It's been sitting there since then, rusting away, but it's still intact."

The Designers gathered around the image. Rook's mouth curved up. "That looks fun."

"I've been studying the schematics, and I think I can get it running again. There's a station that intersects with this line about a five-day journey from here. If we board the train there, get it started, and clear the tracks, we can ride it a few hours to get us pretty close to the Barrens. It'll save us weeks of travel through the unprotected zones."

There was silence for a moment as the Designers watched the speeding train. Rayne reached for the memories of what she learned about them before the Great Divergence. Even without her Thread, fragments of knowledge surfaced from Games she had played.

Roads and rails used to connect in a gigantic web across the continent, delivering food and all kinds of things that people needed. That was before they reorganized into separate, self-contained Arks. Now there were eight sovereign states, each capable of sustaining themselves without importing anything from further away.

"This train was one of several running at the time. This line was called"—Cha paused the image, reading the script on one of the carriages—"the Liberty Express. It was the one that ran closest to here, and passes within a few miles of the Barrens." She flicked her fingers, and the train unfroze again.

She zoomed the image out. Rolling alongside the train were fields of waving grass. As they watched, several low buildings appeared. Ramshackle huts and farm stands, it looked like. Then more buildings—houses, entire neighborhoods. Taller, larger structures showed up, and suddenly they were on the outskirts of a city.

"So this was a hundred years ago?" Rook waved his hand at the images on the Thread. "What's it like now? I never heard about tracks near here. And where's the train?"

Vic leaned forward. "Cha, slow it down."

The image moved slower, the streets stretching out. The buildings came into focus as the image moved, their walls and roofs stretching out like a grand quilt, patchworks of color and light. Windows peered back like sleepy eyes as the train rolled along. The towers made of metal and glass were much taller than anything Rayne had seen in her lifetime.

Then the train's metal tube slipped into a hole in one building, and the image went dark.

That was it. Rayne waited for Cha to start the images again, to show them where the train ended up, but Cha just sat there.

"It's so sad to see it this way," Rook said. "The way the cities used to be. Before."

Rayne brushed her hand over the dark Thread, willing it to move. It didn't. The cities had been grand, it was true, but the people living in them had miserable, hustling, violent lives. Not like people in the Arks.

"Well, we wouldn't have to travel that far," Cha said. "All the way into those old tunnels. The Pine Barrens Ark is a good distance away from that."

Vic looked away, his jaw set.

"All right, this is what we're going to do." Rayne stood up from the couch. All eyes swiveled to her. She felt Vic's eyes on her.

Her resolve rose, sending fresh warmth to her fingers. Getting on this train to the Pine Barrens Ark was the right thing to do. She knew it. They would find out what happened to the people in the Pine Barrens, and reinstate hers and Vic's Threads. She was going to do it alone if she had to.

"I'm going to find the Guild of Seers and ask them to reconnect my Thread," she said, holding Vic's eyes with her own. "I don't know where they are, but I'm going to keep traveling until I find them. This train—" She pointed at the dark Thread.

"This is what we're going to use. To travel overland. If there's enough of it left."

"Rayne..." Vic began.

"I'm doing this," she said. "I'm traveling to the station and getting on this thing. And I'm not stopping until I get my Thread back."

"Rayne—"

"We'll need to prepare," Cha cut in. "I can get started reviewing all the data we have on the Liberty Express and whatever infrastructure is left behind. There was more than one train line, right?"

Rook bobbed his head, already speaking softly to his own Thread.

"So we're going to map it all out. What's still operable. What's not. And the route we're going to take to get to the Barrens."

Mo touched his temple. "On it."

"I don't think you should do this," Vic said.

"Why not?" Rayne crossed her arms.

"Whoever did this is still out there. Could be, anyway."

Rook paused and glanced up.

"I don't need your permission to go," Rayne said. "We've always worked together. We have each other's backs. So I know you'll support me on this."

Vic's mouth twisted. "Stop this. You don't even know what you're saying."

"I do. I know those people need us. Something terrible happened to them, and they need help. No one else is coming. No one else even knows what happened."

"You heard the Seers today." Vic shot to standing. "They aren't on our side. Maybe they never were. Something's gone wrong with their data. They haven't gotten clear guidance. I'm not going on a stupid adventure hoping the Guild is going to be any different."

Rayne stared at him. Small pieces of her heart popped off, dropped through her body, and broke in shards at her feet. *A stupid adventure? It's like he doesn't care about me at all.*

"The only way we're going to get our Threads back," Vic said, "is if we take them back. Using force if we have to."

All the Designers stopped moving.

"What exactly are you proposing?" Cha asked.

"It's simple." Vic ran his hands over his dark curls. "We get the code Ana wrote. The code that appeared as that piece of clear quartz. You know. The crystal Vennor used in the last Game."

Briz raised their eyebrows. "The code that killed Cas? Killed Trueno, the Seer? And nearly killed the rest of us?"

"That one." Vic spoke in a rush. "But we don't actually use it. We only need the code to convince the Seers that we aren't backing down. That they need to reconsider their decision and what data the NEWRRTH's feeding them now. Where it's leading them."

"That's your plan?" Cha said. "Threaten the Seers with their own code?"

Rayne licked her lips, suddenly parched. "I'm not doing that."

Vic's face softened, and he reached out a hand to her. Rayne took it, and the anxiety crushing her heart eased a little. Vic cared about her. About their future. He was just doing what he thought was best. Going about it in his own way.

"I'm not doing that either," Cha said decisively. "I'm with Rayne."

"Vic has a point, though." Rook bent his head toward Vic. "We have to do something."

Briz started pacing again. "This *is* doing something."

"I'm not saying it's guaranteed to work." Vic sat down again, pulling Rayne beside him. "But I won't travel all around the unprotected territories on some speeding death trap to see if someone else can fix this. We have to do more than trust the Seers. We have to take control ourselves."

Rayne

RAYNE WOKE out of a dreamless sleep. She lifted her head and winced.

She'd fallen asleep on the couch, her body stiff from lying in an awkward position. She tried to stretch, but it only made the pain worse.

Vic was speaking nearby, low and tense. "She won't listen to me, and you're not either." His voice came from the kitchen. Rayne recognized his mother's voice, too, but couldn't make out what they were saying.

She got up slowly, feeling every ache and soreness in her body as she moved. No answering pulse of endorphins came from her Thread.

That was it. Another night I spent without it.

She passed Mo working with his own Thread on a pile of pillows in the corner. His eyes were bloodshot. His hands moved fast, and he muttered to himself, occasionally tapping his right temple. Briz and Cha were nowhere in sight. Rayne guessed they had either crashed in her bedroom or had been working in there all night.

Stumbling into the kitchen, she saw Vic next to Rook against the windows. A hologram of his mother, Healor Lynn, hovered between the two Game Designers. Rook had a pained look on his face, like he didn't want to be in the middle of this conversation. But without a Thread, Vic needed him to place the call.

"You have to help me do this," Vic was saying to his mother. "You're the only one with access to all the data on Freya's Path. We need them again. Especially with this cracked stunt Rayne wants to pull. You know she won't back down on this."

Rook's eyes widened, and he jerked his chin. Vic turned and spotted Rayne standing in the doorway. He closed his eyes and ran a hand over his hair. "I didn't mean it like that. Gods. Sorry about waking you up like this."

Rayne took a breath and stepped into the kitchen.

Healor Lynn's hologram sighed heavily, then broke into a smile.

"Good morning, Rayne. I see you've joined the land of the living." H. Lynn's eyes sparkled, but Rayne noticed the purplish circles underneath. H. Lynn must have been just as stunned as she by the Seers' verdict. Her only son had his Thread ripped away. What would their family's future look like now? And what would Rayne's own mother go through when she learned of the Seers' verdict?

Rayne could picture Kai's disappointment. Her mother always believed in Rayne's extraordinary talent as a Designer. After her father died, however, Kai had retreated into herself and left Rayne to her own devices. Rayne could remember the times she spent alone in their cottage, realization dawning that her mother would be spending another night in her precious greenhouses. There was always important work for Kai at the

Orchard, and after a while Rayne stopped expecting her mother to check in every day. Rayne wanted to believe her mother still thought she was special, but sometimes couldn't help feeling like she was just fooling herself.

It didn't matter, anyway. Kai was oblivious to the Seers' verdict, and Rayne feared she'd remain that way for a long time.

"Good morning, H. Lynn." Rayne took a breath, grimacing again at the aches in her body, and skirted Vic to get to H. Lynn's image.

"Rayne, please, I didn't mean anything by it. I swear." Vic reached an arm out. Rayne ignored it.

"How are you feeling today?" H. Lynn peered at Rayne, narrowing her eyes. H. Lynn missed nothing. The music of the Haven tinkled behind her, attempting to create an aura of peace, which Rayne didn't share at the moment.

"I'm very sorry for you both," H. Lynn said. "This is so much more devastating than we expected. Vic is having a hard time adjusting."

Vic jutted his lower jaw. "It's tough. But we have a plan. Right?"

Rayne leaned her head on Vic's shoulder. He slid his arm around her waist and pulled her close.

Rook rolled his eyes.

"Hey, I'm sorry," Vic whispered into her ear. "I shouldn't have said that before."

Rayne's annoyance lingered for a moment. But she couldn't be mad at Vic. Not with his arm around her and his breath warm on the top of her head. Not when he was so heartbroken himself.

"I don't want to be the bad guy here," Rook said. "But can we wrap this up? We have a lot to do today."

H. Lynn leaned in. "Rayne. I know what you're about to do, and I want to commend you."

Vic let out a half-shriek. "I just told you it's a ridiculous, dangerous plan! What are you doing?"

"The outbreak." H. Lynn's eyes shifted. "The numbers are not good. I know it's the last thing on your minds right now, but we're nearly at capacity at the Haven. They're building a temporary annex to house more people. We're not any closer to understanding what's causing this, or even if there's a common infectious agent. Our transports are running around the clock, bringing people here."

Rayne nodded. She knew the outbreak was getting worse. People started calling it the rig, a play on how stiff people got when they became infected. But didn't the Thread always resolve these kinds of crises? It guided the Healors to optimize public health and helped them manufacture medicines to protect from similar pathogens in the future. Since the extinction of viruses, the Arks hadn't seen a pandemic for years.

Vic's face tightened. "I don't know what that has to do with us."

"There's discussion of a quarantine in the Ark. You know what that is?" H. Lynn lowered her voice, glancing behind her.

Rayne's pulse quickened. She recognized that term. *Quarantine.* She didn't need her Thread to explain it to her.

"I remember learning about that," Rayne said. "But how would a quarantine affect us? We can still work in the virtual."

"You'll have to leave now, if you're going to leave at all." H. Lynn let out a sharp exhale. "We're about to have a meeting to understand all the factors involved in the outbreak." She trailed off, her gaze becoming unfocused. She was listening. "Oh," was all she said, suddenly crestfallen.

"What is it?" Vic dropped his arm from Rayne's waist. "What's going on?"

H. Lynn flicked her gaze back to Vic and Rayne. "You don't want to know," she murmured. "It's just more data on how people's bodies handle the rig—the outbreak. Their brain activity is pretty minimal." She gave a brief shake of her head. "Please, Vic, leave with Rayne. Get out of here. You don't want to be around if this outbreak gets worse. *When* it gets worse."

Vic threw his hands over his head. "I'm not leaving. I'm going to find that code. I told you."

H. Lynn drew herself up, pressing her lips together.

Rayne spoke first. "Let's consider this." She gripped Vic's arm. "You could work on the code on the way to the Barrens. You don't need to stay here." It was terrible to pressure him this way. She knew he didn't want to leave. But why stay, especially with a looming quarantine?

Vic shook his head. He looked like he was about to say something, then pulled his arm back and stormed out of the room.

He nearly bumped into Briz. Briz put their hands in the air, flattening against the wall to let Vic by.

Rook groaned. "I'll go."

H. Lynn's hologram flickered, her face sad, resigned. The call ended, and Rook took off after Vic.

Briz took a tentative step toward the windows. "What was that?"

"Just Vic being Vic," Rayne said. Vic had been trying to protect her from something, but then he had pulled away— almost as if he didn't want her around. Why did it have to be so complicated? Why couldn't things just be simple between her and Vic?

"Come on," Briz said. "Leave him." They watched Rook disappear down the hallway after Vic. "We have something to show you."

Rayne followed Briz into the living room. Rayne considered what H. Lynn said about how quickly the outbreak was spreading, and how little they knew about it. Goosebumps worked their way up her arms. She didn't want to think about what would happen if Vic stayed here during a quarantine.

Cha and Mo stood by the couch, their backs turned. An image glowed between them. It was a Designer's map, a three-dimensional visualization of progress through a Game. Rayne longed to see it, but before she drew close, they shut it down and faced her.

"We've been practicing," Cha said. She put a hand on Mo's shoulder, and smiles spread over their faces. "Mo spent all night with his Thread working out a path through the rail lines. Which ones we need to follow in order to get closest to the Barrens."

Mo blushed. "Not that hard. Just had to write a simple algorithm."

"And Briz here—" Cha moved closer to her friend, who beamed. "Briz figured out how to get to the train closest to us. Where the station is, and how to power up the tracks."

"It's wild, you know?" Briz said. "That people used to get around on those things."

Luci bumped against Rayne's hip. "Crumbs all over the place. Step back."

"Hey, Luci." Cha scooted over so Luci could swipe the table. "You know you helped us, right? You gave us the idea of finding those robotic track cleaners. So the tracks will be clean for when the train needs to get by."

"I know," Luci said. "You don't have to keep telling me."

Cha snorted. They watched Luci back up and whir away, its cleaning pad in the air.

Rayne shivered again, this time with nervous anticipation. They were doing this. They were traveling to the Pine Barrens Ark on a high-speed maglev train. One that hadn't run for decades.

"And Cha," Briz said, giving Cha's hip a playful bump. "She's champing at the bit to drive that thing."

Cha grinned. "I may be excited about that."

For the first time in her life, Rayne had been an outsider in Game design. She had slept on the couch, worrying about her own problems, while they all worked.

"Thank you," she said. "You know, for getting all this done. For me."

"Which brings us to a bit of a sensitive issue." Briz guided Rayne to the couch and sat down next to her.

"I know. It's about Vic," Rayne said. "You don't want him to come with us."

Cha and Briz exchanged glances. "Hey, now," Cha said, dropping on the couch on the other side of Rayne. "I wouldn't put it like that."

Briz cocked their head. "He has his own plan. We're not part of it."

"But we're not letting him do this on his own," Mo said, excitement in his gentle eyes.

Rayne felt a surge of relief and admiration for her friends. They would bring Vic with them, then.

Briz gave a small shake of their head, anticipating Rayne's train of thought. "We don't think Vic will come with us. We're splitting up. Mo and Rook are staying here with Vic. Give him access to their Threads. See where his investigation into the crystal code goes."

"It's better this way." Mo shrugged. "We'll have more to work with. If you all don't—"

"And Cha and me," Briz said, interrupting Mo. "We get to be explorers on the greatest ride ever. Set out for lands unknown. With you."

Briz reached around to ruffle Cha's already-frizzed hair. They both leaned into Rayne.

Rayne was still. It was too much to process. Her friends' resourcefulness surprised her. She felt sad that they were going to split up and resigned to the fact that she and Vic would be separated.

She gave a weak smile and nodded her head in agreement. "That sounds like a good plan."

"You know it is," Briz said. "Hey. We're here for you. You know that."

Rayne nodded again. Pressing the tears out of her eyes, she braced herself on her friends' knees to push herself to standing.

"Thank you." Rayne faced them. "I'd stand here all day and hug you all, but we need to leave. Now."

WET SPRING_

Rayne

THEY SAID their goodbyes that morning. Rayne leaned against her Tree for a moment before Vic found her.

Vic wrapped his arms around her. His chest was warm against hers, and she felt his heartbeat through his jumpsuit. Rayne closed her eyes and took a deep breath, savoring the moment.

"I'm sorry, Rayne," Vic whispered into her ear. "I wish I could come with you."

Rayne pulled away from him, intertwining her fingers with his. "We're going to get our Threads back."

"I know." Vic's eyes searched hers. "Don't be afraid to use it. The flare."

"I won't."

The emergency flare, Cha called it. She built it right into the D-boards so any Designer could access it. A way to signal the other Designers for help, should that be required. But Rayne and Vic knew that they'd never be able to touch it. Only a person with a Thread could access the D-boards. The flare wasn't for them, but for their friends.

Rayne smiled, trying to hide the tears in her eyes. "I'll be back before you know it."

Rayne, Briz, and Cha walked for three days before it rained. Even carrying packs filled with food supplies and bedrolls, they made good time. The steady weather helped. The days swathed them in dappled sunshine. The ground was soft underfoot, the air clear and singing with new life.

The Thread guided them to homes scattered in the hills when it came time for rest and replenishment. When they found a neighbor willing to take them in for the night, they spent a peaceful evening together. They hid nothing from the people they saw along their route. Strangers greeted them, recognizing Rayne from the Seers' pronouncement. If they felt pity or disdain about her lack of connection to the Thread, they didn't show it.

On the fourth day, dawn broke under a purple ripple of clouds. The three of them rose early, packed their sleeping things, and left before their hosts woke up.

They trekked up and down slopes that grew steeper as the morning wore on. By midday, a cool forest closed around them. Tangled vines dripped from the maples and oak trees. Rayne instinctively avoided them. Her mother's warnings about poison ivy echoed in her memory.

When a misty wetness materialized on Rayne's cheeks, it jolted her out of her daydream. She had been thinking about Vic, wondering if he was okay. Since losing her Thread, her thoughts had become as tangled as the vines. Questions lodged deep in her mind, spinning sticky webs.

Why does Vic believe finding Vennor's crystal code will get his Thread restored?

What happens if they get to the Pine Barrens and can't find anyone to help them?

Is he missing me right now?

She tipped her face to the sky and sucked in the raw dampness. Cha and Briz tapped their temples, probably checking the Thread's weather predictions again. A downpour would soak their bags and ruin their firestarters.

"We should find shelter," Cha said, breaking the silence.

"This way." Briz abruptly turned into the underbrush. "The Thread says there's a bridge up ahead, and we can get under there before the rain gets worse."

Rayne ducked into the thicket behind Briz, holding back a briar for Cha. "Thanks," Cha said, brushing her gloved hand along the bramble as she passed underneath.

A crow let out a jangled cry. Rayne straightened, her hand frozen halfway to her temple. Then she remembered. She couldn't log her wildlife sightings in her Thread anymore. Cas would be so disappointed. Her species archive would have a gap, made longer by each day she didn't have access to her Thread.

She ducked into the brush again, hurrying to keep up with Briz.

The crow cawed again, closer.

"She's laughing at us," Cha said, following Rayne through the prickly bush. "She wants to see if we'll make it to the bridge before we get rained on."

The crow answered with a low, throaty call.

Rayne stopped and craned her neck. Where was that bird?

"Hey, what are you doing?" Cha nearly ran into her. "I want to get out of this drizzle."

Rayne made her way clear of the thorns, scanning the tree branches above them, but couldn't see where the bird was. It sounded like she was directly above them. "I know. I want to stay dry, too. I just want to see that crow."

Out of the corner of her eye, black wings spread wide, an impossible span lifting into the sky. Before Rayne got a clear view, the crow disappeared into the clouds.

"Oh!" Cha saw it, too. "That was a big crow."

"Come on!" Briz waved to them from the top of the next ridge. "The bridge. It's over here."

Cha gave Rayne a gentle nudge on the shoulder. "You okay?"

We need you. The thought bubbled into Rayne's consciousness. The words blazed in her brain, bright and foreign. *We need you.*

We need you? What does that mean?

"Yeah, we're coming." Rayne forced her legs to move forward.

We need you. The words lodged in her chest. They felt warm there, comforting. Where did they come from?

The rain picked up, lacing Rayne's cheeks and making round sparkles on her mittens. What had she been thinking about, just before that phrase came into her mind? Vic, the weather, her mother's warning about the poison ivy. The crow.

Her mother. Kai. Fresh warmth shot through her core, and Rayne stifled a gasp.

Kai needed her. Rayne didn't know how, but she could swear the message came from Kai.

How could her mother say anything? In her unresponsive state, was Kai aware in some deep place? It could be possible that her mother sensed what was happening to Rayne, and somehow, though it gave Rayne pause, had sent a pulse of love.

Rayne let the tears come, hot under her lashes.

She stumbled up the rise where Briz had been standing a moment ago, eager to get under the bridge and away from the gathering wetness. But there was no one there. No bridge, no Briz or Cha, just more trees in every direction.

Turning, she called out. "Briz?"

Cha had been behind her just a moment ago. Hadn't she? "Cha? Where'd you go?"

No answer. Rayne clutched the straps of her backpack, turned one way, then the other. The underbrush clapped softly as the rain started.

Oh, crap. I'm lost in the woods in a cold rain without my Thread. It was almost funny.

A noise came from behind. A scuffling. Rayne spun toward the sound. Twigs snapped and leaves rustled. A large body moving over the ground. Rayne squinted at a sprawling green yew. One branch swayed.

Rayne bolted, her heart slamming. Her legs pumped over the rocks and dirt. Her backpack jostled heavily, breath coming in massive gulps. For a split second, Rayne saw herself free from the dead weight of the pack, springing forward with new speed. But before she could drop the bag, there it was.

The bridge.

It was a crumbling structure, half caved in. Moss grew in drifts along the timber sides. "Hey!" she shouted. "You in there?"

Without glancing behind, Rayne shuttled herself into the opening at one end. What had once been a graceful archway was a yawning cavity surrounded by boards blackened with decay. She leaped over a gap where several slats had fallen through, revealing a steep decline underneath. She landed off-balance, stumbled, and fell to her knees inside the old covered bridge.

"Rayne! Down here!" It was Briz.

Rayne whipped her head around, but the inside of the bridge was empty. Dark. She shifted onto her haunches. The slats creaked underneath her weight.

"Down here! Look down," Cha yelled. Rayne peered through the gaps in the floorboards. Then she saw them waving to her from below. Far below. How had they gotten down there?

"Go outside and around," Briz called. "Outside the bridge, there's a path. Take it down."

Cautiously, Rayne pushed herself to standing. Retraced her steps. When she stepped over the gap in the boards, she hesitated. Poked her head out of the entrance and looked left, then right. There was no one following her. What did she expect? Nothing lived in these woods. Not anymore.

The rain came down harder now, making a steady shushing sound in the trees. With relief, Rayne spotted the muddy path she had missed earlier. It branched away from the mouth of the bridge, dropped underneath the structure, and switch-backed down the hillside. Rayne took it as quickly as she could without slipping in the muck.

The path ended in a clearing directly underneath the bridge. The bridge itself, along with jagged outcroppings of rock along the hill, made a swath of protection from the wind and rain. It was relatively dry.

Cha squatted next to a pile of twigs, flicking sparks into a puff of tinder.

"There you are." Briz dropped an armload of sticks next to Cha. "I didn't know you were so far behind."

"I wasn't." Rayne shrugged out of her pack. "I was with Cha. Until I heard..." She glanced up the path where she had just come.

"You heard what?"

Rayne patted her thighs, smoothing the tops of her pant legs, which were completely soaked through. She shivered, dropping her bag to the ground.

"Nothing. I thought I heard something moving in the bushes. But it was nothing."

Cha glanced up. "What was moving? What did you see?" A look of alarm crossed her face.

"Let's get that fire started." Briz brushed bits of lichen from their arms. "We need to get warm and dry out."

Cha returned to her fire starting, giving a yelp when a lick of smoke and flame materialized.

Rayne blew the air out of her lungs, catching her breath. She walked with Briz away from the fire. "Tell me what's living out here. In these mountains. I want to know."

Briz cocked an eyebrow. "You going to help me get more firewood? I think we're going to set up here for the night." They turned to Rayne. "If something doesn't attack us first." They cackled.

Rayne gave Briz a little push. "Don't make fun of me. I had a moment, that's all."

Briz wasn't done. They jumped at Rayne, hands in the air. "BOO."

Rayne flinched. That set them off laughing again.

"Not fair. You know I don't have my Thread to flush my adrenaline. I'm jumpy, that's all."

"Fine, fine," Briz said, chuckling. "It's not fair. But it's still funny. Come on, there are some sticks over here."

Briz and Rayne stepped out into the rain and returned to the clearing with two more armfuls of damp wood.

Cha crouched next to a pyramid of sticks over the smoking tinder. "The Thread showed me how to do it. Dry out some of the kindling."

Rayne dragged her pack closer to the fire and sat on it. "We won't survive out here without your Threads." She removed her mittens and held them in front of the flames.

Briz sat down on the packed dirt next to her. "I was thinking the same thing." They reached into their bag and pulled out a gamescreen. "If we keep making good time, we're only a couple of days away from finding the train." They turned it over in their hands. "We need to be ready. To drive it."

Rayne twisted her wet mittens and held them closer to the fire. Her fingers tingled with returning warmth.

"I'll keep an eye on things here while you play." She glanced over at Cha, who poked at the fire with a stick. "Go ahead. You both should practice. I won't be any help. With the driving, I mean."

Cha tossed the stick into the fire and came to Rayne, giving her a half-hug. "You're doing great, you know, getting through this. Once we get your Thread back, you can play the train driving Game all you want."

Rayne snickered. "No way. I'm never playing that Game. It's for the two of you. You can have all the glory."

Briz smirked. "I'll never share my glory."

"I know," Rayne said. "Just as long as you actually learn how to drive that thing, and don't kill us."

Cha pulled her gamescreen out of her bag. "Ready?"

She and Briz lay down together, getting as comfortable as they could on the ground. Cha pulled her bag closer, and they put their heads on it, slipping the screens over their eyes. "Going in."

Rayne watched them submit to the Game, their bodies going limp. Her thoughts jumbled and fizzed. No matter how she tried to make sense of the day's events, nothing calmed her.

She picked up Cha's stick and stirred the fire. She did know one thing. No one was coming to help them. They were on their own. Freya's Path, her mother, even H. Lynn—the people who had guided them before—were silent, gone, occupied with their own troubles.

Her gaze remained on her friends' motionless forms until the fire's shadows had grown deep.

A RIDE_

Vennor

VENNOR GRASPED the railing and descended the last flight of
steps. The high-rise had a single functioning elevator, so after
the gathering on the upper floor, Magna's people opted to use
the stairs on their way down.

Her feet touched solid ground on the first floor and Vennor
let out a sigh. Gedeon put his hand on her lower back.

"Don't touch me." Her lower back issued a warning pang.
Soon, if she didn't stretch, the ache would shoot down her right
leg. It wouldn't stop for days. Without a Thread to moderate
the pain, her sciatica was an excruciating condition.

Gedeon increased his pressure on her back. "Come now,"
he said. "You don't mean that. We share blood."

She swatted him away. "I don't need your help."

Vennor straightened her coat and walked toward the exit. A
crowd of people—all rebels from the meeting upstairs, Vennor
assumed—milled around her, but she moved through them like
a ghost. They parted and let her pass. After the stunt that
Magna pulled, announcing that Vennor was going to join their

rebellion, they all knew her face, her personal story. And that she was a Seer of the Atlantic Ark.

"You do need my help, though." Gedeon's voice was smooth. "You need me to make introductions. Meet the right people. Help you get started with your work here."

"I already told you," she said. "I'm not helping you with this... situation."

"It's not really your choice." Gedeon's fingers tightened on her back. "You're part of us now. You don't get to refuse what is asked of you."

"I didn't choose to join *this*." She yanked her body away. "I'm not part of your rebellion. I won't help you hurt anyone."

"My sister." Gedeon bent close to her ear as they walked. "You don't want to upset Magna, do you?"

As far as Vennor was concerned, Magna was nothing but a power-hungry woman who used people for her own gain. Vennor didn't care about upsetting Magna, but she feared what Magna might do if Vennor refused to help.

Magna didn't have access to the deep intelligence and perspective that Vennor did. Being in the Legacy Settlements her whole life, Magna didn't understand the power of peace. How the Arks had been created to bring harmony to all living in them. How the NEWRRTH guided every person to their own perfect version of comfort and contentment. Nothing to strive for, no part of their existence left to chance.

Unlike the Settlers, who clawed and gripped their way through life, all in blind faith to an indifferent fate.

Magna didn't have the subtlety or the discipline to pull off an attack on the Arks. Vennor would make sure of that. She just needed to figure out how to distance herself from this rebellion first.

"I don't care if Magna is upset." She exited through the front of the tall building and took several steps onto the sidewalk, sucking in the cool air. The freshness made its way deep into her lungs, clearing the tension in her chest. Gedeon kept pace beside her.

"Oh, but you should care." He gripped her arm.

"Don't." Vennor wrenched away, but Gedeon grabbed her other shoulder, his hands digging into her muscles, drawing her close. He flicked his head once, his eyes trained just above her head.

She followed his gaze. A gray-clad man with a shaved head and a black beret stepped onto the sidewalk, closing the distance between them. The black strips of fabric over his ears and mouth made him look like an insect. He nodded to Gedeon. A hand came up, clutching a piece of cloth.

Vennor reared back. The man tossed the hood over Vennor's face. Everything went dark. A hand came over her mouth. The roughness of the fabric pressed into her cheeks. Vennor shook her head from side to side, a scream building in her throat.

Voices approached, surrounding her. Terror flared down her spine. Hands lifted her straight up. Her feet left the pavement. She kicked at the air once, twice. The men's hands—she heard only men's voices—ran over her body as they grappled for purchase, then propelled her quickly forward.

Something hard bumped into her knees. Metal? The men twisted her legs, pushed her down, and she cried out. They pried one leg away from her other one, and she straddled a cold, padded seat. An engine started, the seat humming underneath her. They shoved her forward, and just before she lost her balance, Vennor smashed into someone's back. They wrenched her hands away from her body and pulled them apart, then around the person in front of her. Wrapping her wrists, she realized they had secured her to this person in front of her who was about to—

Her head rocked back as the engine roared and rocketed forward. She instinctively tightened her grip on the person's torso to avoid falling off. Her wrists were bound and her body pressed against the driver's, her cheek resting on a broad back. She held her breath.

The scooter's engine revved like an enraged beast. The air trembled as they picked up speed. Wind whipped through her hood and made her eyes water.

The scooter tipped left as it took a turn. Then another turn. Revved straight ahead. Swerved again. Vennor lost all track of their direction. Sounds of talking and laughing came and went, as if they passed through throngs of people. Once or twice, there was a shout of anger as they came upon someone who wasn't expecting them.

The wheels skidded around sharp corners, spitting up water and gravel. The high-pitched shrieking of the engine dragged through the air, echoing off buildings on either side of them.

They were riding deeper into the city, she guessed. Toward the waterfront.

Vennor was a rag doll, her body bouncing and swaying on this machine. She flattened herself against the person in front of her, tightening her embrace as they hurtled to an unknown destination.

The scooter jerked over a hard lump. For a second, the wheels caught air. Vennor's stomach flipped, and she whimpered, her legs squeezing into the seat. They came down hard, skidding slightly. The sound of the scooter's echo became different. More hollow. Vennor took a breath to calm her roiling belly and listened.

Water. Yes, she definitely heard sloshing waves. The engine buzzed over something that wasn't a brick roadway. It was smoother, quieter, and angled them up. She squinted through the hood, but couldn't see a thing.

The driver slowed, and the scooter tipped down. As if they had just crested something like an archway.

A bridge.

The muscles clenched in Vennor's belly. She knew where they were heading. They were driving to Blackwater, the part of the city that had succumbed to the tides long ago. It lay in ruin, half submerged in brackish water.

As a child, Vennor explored the waterlogged buildings of Blackwater, but never enjoyed being among the submerged skeletons of the past. It was too sad, too creepy. And it reeked of rotting filth.

The scooter took a few more turns, then slowed. The engine dropped to a whisper, and the driver sat up straighter.

They stopped. Vennor let her breath out, unaware that she'd been holding it. Hands scrabbled at her wrists, untying them. When her arms were free, she slipped to her right, unable to balance. Her right foot brushed the ground and her knee buckled.

Arms reached around her before she crumpled.

"There," a voice said. "I got you."

Someone whipped the hood from her face and she squeezed her eye shut against the brightness.

Blinking, she let her eyes adjust to the light. Before her lay a cobbled courtyard, littered with debris. A hulking stone building surrounded them on three sides.

But it wasn't the building that caught her attention. It was the sickly smell of sea air mixed with putrid decay, and the sound of waves lapping against ancient stone walls, that told her what she had already suspected. They were in Blackwater.

"Here, this way."

The driver stepped away from the scooter and supported

her with an arm around the waist. Black strips of wool wrapped around his face, so Vennor couldn't tell if she'd seen this man before. His voice didn't sound familiar.

She tightened her lips, determined not to say anything as they hobbled along. Where was he taking her? After a few steps, Vennor regained her balance. The strength returned to her limbs. She pushed the man's arm away and stopped.

"Come on," he said. "We're going in." He tipped his chin toward the center of the building.

An imposing staircase spread before them in the courtyard, leading into the entrance between four marble pillars. Or what Vennor suspected were pillars underneath layers of twisting plant growth.

She hesitated too long, and the man clicked his tongue with impatience. Then he grabbed her elbow and forced her forward.

They stepped through the courtyard over pieces of broken glass and stone. Vennor tried to avoid twisting her ankles as the man propelled her toward the stairs. She didn't want to think about what was waiting for her inside. About what they were going to do to her to convince her to join their rebellion. She resolved to herself that no matter what they did to her in there, she would not cave in to their demands. They would never persuade her to turn against the NEWRRTH, or the Atlantic Ark.

They came up short against a concrete barrier. A single tree, gnarled and bare, curled over the structure. Only it wasn't a tree, Vennor saw as they drew closer.

It was a statue. The driver let her elbow go and placed both hands onto the base of the statue, over a deep green coat of moss.

She craned her neck, her jaw dropping open. Above the

base rose a life-size replica of a horse and rider. The figures were a mottled green, peeling in places, with vines twining around the horse's legs and neck and sprouting from beneath the rider's arms.

The scooter driver bent forward, palms against the crumbling concrete, and murmured. Vennor couldn't take her eyes off the rider, cast rigid in copper, who seemed to ripple with life. Even through the layers of grit and rust, Vennor recognized the rider's stance. The legs hanging straight down on either side of the metal horse, signifying stillness. His arms thrown wide. Head tilted back to the sky. A piece of the rider's jaw had fallen away, but his form was still magnificent.

The horse and rider stood forever at rest, making their invocation to the heavens and marking the entrance to the old exhibition hall. She knew this place.

The Fine, they used to call it. After the single word still legible etched on the stone above the columns. Her eyes flicked to the staircase, following it up to the entrance. Searching above for the words once visible there. But the brambles had grown over the markings, erasing them.

The driver finished his muttering and came toward her.

"You were saying it. The protection." Vennor broke her own promise not to speak. The shock of standing in front of the Fine again erased her earlier resolve. The words of the protection prayer, the crumbling concrete facade, the horse and rider statue—they were ghosts from another lifetime.

The driver cocked his head in acknowledgment. "Always do."

He nodded once before turning and taking the stairs to the entrance. Vennor followed, her head spinning. As she reached the bottom steps, Vennor couldn't shake the feeling that they were being watched.

She felt a stirring inside her, a flame of determination to fight for what was right. Glancing back, finding nothing, she quickened her steps to the exhibition hall with the driver.

Vennor

VENNOR PICKED her way up the crumbling steps. As she drew closer to the entrance, she noticed a waxy green line just above the front doors. Dried algae? It appeared at the same height all the way around the perimeter of the U-shaped building.

The tide line.

By the looks of it, the water had traveled up the staircase and flowed into the building itself, rising high enough to submerge the first floor. Vennor wondered how long ago that had happened. And if it still did.

The front doors were splintered and warped. With a glance at the driver, Vennor reached up to touch one. It squealed in protest, but after a hard push, hinged open. Vennor slipped inside.

The odor of brine and dust rushed up her nose. Vennor covered her mouth with the back of her wrist and pushed on. She entered a narrow chamber that faced a long, pockmarked wall. Turning, she checked for the driver. He wasn't behind her.

A noise up ahead. Vennor's head snapped around, her senses on fire, listening with every cell. Carefully, she moved forward. Edged past a sprawling desk, overturned and covered with dirt and shards of glass.

She wouldn't let Magna and her people frighten her. She knew what this place was, and why the Settlers brought her here. Such basic scare tactics didn't faze her. She'd seen too much in her lifetime, knew too well how people relied on threats and violence to get their way. True danger didn't lurk in the dark. It lay in the hearts of unenlightened souls. In people who used force to get their way without a care for the highest good of all.

Peering around the wall, Vennor walked through a short hallway that emptied into a vast room. She stopped, momentarily overcome by a wave of rotting sweetness. Eyes tearing, she squinted into the dimness.

The room's edges disappeared in shadow. Chunks of ceiling hung down precariously. Paint peeled off every surface and patches of corrosion colored everything in shades of brown and yellow. Broken pipes leaked into pools on the floor. Cobwebs hung everywhere.

"Show yourselves." Vennor's voice disappeared into the room's vast interior. "Let's get this over with."

No answer.

Taking a shaky breath, she started forward. Her shoes crunched on bits of glass and stone. She sloshed through puddles of water. She didn't see anyone, but heard a noise from the back of the hall. A scuffling sound.

"Over here." A voice sounded from her right. "Come this way."

Vennor's breath came faster. The air was heavy and damp, and she couldn't take a full breath.

She wasn't afraid of them. Not really. She had no reason to

be. She was a seasoned Seer with years of training. The Settlers' rebellion was no concern of hers. And being taken here, to the Fine, was an annoyance. Nothing more.

Quietly, she approached the center of the room, listening. A round pedestal rose from the floor, positioned beneath an arched opening. From a distance, it looked like a pile of rubble.

Vennor walked up to it, drawn by a desire to know what lay hidden among the debris. It was an imposing seated figure, cracked all over, carved out of pale stone. The figure wore a stiff headdress that covered its oddly narrow shoulders. Its hands rested on bent knees, the fingers broken off.

Egyptian statue of the Middle Kingdom, her memory supplied.

She'd seen it before. She reached out and touched a stone knee. It had shattered, but still held together by an unseen force, glowing with a patina of age. Ancient and revered, it had survived the years. Resilient. But not without lasting scars.

She glimpsed movement.

"Come out," she called. "It's obvious you're here."

There were a few streaks of light in the back of the hall. She followed them, stepping over broken ceiling tiles and jagged pieces of stone. She nearly tripped over a rusted metal beam but caught herself on the wall. Her hands left a smear of grimy fingerprints.

She rounded a corner and saw the stairs leading down. She steadied herself against the wall but pulled back when it turned squishy. The stench was of a putrid rot and she suppressed a gag.

Just before the darkness swallowed her whole, she reached the bottom of the steps and found herself in a large rectangular room. Light came from a row of windows high along the right side of the space. Pockets of plaster lined the walls of the room, all the way around, each with an empty pedestal in it. A pile of metal shelves lay in a heap, smashed against the wall.

Otherwise, the space was empty.

"Stop playing games with me." She turned, trying to catch movement again. Her voice echoed in the stillness.

"Games." It was Magna. Her voice came from everywhere, but no one place in particular. "Isn't that what you like to play? In the Arks, I mean."

Vennor prickled with irritation. She wouldn't take the bait and defend the purpose of the Games to this woman.

"I'm going." She turned toward the door.

"Not that easily, you're not." Magna's voice was closer. "You need something from us. I understand that. Before you agree to help our movement. You need to understand what our people are going to accomplish. And I'll give it to you. As a token of my appreciation for your talents. It's... well, it's what you've been searching for ever since you left us. All that *research* you've been doing. Trying to protect the world from violence. You're not that hard to figure out, after all."

Vennor froze. "I don't know what you're talking about."

"You're lying." The voice was soft. Approaching. "Your eyes tell me that much."

Vennor sensed movement again. A figure emerged from the shadows and stood in the middle of a puddle on the far side of the room. A woman with a black hood pulled over her head. Her eyes glowed.

"Magna." Vennor kept her voice calm, though her fingers twitched. "What do you want with me?" She clenched her fists, digging her nails into her palms.

"What do I want?" Magna tilted her head. "I'm going to tell you what *you* want." She opened her arms. "And what everyone here wants."

"Get to the point," Vennor said.

Magna tipped her head, hood slipping back, and let out a throaty chuckle. "Get to the point! Isn't that the most Atlantean thing to say? With all the technology you have in your bodies, pulling all that juice inside you, so that every answer is a nanosecond away from appearing in your over-networked brains." She clapped her hands together, bringing them into a prayer position under her chin. "That is just the most appropriate thing."

A lick of uncertainty twined through Vennor's chest. Why did Magna bring her here?

"And of course, we will." Magna's voice grew louder. "*Get to the point.*" She stalked closer. Her eyes were cold, her face hard. "Peace. That's what you want, isn't it? The everlasting comfort of peace. No more bloodshed. Anywhere. Ever again."

Vennor's mind worked. Of course she wanted peace. But peace didn't happen on its own. People needed guidance. That's what the Thread was for. That's why they played Games: to learn. Their ancestors, like the Settlers, didn't know how to harness the lessons of history. They made the same mistakes over and over again.

"You're thinking right now about the necessity of your precious NEWRRTH," Magna continued. She was so close Vennor saw each strand of her braid, the silver pieces glinting at the end. "How much you need it. How there's no other way for people to live together on this planet. That every other way has failed."

The dust coated Vennor's throat, making her cough. "That's not—"

"It is." Magna walked in a slow circle around Vennor. "But you're wrong. We don't have to rely on anyone else's intelligence to know what to believe. And that's what I'm about to show you."

A trickling sound came from deep within the building. It

was so faint Vennor wondered if it had always been there in the background.

"Here's what we're going to do." Magna's eyes sparkled, a smile spreading across her face. "You're going to discover something tonight. About yourself. And the real world."

Suddenly, a dark stain appeared on the floor. "What's that?"

Vennor took an involuntary step, reaching to steady herself on Magna's arm. But Vennor's hand passed straight through Magna's body.

Vennor's mouth hung open. "You're not here."

Magna's image flickered and sparked, then steadied. "Very good. I see you'll be a quick study."

"But how did you..."

"Learn how to do that?" Her smile turned into a smirk. "Technology has its place. And we make good use of it here. Just not inside our bodies. And not to crush our free will."

This was new. Settlers using tools they long shunned.

The trickle became a splashing. A deep groan came from the other side of the wall. Vennor retraced her path to the staircase in time to see the door at the top vibrating, as if struggling against an unseen force. With a tremendous squeal, it jerked forward and locked into place.

Black liquid rushed underneath the doorframe, splashing down the stairs, coming in from cracks along the walls, pooling at her feet. She backed up, searching for a step or a table, anything elevated, where she could escape the spreading wetness.

"I know what you think you're doing." Vennor's hands found the wall behind her. "You think I'm afraid of you? You think you can threaten me into joining your rebellion?"

"Threaten you?" Magna's virtual form followed Vennor to the wall. "We wouldn't do that. You're in a precarious position.

But things can change quickly if you want them to. All you need to do is ask."

Vennor tucked herself into one hollow that lined the walls. She wouldn't dignify Magna with a response. Her ankles blazed with cold as the liquid—water, Vennor supposed— lapped over her shoes. The air carried a damp, salty brine.

The pedestals. They were in every alcove. She inched along the wall until she put her hands on one. It was hip-height with a flattened top. Just wide enough, and heavy. It would hold her.

Clenching her teeth, Vennor hoisted a knee to the top of the pedestal. The stone did not shift. Placing her weight on her hands, she pushed herself off the floor and touched both knees to the stone. With effort, she shifted onto her feet. Balancing, she stood up.

As she straightened, Vennor had a new vantage point. Backed into a rounded alcove, she couldn't see much on either side. But with the added height of the pedestal, she had a good view of the windows lining the upper portion of one wall. Several had shattered, leaving gaping holes. To the outside.

The windows were far up, too high for her to reach, but Vennor had what she needed.

A way out.

Rayne

RAYNE'S DREAM pulled at her. It was one of those deep ones that felt more like a memory. She was speaking with her mother, whose long gray curls hung wispy over her shoulders. Kai leaned close to Rayne, her hands around a cup of hot tea. She spoke fast.

"Slow down," Rayne said in her dream. "I can't understand what you're saying."

Kai's words kept tumbling out of her, with no pause between them. "It's your Thread. Your Thread is in danger." Her rose thorn necklace lay flat against her neck.

Rayne shook her head, trying to understand. "What?"

Her mother continued to speak, faster and faster, her voice rising. "You need to hurry. You don't have time." Her mouth twisted into an expression Rayne knew well. Frustration.

"Ma, what's going on? Why are you so upset?"

Flecks of spittle flew from her lips. "It's your Thread. You have to open your eyes, find them. Find me!"

Rayne stood up, backed away from her mother. Her mother's form slipped into something else, her skin turning shiny and taut.

"You're not my mother." Rayne took a step away. "You're not Kai. Go away."

Kai's nose became flat and wide, her eyes turned into slits. Long, spiky fur covered her face. A long tail whipped around her like a bristle brush.

"Please, don't do this." Rayne's body crumpled. She turned to run, but her legs wouldn't move.

Her father appeared then, his eyes the same as her mother's. Feral. Wild. A snarl contorted his face. He sprang toward her.

Rayne fell away into the darkness.

Her eyes snapped open into the gray dawn. She sat up, heart hammering, and scanned the camp. Cha and Briz were asleep next to the smoldering fire.

She uncurled her fists. Placed a palm underneath her collarbone, and took a couple of deep breaths. The air carried the scent of wet pine and frozen soil.

Her dreams had gotten more vivid, more intense, since losing her Thread. She remembered most of them. They were usually weird. But not as scary as this one.

She pressed her eyes closed, trying to clear the image of Kai transforming into that thing. That *beast*. And her father too.

Pushing out of her blanket, Rayne edged away from the clearing and her sleeping friends. She clasped her long coat against the morning chill.

She needed to find a place to relieve herself. Then she'd get the fire going for their morning meal. The rain had stopped, so it would be good to make the most of their travel day.

The fog hung heavily over the forest, obscuring all but the nearest trees. A layer of ice draped over the tree branches, giving them a sparkling, delicate appearance. The forest was still, with only the soft crunch of her boots and the occasional drip of melting ice breaking the silence.

Rayne crouched near a tree. After she was done, she stood and stretched, the earthy scent of the forest filling her lungs. She turned and walked away from the tree, her hands stuffed into her coat pockets.

She was nearly back at camp when a noise to her right made her stop. A twig snapped. She turned slowly and looked over her shoulder. The fog swirled, but she saw nothing.

"Hello?" Her voice sounded too loud. She scanned the trees. They were close enough together to block the sun, but not close enough to form a canopy. A rutted path, one she hadn't noticed before, ran alongside a clump of trees. "Is anyone there?"

Something moved to her right, just out of her line of sight. Her breath caught. She turned back around. Someone was there.

She tried to sprint away, but her legs were hollow and shaking. The fog created a wall between her and whoever was standing there. She couldn't make out any details. A man, maybe? She couldn't tell. Her heart thudded.

Her dream came back in blocky fragments. Her parents' snarling faces. Fierce yellow eyes boring into hers. Fur standing on end.

A crashing through the underbrush. "Hey! Rayne!" It was Briz, zigzagging through the pines. Rayne's feet sprung into action, propelling her toward her friend.

Rayne nearly crashed into Briz, grabbed for their arm and kept on running, dragging Briz with her.

"Whoa, hey, are you okay?" Briz stumbled behind Rayne.

"Come on!" Rayne let go of Briz and flew toward the clearing. Rounded the corner to their camp under the bridge. Saw, with fresh eyes, the wall of rock behind their sleeping area.

They had slept in a cozy, dry spot under the bridge, but the rock penned them in. They were sitting targets for anything that wanted to trap them there.

Cha glanced up from her place by the fire. Her hair was disheveled and her eyes widened when she saw Rayne. "What happened?"

Rayne didn't answer. She raked her fingers through her hair, trying to focus, to calm down. Kai's dream-words rang in her ears: *Your Thread is in danger.* She remembered the feral look of her parents' faces. The beast loping toward her. She could feel its hot breath on her neck.

"Rayne!" Cha stood, her voice sharp. "What's going on?"

Rayne slumped against a tree. Tried to get her thoughts out. "I heard something behind me."

"What did you hear?" Briz jogged up behind her, breathing hard. "What happened?"

"We have to go. We're sitting ducks here." Rayne scrambled to her sleeping blanket and started shoving her things into her pack. "I heard something in the woods. Someone's watching us."

"What?" Cha's voice was shrill. "Why didn't you tell us?"

"I'm telling you now. Come on." Rayne threw the blanket off her sleeping bag and stuffed her belongings back into her pack. "There's someone out there. Or something. We need to go right now." Her hands shook as she worked her sleeping bag into its sack.

Briz moved to the fire pit, and thoughtfully shoved at the sooty, gray ashes. "The ridge is just up ahead. We can regroup up there, figure out what's going on."

Cha's mouth tightened. "If someone's here with us, aren't they going to follow?"

Briz shook their head, eyes on Cha. "We keep on going. Like we planned."

Rayne shook her head. It wasn't the smartest option to stay on their planned track. They'd be easily followed. Or was it better to get to the train as quickly as possible?

"The Thread'll help us." Cha touched her temple and spoke a few words of instruction. "Guide us along a route today that ensures no one can track us." She reached for her pack, just as Rayne finished stuffing hers. "See? All taken care of."

The sun appeared then, spreading a pale pink light over the forest. Rayne scanned the trees. She couldn't sense anyone out there.

"Okay. Let's go."

Briz picked up their bag, kicked a final spray of dirt over the fire, and stepped into the forest. Rayne and Cha followed, packs hoisted to their backs.

As they walked, Rayne flicked her eyes to the right and left, ready to flee if danger returned. But, as the sun rose higher, the only sounds were the drip of ice melting from the branches and the scuff of their boots over the hard ground.

They weren't followed. When they reached the ridge, Rayne stopped and looked back. Pockets of fog huddled around the trees, obscuring most of the forest they had just climbed out of.

"Let's keep going." Briz's voice was firm.

Rayne nodded. With another deep breath, she turned away and started walking. She didn't look back again.

THEY STOPPED for a midday meal among a collection of granite boulders. Cha unpacked a small spread of provisions. Rayne found a spot to sit on the lichen-covered rocks and took a long drink from her water bottle. She accepted a roll of lettuce, rice, and fig from Cha.

Her stomach rumbling, she devoured the roll in three large bites. Licked her fingers.

"Do we have any more of those? Or the bars we had yesterday?"

Cha pushed a bite of roll into her mouth. She held up a finger, *wait*. Leaned down, and rummaged in her pack.

Briz kept glancing at Cha. Chewing their rice, they looked at Rayne. "There's something we should talk about."

Cha looked up, her hand around a linen-wrapped bar. She handed it to Rayne, her cheeks coloring.

"Do you know what it was? What I saw back there?"

Cha blinked. "Oh. No."

With another glance at Cha, Briz spoke. "This is hard to say." They cleared their throat. "It's about the stability of your perception. We think you might be over-interpreting the sights and sounds around you, reaching for what isn't actually there."

Rayne stared at them for a moment. "What?" she finally said.

"Look, it's nothing bad," Cha said quickly, holding up her hands. "It's a common thing, apparently. Lots of people experience phantom sensations after a Thread gets terminated."

Rayne felt a wave of embarrassment wash over her and she looked away, not wanting to meet Cha or Briz's gaze. She knew they weren't saying this to be mean or patronizing. They were just being honest and looking out for her safety. But it still stung.

"You're saying I'm imagining things," Rayne said. "Making them up."

"No, definitely not," Cha said, reaching for Rayne's arm. Rayne shrank away.

"We know you're not doing it on purpose." Briz took another bite of their roll. "It's just a physiological thing. Well, maybe psychological. Your nervous system's relied on the

Thread for so long, you're re-learning how to interpret your own sensory input now. And there can be certain side effects when your Thread's suddenly dark. You've heard about—"

"All we're saying," Cha interrupted, "is that we're going to run some calming sequences with you, so you don't have to feel hyper-aware and anxious all the time."

"I'm not hyper-aware." Rayne's mouth twisted.

"Maybe hyper-aware isn't the right word," Cha said. "Just... accept our help here, okay?"

Great. They think I'm losing touch with reality.

Cha frowned, as if catching herself. "It's just some meditation stuff. And other things. We want to make sure we ground your thoughts in reality." She paused, searching for the right words. "And that your imagination isn't running wild."

Rayne tried to push her thoughts away with a deep breath. It made sense, in a strange way, what they were saying. She had noticed a change in how she perceived things ever since her Thread had been silenced. Colors seemed brighter, sounds sharper, emotions stronger—and it was both comforting and confusing at the same time.

She wondered if Vic was seeing and hearing things, too. She'd have to ask to call him later.

"But I heard something back by the bridge." Rayne dug her fingers into the rock underneath her. "I'm sure of it. I wouldn't imagine something like that."

Briz nodded once, chewing. Cha kept her gaze on her hands. Neither looked at Rayne.

"Wait. You think that wasn't real? What I heard? What I saw?"

I'm a liability. I'm going to hold us back and jeopardize this entire journey.

"There's a lot we don't know about being unconnected

after a lifetime of having a Thread." Cha kept her voice soft. "But we know hallucinations happen. They're likely, even."

"Hallucinations?" Rayne leapt to her feet, the bar in her hands tumbling to the ground. "That's what you think I'm having?"

"Hey, it's all right. We're not saying it's a deal-breaker, okay?" Cha put her food down and stood, moving toward Rayne. "We're still doing this. We need to get to the Pine Barrens. To investigate your appeal, and to understand what happened there. Our people and the people of the other Arks need to know what really happened there." She tilted her head, lips pursing. "And we need you to be sure about what you're seeing. Given the speed we'll be traveling."

"We need you calm and focused, is what she's saying." Briz joined them and squeezed Rayne's shoulder. "Cuz you're going to be our lookout. When we start driving that train."

Rayne

RAYNE'S PALMS were slick with sweat, her thoughts jumbling, as they packed up the food and started walking along the ridge.

She tried to focus on their surroundings, on the sounds of the wind and the uneven surface of the rock ledge beneath her feet. Her legs ached and her back hurt. Her mouth was dry, her lips cracked and sore. Her throat was scratchy, too.

But she was having trouble paying attention. Her thoughts kept drifting back to the sounds she'd heard the day before. She couldn't stop thinking about the crackle of leaves, twigs snapping, and the certainty of someone *being* there. Two golden eyes watching her.

Once, she saw a flash of movement down in the valley below. A figure running between two large rocks. She squinted, trying to get a better look, but couldn't tell what it was. If it had been a person or an animal, or nothing at all.

What if I can't trust what I see and hear? Where does that leave me? She ached to talk to Vic. Was he having the same symptoms? Was he just as confused as she was?

Cha and Briz had been attentive and kind, even when she'd snapped at them at one point when she'd wanted to stop for a rest. After that, they all stayed quiet.

The sun was low in the sky, the air still and cool. They'd been walking for hours, and they still hadn't reached the bottom of the ridge.

Suddenly, Briz stopped and pointed. "Look! Over there. I can see the water."

The blanket of granite they had been walking on stretched out in front of them, jagged and imposing. But a short distance away, the path sloped down, disappearing into a group of trees. Through their black trunks, Rayne glimpsed a silvery blue. The lake.

With their destination in sight, they picked up their stride. As they descended the ridge, Rayne saw choppy white waves all over the water.

The trail changed underfoot, becoming loamy and springy, as they left the ridge and entered the small glen of pines.

"See? Beautiful, right?" Briz said, smiling.

"It is kind of pretty," Rayne said. Her chest relaxed a little at the sight. It was beautiful. The warm pine scent filled her lungs, rich and sharp. She kept glancing at the lake. She'd never seen a large body of water in real life. As they moved through the trees, Rayne cycled through her memories about Games involving lakes or oceans. She had played a lot of Games where she had been on boats, visited waterfalls, swam in vast gentle seas. But those Games didn't compare to seeing the real thing.

They were so close now. Once they got to the train station, and got the train moving, it was just a few hours' ride to the Pine Barrens. What would they find once they arrived? And how much longer until she got her Thread back—if at all?

They wound through the trees, listening to the water

lapping over rocks and stones. The breeze picked up. The air became heavier and sweeter.

A row of squat buildings came into sight along the water's edge, their facades peeling and faded. One was collapsing into the lake. Some buildings bore the symbol of the train, a red circle around a white eagle, its wings spread wide.

"It's a little hard to get right down to the water," Cha said. "But we'll get pretty close. The train's over there." She pointed at a taller structure tucked behind the buildings along the shoreline. Rayne recognized it from the images they had gone through before leaving.

They followed Cha down a narrow path through the trees and out onto a patch of flat rock. "We'll stay here for the night, get dinner, and some rest. Tomorrow, we'll start preparing to—"

"I don't think so." Briz brushed past them, smirking. "We made it this far. Let's go see the train. Come on!"

Cha rolled her eyes. "You think they could be patient for once?" After a moment, she grabbed Rayne's hand, her eyes twinkling. "Okay, let's go see it at least."

They dodged through a string of boulders along the water's edge, then walked past the falling down buildings. Close up, they were in worse shape than they looked from afar. Black holes for windows, ripped siding, and debris all over the place. The emptiness and waste made Rayne's skin crawl.

The sun blazed low and orange as it set over the lake. Rayne shivered as a trail of cold air snaked down her neck. She drew her coat around her, concentrating on the soft splashing of the waves against the rocky shoreline.

The train station stood taller than Rayne remembered from their planning sessions. It wasn't at all like a warehouse at the Orchard, which Rayne had initially pictured. This was more than twice the size of any building she had ever seen. And it was ornate.

The sloping roof was made of overlapping hexagonal metal panels. A curved entryway dipped over stone blocks the same color as the granite they'd been walking on. All the way around, its walls were tagged and decorated with graffiti. A row of dirty windows above the entryway were sealed tight.

The front doors were open, though, and Briz was already inside. Rayne heard a whoop, then a laugh, then more whooping. Rayne and Cha passed through the stately archway side by side. Briz stood at the end of a raised concourse, eyes wide and arms outstretched.

The station was cavernous. The ceiling arched at least thirty feet overhead. In the middle of the ceiling, a massive, rounded skylight let in the sun's last light. A wide walkway spread before them, gleaming white, and painted with an outstretched eagle encircled in red.

Cha laughed. "Well, I guess we're ready to go."

Rayne's heart sped up a little, just at the sight of everything that lay before them. She had seen the interior of the station in the images the Thread generated, but it was still so much larger and more elegant than she'd imagined.

Three trains sat on their tracks like sentinels, their silver-blue exteriors gleaming in the dim light. Vehicles designed to transport people and goods across hundreds of miles. They were beautiful, sleek metal contraptions with low, sloping noses. Narrow cars disappeared into the shadows at the edge of the building where the tracks exited into the open air. The sides of the cars were made of matte black metal, but the tops were glass. Their sleek silver bodies appeared as if they could take flight at any moment.

The air held a faint scent of plastic and electricity. And something pungent, feral. It made Rayne's nose twitch.

"Do you see this? It's incredible." Briz jogged down the tiled walkway, their pack bouncing. The three trains were identical except for the emblems painted on their cars. Briz checked each train. Nodding, they approached the train parked in the middle. Liberty Express read the script on its side. Just like they had seen in their Game.

Stepping down onto the track, Briz drew close to the Liberty Express and ran their hands along its side. Rayne watched, feeling a little dazed.

"It's been here for years, untouched." Briz's voice echoed in the cavernous space. "It's like time stopped for this place."

"Look at these hulls," Cha said. She followed Briz to the train and placed a hand on its steeply sloped front. "This engineering is incredible. You know what it took to build this?" The two of them bent and murmured together, walking around the nose, conferring with their Threads.

Rayne took in the space. Her gaze followed the intricate markings on the walls, a pang of homesickness flaring. The same graffiti was inside the station, and it reminded her of the pit paintings inside their neighborhood's shelter. During the times they took refuge from violent winter storms, Rayne often walked the underground tunnels to find all kinds of colorful markings on the walls. It surprised her how similar the styles were.

But then something else caught her attention. Across the room, an odd shape appeared where the graffiti descended into shadow. The bright colors on the wall dimmed, then shifted. Rayne took a step forward, then several, tilting her head this way and that to puzzle it out. Yes, the shadows in the far reaches of the room were definitely moving.

She froze, unsure if she was really seeing movement or if it was just her imagination playing tricks on her. Was she hallucinating again? She wanted to call out to Cha and Briz, but she couldn't make any sound come out of her mouth.

"Shit!" Briz's voice carried across the room. "It's busted!"

Rayne's knees unfroze, and she bolted toward the platform. Briz and Cha stood on the other side of the train car.

"Hey," Rayne said. "Hey, I might have—"

"It's all banged up here." Briz walked along the other side of the car, disappearing from sight. "Completely busted up. Crap."

Cha cupped her hands around her eyes and flattened her nose against the train's windows. "Yuck," she said. "Do you see inside?"

"Shit!" Briz said again, banging their fist against the other side of the train. "This door might not be functional. Come here, let's see if we can get it open."

Rayne took the step down to the track and followed Cha around to the other side of the train. They paused at the sight of several large scratches along the train's side. The metal was dented in places, the hull scratched. Long, jagged scrapes slashed along the metal. Whatever happened had left the compartment door crumpled.

"What is this?" Cha dragged her hand along the deepest of the scratches. "What did this?"

"Hell if I know." Briz tapped their temple and asked their Thread to explain their options. While they listened, Cha snapped her head around.

"Did you hear that?" she asked.

Rayne held her breath, chills racing down her spine. She strained, but heard nothing.

Briz dropped their pack and unzipped it, cursing. "What kind of tool?" they asked their Thread. Their arm disappeared into the open bag, rooting around.

"Sh." Cha held her hand up.

Briz stilled, hand still in their bag. Their Thread went quiet.

A low growl floated through the air. It was so soft Rayne wasn't sure she heard it at all. The hairs on the back of her neck stood straight up.

Cha's hand shot out to grip Rayne's forearm. She put a finger over her lips, unnecessarily, in a shush gesture.

Briz pulled their hand out of their bag, holding something small and wrapped. Quickly, they closed the pack and slung it over their shoulder. The three of them backed away from the train, eyes searching the dim building.

"I'm not imagining that, am I?" Rayne whispered. "You heard it."

Cha's eyes were wide. She nodded, her fingers tight around Rayne's arm.

The growling came again, louder this time. Rayne couldn't tell what direction it was coming from. She glanced up, not knowing why. There was nothing but criss-crossing steel beams above them. A sliver of rising moon showed through the huge skylight. How many ways could they get out of this building? Her gaze went to the front entrance, to the doors they had used to get into this vast place.

There was an unsteady clicking sound, and thumping. Whimpering and whining. Dark shapes moved against the walls and got closer, then closer still. Four-legged animals, Rayne saw, dogs or wolves or something else; their eyes shone in the darkness. Suddenly, the air filled with a chorus of snarls.

Rayne could hardly breathe with fear as she stumbled backward, her gaze shifting between Briz and Cha for guidance. "It's the ferals," Briz whispered. "The half-wolf mongrels that roam the outskirts of the forests down here. I thought they'd be long gone."

"What—"

But Briz was already running full-speed ahead, their face a

mask of terror. Feet pounding against the tiled floor, they fled along the dark tunnel leading out of the station.

"Run!" Cha grabbed Rayne's arm and yanked her forward, both of them breaking into a sprint behind Briz. Rayne didn't dare look back at the predators that followed them out of the shadows.

SPEED_

Rayne

Rayne thought her heart would burst as she did her best to keep up with Briz and Cha alongside the tracks. She couldn't hear anything but her own ragged breathing. Rayne sensed the terror of Cha and Briz beside her, but they all kept running, never daring to look back.

A shape materialized at their side, veering toward their legs. A meaty snarl ripped from the creature's throat. It leapt. Rayne crashed to a halt, banging her body against the hull of the train, and threw her arms up over her head in an instinctive move to protect her skull. Beside her, Cha shouted and lost her balance, landing in a tangled heap beside the track.

The animal swerved around Rayne, jumped over Cha, and barreled forward. It went straight for Briz. Briz, long legs still pumping as they ran away down the track, clutched something in their right hand.

Another growl behind them sent a shot of adrenaline through Rayne's core. There were more animals coming. She pulled Cha to standing and took off with her again, trying to catch up with Briz. An animal let out a loud bark and snarled behind them. How many were there?

The train. They had to get inside the train.

Cha had the same idea. "Show us the doors," she told her Thread, breathlessly. "The ones that work. We need to get inside."

"Briz!" Rayne shouted. "Briz, the doors! We need to get inside!"

Briz gave no indication of hearing. They ran farther and farther away, heading for the end of the building that emptied its train tracks into the night air. Rayne's fear spiked. Briz needed to stay with them, get inside the train, so they could all leave together.

Galloping shadows trailed right behind Briz. Briz held their right hand high, almost as if they were protecting something inside it.

With a jerk, Briz pivoted to the right. An animal jumped, its body twisting, and snapped at Briz's hand. The creature missed. With a vicious snarl, it tumbled to the ground.

Cha slowed, putting her hand on her temple, listening.

Good, Rayne thought. *She's getting instructions from the Thread.* Without warning, Cha stopped short, then ducked. Yelling Rayne's name, she put a hand across Rayne's chest as if to tell her to slow down.

The weight of an animal crashed into Rayne's legs. She fell, clapping her hands and face on the rough pavement.

Wet sounds filled the air. Paws scrabbled at her calves. Rayne pushed herself to all fours, twisted her body around. A feral dog held the ends of her coat in its muzzle, twisting its snout back and forth, ears flattened, making gurgling growls. It was huge and muscular with matted fur. Glowing yellow eyes bore right into Rayne's skull.

Rayne tried to wrench the coat free. The animal, surprised, let go and snapped, throwing saliva on Rayne's cheeks.

Cha stepped forward and put her hand over Rayne in a protective gesture. "Back off," she said to the animal's face. Her voice cracked. The feral growled, hackles raised, but didn't move. Spittle dripped from its jowls.

Rayne froze, pushed up on her elbows, panic swirling through her body. A chorus of clicking and snarling began as other ferals appeared, trotting toward them and gathering behind the first. Rayne wanted to scream, to fight the animal on top of her, but Cha spoke again.

"Leave her." She said it firmly this time, her eyes locked onto the animal's. "Go away. *Go.*" She towered above it, her mouth a thin line, her hand still out in front of the animal's face.

The feral snarled, lowering its head.

Cha dipped her head a fraction while keeping her stance intact. "It wants. The food. In your pack." She spoke each word slowly, quietly. "I'm going to distract them. You'll leave your pack where it is. Then get up. And run with me."

Rayne barely had time to nod in acknowledgment before Cha brought her hands together and clapped once, loudly. A couple of ferals flicked their gaze in her direction. Cha clapped again, training her focus on the animal that pinned Rayne to the ground.

A scream, shrill and human, tore through the building. Rayne and Cha's heads snapped to the sound. The ferals scattered, their eyes darting in all directions. Rayne scrambled to her feet.

Without a word, she and Cha broke into a sprint toward the source of the scream. The feral dogs gave chase, snapping at their heels as they ran.

Briz. Briz was in trouble. Rayne's breath came in sharp

bursts as she flew down the concourse. A nameless, desperate plea pounded through her head as she ran toward her friend.

Oh please oh please oh please—

A crash echoed off the stone walls, followed by another high-pitched scream.

"Briz!" The words tore from Rayne's throat. "Where are you?"

"Over there!" Cha shouted. She leapt over the center of the concourse and a long row of dusty metal benches. Rayne followed, her long legs clearing the benches in one leap. They approached the far train, the one resting on the tracks on one side of the building. It wasn't their train, Rayne thought, but there was one thing that made it the most welcoming sight in the world.

A wide open compartment door on one side.

"Briz!" Cha ran straight across the platform, skidding once on the shiny tiles, but righting herself. Rayne followed, searching up and down the track until she located Briz, who stood flattened against the train, just a few cars down from the train's open door.

The animals swarmed past Cha and Rayne to join the ferals gathered around Briz. Ten or more animals focused on Briz's dark form, low growls and sharp whines cutting through the air. Briz leaned back into the train's side, holding their hand high. Rayne's head swam. What was Briz doing?

The animals had gathered around them with menacing hums and snaps. Without warning, Briz pushed off from the train into a lunge. At the same time, they tossed a piece of whatever they had taken from their pack toward the animals in front. They held their other hand out in what seemed like a gesture of peace or surrender.

Three or four ferals pounced on each other, yipping barks

interspersing with wild snarls. After a few tense moments, Briz dropped more in a different spot. The rest of the animals began grappling with each other.

"The food," Cha said. "Briz is giving them our food."

Briz looked up from the fighting, locked eyes with Cha, and nodded once.

Cha tensed. "Get ready," she whispered. "We're going inside."

"Into *that* train?" Rayne couldn't fathom how the three of them would get past the snarling pack of wild dogs to access the train's door. It was the wrong train, anyway.

With a flick of their wrist, Briz tossed the rest of the food across the platform, over the animals' heads. The ferals turned and dove after the package, scrabbling and yipping all around each other.

As soon as the animals went after their prize, Briz broke into a run toward the open door.

"Now!" Cha pulled Rayne into a sprint along the platform. The train compartment door was only a few yards away. Rayne spotted the dark interior of the car. She pushed herself faster, her heart pounding. The group of ferals closest to the doors finished their snack and raised their snouts in the air. They locked onto Briz running from them, and paws pattered into motion. One of them tripped and yelped. The rest gained speed.

With a leap, Briz made it to the door. They turned to grab the handle. A feral dog, its feet skidding on the tile, smashed into the interior of the train behind Briz, knocking them forward into the compartment.

Rayne came to an abrupt stop, ready to lunge into the car to help her friend, but Cha grabbed her arm, holding her back. "Just get inside!" she spat. "Get on the train!" She shoved

Rayne forward into the open compartment. Rayne scrambled over the threshold, nearly falling on her face.

She turned to help Briz, but Cha pushed her in farther, following in close behind. With effort, Cha yanked the door shut. The lock slid into place with a rasping clang.

Fierce thuds sounded outside as the animals threw themselves against the closed panel. They heard snarling and saw bits of fur flying in front of the compartment's window.

Cha backed away from the door. She felt her way along the darkened compartment. "I'm going to find the command panel. Stay here and help Briz."

Rayne spun around to face the back of the train, squinting into the dark. Briz lay sprawled on the floor in the corner, their eyes wide. A single feral crouched in the shadows. Briz raised their arms, ready to ward off the feral that had knocked her down. The animal had backed off, but crept forward now, its ears lowered and teeth bared. A sour smell came off it.

Rayne tensed. She took a step toward the corner where Briz lay. Slowly, she let her bag drop from her shoulders and grasped the straps in her hand. The feral ignored her. She took another step. The dog made an indistinct sound in its throat, but didn't take its eyes off Briz.

She was close enough now. As quickly as she could, Rayne unzipped her pack and reached in. Her hand closed around a piece of dried cranberry biscuit. She pulled it out.

The feral whipped its body around. Gritting her teeth, Rayne extended the biscuit to the animal. Her hand shook. The feral stared at her for a few seconds, then took a step toward her. Rayne held her breath, expecting it to lunge any second. After a few more steps, the feral lifted its nose and took a sniff. Rayne couldn't control her shaking hand any longer, and dropped the biscuit on the floor.

The dog's ribs showed prominently, its fur matted and

dirty. It darted forward and swallowed the biscuit, its eyes on Rayne.

Backing up and reaching again into her bag, Rayne got another piece of food ready. She held it out. The feral's eyes became slits, its mouth pulled back to reveal sharp, yellowed teeth. Rayne dropped the second biscuit, this time a little further away from Briz. The feral snatched it up.

Just as Rayne reached into her bag again, the feral gave a soft whine. Then it dropped its head and licked something near its chest.

Rayne's gaze followed. With a pang of surprise, Rayne noticed the animal's swollen belly. It was much larger than she would have expected for a half-starved creature. It looked uncomfortable. An injury?

No, a pregnancy.

Rayne's mouth twitched. The Principle of One floated through her mind. *We are One. We are One.* She thought of Cas and his stubborn determination to help anything furry and lost. A ribbon of tenderness wound its way through her chest.

Briz got to their feet, cradling one hand against their chest, and circled behind the animal. The dog half-turned to give Briz a low growl, but trained her focus on Rayne. The dog's eyes locked onto the third biscuit in Rayne's outstretched fingers.

"That's it," Rayne said. She kept her voice soft. "It's all right."

Rayne sensed Briz's glare. Out of the corner of her eye, she saw Briz raise their pack to their shoulders.

Just then, the lights in the compartment blinked on and brightness flooded the interior of the car. Rayne dropped the biscuit to the floor. The dog lunged. Briz swung their pack at the animal.

The pack whooshed over the dog's head. In a flash, the dog snatched the food from the floor and skittered into the corner.

"No!" Rayne raised her arm in front of Briz just as they started to swing their bag again, aiming for the animal's head. Rayne pushed them all the way back against the far wall of the compartment. Briz's face contorted in confusion, and they let go of their pack.

A zippering sound made them both look up. The air crackled. Rayne detached herself from Briz, who had fallen to the floor, wincing, with one hand pressed against their chest.

"Wait," Rayne said. "Just stop. There's no need to hurt her."

A grinding whine came from the bowels of the train. The dog dropped to a crouch, her eyes rolling in her head. The sound reverberated like an ache inside Rayne's bones. Her throat went dry and a metallic taste filled her mouth.

The noise crescendoed. It powered itself up, gaining energy and pitch until it became a wailing screech. Pressing her hands over her ears, Rayne searched in vain for the source of the racket.

When the train lurched forward, they lost their balance at once. The two humans and the dog tumbled over one another, bouncing and fumbling backward along the aisle. Rayne wasn't sure who yelped the loudest.

The dog was the first to recover. Like lightning, she righted on all fours and wriggled underneath a seat by the windows. Briz came to their knees, one hand flat on the floor. Their hair dangled by their cheeks, a dazed expression on their face.

Rayne pulled herself to standing using a metal pole bolted to the compartment's ceiling. Gripping the cool steel rod, she tried to find her balance as her body rocked in rhythm with the train. She was near a window. Glancing out, she saw the pack of ferals in the station bolting away, their tails disappearing into the murky gloom.

The station moved slowly by. The rows of metal benches,

the graffiti-filled walls, the steel beams in the ceiling. All of it gliding past like an old-time movie.

Rayne corrected herself. The station wasn't moving. It was the *train* moving out of the station.

Movement. Motion. The train.

They were on their way.

WATER_

Vennor

Vennor fought the urge to panic. She had to stay calm. Think.

The floor swirled with water, the high tide rushing in. She needed to get out of there at once. The upper windows were an option—but the more Vennor considered it, a poor one. She would have to wait until the water filled the room enough to carry her through the broken panes. Then all she could do was hope she didn't nick an artery on the way out. And where would she land once she pushed through? There would be terrible currents on the outside of the building as the tide spilled out. She could get swept away into an even more perilous situation, possibly into the open ocean. Vennor shivered at the thought of struggling in the dark, freezing brine until she drowned.

The water gurgled and sloshed as it rushed down the steps. Vennor surveyed her surroundings, looking for anything that could help her.

"You don't know what to do." Magna's voice was a menacing whisper. "This situation will not improve for you. It's going to take all you've got to save yourself."

Magna's aspect, a shadowy form against the wall, stood with her arms crossed. Her lower legs appeared to hover just above the murky waters. Vennor's gaze darted between the broken windows and the pedestal she stood on, trying to calculate her escape.

It was useless. Her thoughts went around in circles, coming back to the same bleak realization each time. She was trapped. She couldn't step down from the pedestal because the water rushed in with too much force. It would already reach her knees if she stood on the floor. Within seconds, it would knock her down, drag her under. There was no rope or ladder in sight. Nothing to grab onto.

"You're a prisoner. Have always been a prisoner." Magna spoke tenderly. "When are you going to see that?"

There had to be a way. Vennor vowed she would not perish here. She would not lose herself in the bowels of the Fine because of one woman's manic desire to control a future she didn't understand.

A wave lurched against Vennor's stone column, sending an icy splash over her ankles. She gasped at the cold. Another wave came right after. At this rate, the water would cover her feet in a matter of minutes. The brackish tide rose like a foaming beast, its surface dark and turbulent. The creaking and groaning of old woodwork echoed through the room. It sounded as if something ancient stirred behind the walls.

Magna stood tall, watching the waters rise toward Vennor's ankles. Her eyes were intense and calculating, her expression almost sad.

"You're letting panic and fear control you." Magna used the same gentle voice. But it sounded closer. "Believe me, I know how you think. But when you join us, you'll see that you can reach past the confines of the body and let faith guide you. Not fear."

Vennor scoffed. How dare this woman presume to know how Vennor felt? Fear did not motivate Vennor. Far from it. If she could connect to the NEWRRTH right now, she'd show Magna that its wisdom was blissfully free of human emotion. The NEWRRTH's logical calculations were based on hundreds of years of human history. Not desire. Not fear. Just facts.

With a surge of anger, Vennor realized Magna left her with no other option. She planted her feet on the pedestal and dug her heels into the stone. She didn't want a rogue wave knocking her off balance. When she felt steady enough, she closed her eyes and cleared her thoughts. It took some effort, but after a moment, she was ready.

She reached out with her mind, searching for the presence of the NEWRRTH. Its aura waited for her, a reassuring warmth like a safety blanket. Quickly, Vennor pulled at its edges, willing its intelligence to enter her body and light up her Thread.

Her hands curled into fists as she prepared herself. The NEWRRTH would calculate the most probable exit from the building, given her current position and the path of the rising waters. She pictured Magna's face lit up in shock, and then rage, as Vennor made her escape. Her Thread would tell her all she needed to know to distance herself from this place, the toxic leadership of this woman, and possibly even how to leave this entire Settlement behind.

The NEWRRTH was just there. She could sense its energy. Relief tingled as she drew the tendrils of the intelligence close.

There was a mighty pop. Vennor's eyes snapped open. She

spotted Magna's form, closer now, holding a white sphere in one hand. As Vennor watched, Magna raised a finger and pressed something on the object. The pop sounded again, then a series of sharp crackles, sending a froth of chills up Vennor's neck and across her scalp.

Centering herself on the stone once more, Vennor exhaled with pursed lips and tried again. Nothing would come between her and the NEWRRTH, the intelligence she spent her life cultivating and studying. She reached for it again, this time pressing her palms against her temples, reaching for the tickle in the back of her mind.

But something wasn't right. The fingers of the NEWRRTH broke apart and fell into darkness. Vennor strained, grasping for its welcoming warmth, summoning it to her Thread. But there was only a yawning emptiness.

This can't be happening.

Vennor tried once more, tamping down her panic. Her teeth ground together as she flailed and floundered in her mind. But it was no use. The NEWRRTH was completely gone. She couldn't sense a trace of it anywhere.

The chill of Magna's calculation settled into her bones. Magna had blocked the NEWRRTH, preventing it from reaching Vennor's Thread.

She was on her own now.

Magna held up her palm-sized device and waved it in the air. She made a forced-sounding laugh. "My little device here neutralizes the electromagnetic pulses coming from the NEWRRTH's nodes. Cuts off all contact with it. Useful for leveling the playing field, so to speak. Also effective in liberating an individual. Or an entire community. Bringing them into the gentle light of the Creator."

Vennor's mouth dropped open. The Pine Barrens Ark. Had

Magna's people used a device like this one to take down the NEWRRTH there, cutting off access to Threads? Sudden removal of one's Thread could trigger psychosis, a break with reality. To do it on a massive scale like that, across a whole Ark all at once, with no support or warning... it was unforgivable.

"You cut off the Pine Barrens' access to the NEWRRTH. You made all those people..." Vennor's voice cracked.

"I see I've surprised you yet again. Now, the people of Pine Barrens Ark didn't thank us. There was some discord. Our methods left something to be desired. That's why with the Atlantic Ark, we'd like to do it differently. With no surprises, no struggles. We have so much in common, don't you see? And I have so much to share with you, my friend."

Vennor bristled. Magna didn't understand half of what she was suggesting. There was no peaceful future without the NEWRRTH. People needed their Threads to guide them forward. And Vennor was not her friend.

"If not friends yet, we're on the same side. Let me help you." She stepped forward, cradling her device to her chest. "The NEWRRTH is dying. It's degrading. It isn't the same, and you know it. You've known it for a while now."

The pedestal under Vennor's feet shifted. Water sloshed over her feet. Her arms flew out to steady herself. Glancing down, she saw the water had covered the entire stone base she balanced on. The water would cover her ankles soon, then her knees. From there, Vennor would either fall into the murky swill and drown, or her heart would stop from the cold.

"You've been too distracted to see the whole truth," Magna continued. "Let me ask you this: the anomaly that penetrated your Games. You never fully resolved it, did you? Who was behind that? Freya's Path? Or someone else? You don't know. That caused a world of damage to your precious Games.

Damage that is being tended to by your fellow Seers, and may never be fully repaired."

Vennor swallowed. Her feet had gone numb. She would not engage with this woman, no matter how desperately she wanted to leave this place.

"And the group called Freya's Path. They infiltrated the NEWRRTH right under your nose. Their existence was yet another rude awakening for you."

Vennor had made mistakes in her life, and this one stung. Trueno tried to warn her about the existence of Freya's Path, and she hadn't listened. She took a shaky breath. Trueno had loved her the best, like no one else ever had. And because of her, he was dead. A hot tear escaped down her cheek.

"That one struck a nerve, I see." Magna gazed at Vennor, calculating.

Vennor was silent. She wouldn't show weakness in front of Magna. She focused instead on the tragedy of the Pine Barrens, the people whose safety and sanity ended when Magna ignited her device.

"The NEWRRTH is disintegrating, and you're too preoccupied to notice," Magna said. "Did you even realize how it corrupted you? It gave you the *data* you needed to go against your own Principle of One. You, of all people! You, who studied the corruption of power across all of human history with the help of the NEWRRTH's intelligence. You who claimed to be devoted to the eradication of violence." Magna's voice got louder. "It was *you* who manipulated the NEWRRTH's code to get your own way. To *kill* in the name of the NEWRRTH!"

But Vennor could hardly hear over the rush of water and the pounding of the blood in her ears. Seawater climbed up her calves, engulfing her knees in liquid ice. She shifted from side to side, her legs singing with the cold.

"I'm offering you a different path. Faith. Freedom. True freedom—where you make choices from love, from life, from a free and faithful heart." Magna touched her breast, where her heart was. "A life that's not calculated by a deteriorating and indifferent intelligence. That's no way to live. It's a prison of your own making. We are choosing differently. We choose freedom. Freedom and faith in our fate."

The stone under Vennor wobbled. Then it broke with gravity as the tide lifted it from its base. Vennor lost her balance and pinwheeled.

"Gods! I'm going to—" Vennor fell. The water surged and drew her downward.

She struggled to touch the bottom so she could keep her face out of the water. But the tide buffeted her body and spun her in circles. Her dark hair ballooned around her eyes. The coldness engulfed her in a quilt of needles.

She kicked and fought against the swirling black. Her head dipped beneath the waves. The brine coated her throat with a sickening salty film. Terror clawed at her, along with a fierce fury at Magna for putting her in this position, for forcing her to defend her beliefs and make choices she would rather not make.

With all the strength she could muster, Vennor thrashed and rose to the surface. She swiped at her mouth to clear the hair from it, and gasped for air. Her breath came in ragged bursts. She needed to get out of this damned water before it claimed her. Her hand caught the stone pillar again, and she held on for dear life. She fumbled for a way to climb back on.

"You're reaching for a solution that doesn't exist," Magna said. Her eyes were flames in the dark. "You're finished, Vennor. The vision you had for the future is gone. The grand experiment of the Arks is done. All you have to do is join me. Join us. We're changing the world in ways you haven't even imagined yet. We don't need the NEWRRTH. We can make the future all we want it to be. *Free.*"

With that, Magna's virtual form winked out, and the room plunged into darkness.

TIDE_

Vennor

VENNOR COULDN'T SEE A THING. There was only the swirling cold, pulling her consciousness down and down. Was she still clinging to the stone pillar? It was impossible to tell. She had lost all feeling in her arms and legs.

With a shred of hope, Vennor reached for the NEWR-RTH. She knew it was there, right behind the veil that Magna's device generated. *Please*, she thought. *Tell me how to get out of here.*

There was nothing. Not even a whisper of energy. Only a void of space where the blazing intelligence should have been. Only this tomb of ice, echoing with Magna's wild declarations of faith and freedom.

But—

A tug. Then a shift in the back of her skull.

It was faint, but it was there.

A spike of adrenaline shot through her jaw and down her spine. Something was speaking to her. Trying to get through.

She must have found a way around Magna's blocking

device. With a rasp, the intelligence clicked into her Thread. It gathered itself into a wave. Crashed through her brain and traveled all the way through to her fingertips.

She was doing it. She was connecting into the NEWRRTH, even though she knew that wasn't possible.

But I'm not connecting to the NEWRRTH, Vennor reminded herself. *I can't be. Its electromagnetic fields are blocked.*

She brought a palm to her temple, sluggish with cold. Something slimy covered her hand, made webbing between her fingers. Was it her own hair?

A splash of seawater lurched over her chest, her toes just brushing the floor. Her head whipped around to get her bearings. It was too dark to make anything out in the room, except for a glimmer of starlight coming from the windows near the ceiling. The broken panes had drifted closer now. Or rather, she had gotten nearer as the water rose. But they were still out of reach.

As her eyes cleared, she saw what had entangled her hands. It was all around her in the churning water.

Torn up sheets of golden-green seaweed floated by her face, wound around her neck, draped over her shoulders. The seaweed was everywhere, brushing and sticking to her body. She probably had pieces of it winding through her thick black hair.

Another shot of energy entered through the back of her neck, traveling all the way down her spine. Her back arched. Despite the stars shooting through her vision, a wild joy gathered beneath her ribs. Before the next wave covered her face, she let out a whoop of glee. Balling her free hand, she clasped the living sea lettuce and pulled it close.

The other Thread. The network she had touched in that Game-cave, just before all of her plans came apart. It was Kai from the Orchard who started that new Thread by activating the living network of plants. The Seers didn't have time to replicate it, but they had collected its data. Was this new Thread an offshoot of the NEWRRTH, or was it something else entirely?

Wherever it originated, it came to her now through the sea lettuce draped over her neck and elbows. It bound her with something below the rising tide, something that seemed to reach out from the depths and embrace her. She could sense its living presence giving her strength through the numbing cold.

She had won. She had found this Thread, summoned it to her, and felt its comforting embrace. It would guide her to safety now, just as the NEWRRTH always did.

A strange rumble vibrated in her skull. Confused, Vennor gave one last kick to what she guessed was the surface. Was this new Earth Thread expanding into the building? Reaching into its walls? She remembered a similar sound when Kai, the woman who had first connected to the Earth Thread, activated it in the Game-cave.

Kai had held the Earth Thread stable for some time. She even created a shield with it, a transparent cloak that protected Freya's Path and the Seed inside a cave. Preventing the Seers from entering and making their activation to upgrade the NEWRRTH.

A flame came to life in Vennor's chest at the memory of Freya's Path. They had stopped her plan from unfolding. They made her fail. Her failure had cost Trueno his life.

The rumble became a whirring. Vennor's connection to the Earth Thread wobbled. She dug her fingers into the seaweed and directed her thoughts away from Freya's Path. She focused on the living green things all around her. The network that connected all the plants on Earth, and flowed through her nervous system to light up her Thread.

The sound engulfed her. It became a pulsing throb, rattling her teeth.

Not inside of her body. *Outside* of it.

The water surged, and she raised her head out of the icy water. Took a gasp of air.

A wave slapped her in the face. Bright lights beat down on the churning water, flashing through the windows.

The room lit up and illuminated everything around her.

A metallic creature appeared outside the building, descending until it hovered just outside the bank of windows. Light streamed from its body, cutting through the night. Its twirling blades turned with a hypnotic rhythm, like a giant metal bird, sending gusts of wind ricocheting over the water.

The panes shook in their frames.

In her studies of war, Vennor had seen many airbirds like this one. But what was it doing here?

The giant metal machine shot its light beams through the night air until one landed on her face like a lick of fire. She turned away, wanting to cover her eyes, but the light stayed on her like a net.

She caught movement out of the bird, something unraveling and dropping out of sight. Then more movement. Something—a shadow—crawled down from the machine. Dangled on equipment hanging out of one side.

Vennor thrashed in the water. The seaweed clung to her like wet wool. Noise and light pulsed and the reedy presence of the Earth Thread faded. Vennor tried to hold onto it, but after another moment, she couldn't sense it at all. Her connection had faded.

It had been brief, but real. She was sure of that.

"Here!" The voice came out of nowhere, startling her. "Here!"

She looked up. A black-clad figure hovered above her head.

With one arm, the person held onto a flexible ladder that went all the way through the windows and up into the machine. The other arm reached out.

"Grab on!" the person shouted, shaking a hand at Vennor.

She lifted her own arm in response, but a crush of seawater rushed over her face. The wave lifted her and she let go, tumbling, losing all sense of direction. Cold liquid rushed into her nose and throat. It stung. Flailing, she pushed herself forward. Or was it upward? She opened her eyes as wide as she could, searching for the surface.

There was the powerful light from the airbird, rippling distantly through the seawater. She struggled toward it.

A sudden pressure gripped her upper chest and squeezed hard. Her body lurched backward at alarming speed. The water tunneled around her face. Her lungs burned, the flesh under her arms contracted, and her vision went dark. She would pass out if she didn't get out of these hellish currents.

Then she was free. The cold air exploded around her as she broke through the surface of the water. She took a long, juddering breath. Her throat and nose were clogged with fluid. She coughed.

When the spasm passed, the thumping chug of an engine burrowed into her ears and jaw, rattling her teeth. Water streamed from her face and hair. She pushed the water from her eyes and saw a brilliant spotlight shifting over the scene below.

She started coughing again, this time noting the wide strap around her chest, digging under her arms. And beside her, hanging suspended in the night air, was that figure. The one who had dipped near her on that rope ladder. They both dangled high above the churning water, spinning at the end of a tether. She nearly vomited.

The person yelled something at her, but Vennor was past the point of comprehending.

Up, it sounded like. *We're going up.*

A violent shiver racked Vennor's body. The air buffeted her sodden body as water continued to stream off her legs. Her legs that were suspended far, far off the ground.

But there was no ground. There was only the tide sloshing against the walls of that room. The room that had been in the Fine. The room she was now quickly exiting.

They slid through the windows. The person navigated their bodies through an opening that miraculously contained no jagged edges, no broken glass. Vennor barely had time to be thankful. As soon as they cleared the opening, the person pushed them away from the building with a little jump. The restraints holding them in place loosened for a fraction of a second. Then the strap around Vennor's chest caught up with gravity and yanked tight. The air whooshed out of her lungs. They fell fast, away from the edge of the building. Down, down. Toward a horrible mess of water and stones and buildings below.

They jerked upward again. Vennor lost her breath once more. They were soaring.

The airbird appeared directly overhead. Its underbelly quivered, and its mechanical wings thrummed in a rhythmic roar. A spotlight winked on and skimmed over their faces.

"You're safe now." A booming voice fell over them from the hovering machine. "Just let our people bring you in."

Vennor had no choice but to comply. What did they expect her to do?

The airbird's tethers descended around them. She waited, she and the person who had rescued her, as two men climbed down the tethers toward them. They were dressed in black clothes, stiff and dry.

The two men each clasped one of Vennor's arms. Someone yanked the strap off her chest. One of them screamed something at her—the words were lost in the wind roaring all around them. She closed her eyes as they pulled her up, up, and over the edge of the craft. The wind and the noise sucked her in.

She was inside.

BITE ME_

Rayne

"LET ME SEE THAT." Cha reached for Briz's arm.

Briz stepped back, pulling it tight against their chest.

"Leave it alone," they said. "It's nothing."

Rayne sat next to Briz in a row of seats behind the driver. She glanced back a few rows at the closed door separating the train cars. The pregnant feral was visible through the translucent plexiglass divider. After rushing into the front compartment with Briz, Rayne slid the dividing door tight, sealing the Designers in the control area.

The animal hadn't budged from her hiding place under the seats. It trembled, too terrified to move.

"What were you thinking, taking your food out for them? You're cracked." Cha pushed herself out of the driver's seat. "It doesn't look like nothing. Let me see that arm, or I swear I'll stop this train right now."

Rayne turned to check out the command panel of the train. The control board arched underneath a long window, the sloping nose of the train. The controls on the board were sparse and primitive. There were three small screens, four red buttons, and a handful of dials and switches. A key dangled out of one lock. It was all illuminated by an eerie blue glow that flickered along the edges of the panel.

Her gaze fell onto an ancient-looking switch near the bottom of the chair that had a shiny red handle sticking out of it. Almost like an invitation to pull it.

"Don't touch it. It hurts."

"Just show me," Cha said.

Reluctantly, Briz lowered their hand. A jagged rip of skin revealed itself on their forearm. Several bite marks pooled with blood, spilling down toward Briz's elbow.

Cha sucked in air over her teeth. "I hope you have a pain sequence running. This is bad. We gotta clean this and bandage it up right away. Come here." She led Briz to the back of the car.

Rayne stood at the controls, brushing her hand over the raised buttons. Was it safe to leave this all unattended while the train rocketed forward?

With instructions from her Thread, Cha searched the side of the car for first aid supplies. She muttered to herself, tapping along the walls and kneeling to search under seats. Kneeling in front of a small cabinet, Cha popped its door open. Clearing a stack of cobwebs, she made a soft noise of triumph and pulled out a white box.

Rayne watched as Cha began laying out supplies to treat Briz's wound: antiseptic wipes, cream, gauze pads. Cha's Thread continued to guide her, providing step-by-step instructions on how to care for the bite properly. Rayne felt a wave of admiration wash over her as she watched Cha work.

The train's hum pitched higher as it picked up speed.

Rayne placed a knee on the driver's chair, leaning so she could see out the large window at the front of the car.

Outside, all was in darkness. But a whine like two chimes out of tune with one another started singing.

"Hey, you all done with Briz?" Rayne asked. "I think we need to focus here."

"Shit." Cha threw something against the wall as she dug through the box. "No antibiotics in this kit. I can't leave this without something to fight infection. This is going to be a nasty one."

Briz kept their face averted.

"Damned ferals." They yanked their arm away, bandage dangling. "I got this. Thanks, Cha."

Cha got to her feet and returned to the controls.

"I sent a brief to Mo and Rook," Cha said. "Told them we're on a different train. They're powering up a new algorithm. We need the track cleaners going. That's their priority." Cha's hand flew over the buttons, making adjustments.

Rayne squinted through the windshield into the darkness. "So we're traveling blind right now? No way to know if the track's been—"

A whooshing thump cut her off.

Rayne crouched. "What was that?"

The train was going fast now, the darkness a blur outside the windows.

Whomp. Rayne squeezed her fists over her ears.

"It's the perimeter tunnels." With a wave of their arm, Briz pointed at the giant sealed windows. "We're moving through tunnels outside the station, powered by a series of electromagnetic fields. It's how we're creating propulsion. You know, moving forward on the tracks."

Rayne straightened. "Oh. You told me that before, I just..."

"It's okay." Cha made a few adjustments on one screen. "Briz, get that bandage on and rest. I'm on first shift tonight."

After the next whooshing thud, the train entered a tunnel

filled with light. Rayne stood and pressed her hand to the window. The laminated pane of glass was cold and smooth. With her other hand, she reached for her temple. She wanted to connect to the train's speed and data fields from her Thread.

But there was only a deep, ringing silence inside her brain.

"Incoming." Briz accepted the call. A holographic projection of Mo appeared, his body shimmering with the train's motion.

"I got the track cleaners going," Mo said. "And we're mapping that alternative route. What the hell happened?"

Cha tilted her head toward Mo's image. "Ferals at the station. There was a whole colony in there and we must have walked into the middle of it. We had to jump onto a different train. Heading"—she consulted the screen in front of her—"south-southeast at approximately one hundred and fifteen miles per hour, and speeding up to peak velocity within three minutes."

Rook stepped into virtual form beside Mo. He wiped a hand over his face, like he was just waking up.

The two Game Designers exchanged glances, then Mo spoke. "The Thread told us this could happen. We didn't think it would, though."

"No time to chat," Briz slid their bandaged arm from view.

Mo nodded, his fingers already working on the blue lines in his wrist. "We've got the data feeds from the train's motion sensors. You'll have to link those up manually on your end. No problem on the new route, it's linking now. You won't get to peak velocity. We're keeping you at a lower speed to make sure the tracks are clear. Oh, there's a big river... lucky. You get to go over a big ol' bridge."

"Tapping into the network of tracks leading away from this station," Rook added, making his Thread visible. "We can use that to determine where the cleaners are and how many are available to—"

"Just get them going, yeah?" Briz said. "We don't want any unfortunate accidents. Just a clean set of tracks and a route that gets us as close as possible to the Barrens."

"Mo?" Rayne stepped forward. "Where's Vic?"

Mo's mouth opened and closed, and his eyes darted to Rook.

Rook raised his palms in a gesture of surrender. "Vic's not here. He told us there was something coming, a lockdown maybe, and he went back. Back to the Center."

Rayne's mouth dropped open. "The Center? Why would he go back there?"

The answer came right away—*to collaborate with Ana on the crystal code*—and heat rose from the soles of her feet to the top of her head. The jealousy was like a fire in her chest, radiating outward to flush her cheeks.

"He didn't go into details with us," Rook said. "But I'm sure he had a good reason."

"Don't," Rayne said. "Don't tell me what he's thinking. I can make a pretty good guess what he's doing there."

Mo's face scrunched up in a grimace. "We tried, Rayne. We tried to tell him it wasn't a good idea. He didn't listen. Kept going on about the crystal code, a way to get back at them, he just went on and on..."

Rayne softened. "It's not your fault, Mo. I know you tried."

Briz clamped a hand on Rayne's shoulder. "Thanks, Mo. Rook. We're going to let you two get on those calculations. Let us know when you have them. I'm making that link into our navigation system here."

The fire drained out of Rayne, leaving her with a lump in her throat.

Mo blinked a few times. "There's something else." His face did that scrunching thing again.

"Spill it." Briz was already pulling up their Thread to work with the train's navigation network.

"They're moving your ma," Mo said. "Out of the holding center."

Anxiety pelleted through Rayne's gut. "What do you mean? Where are they taking her?"

"She's going to the Haven," Mo continued. "But they're so full up at the Haven, they're opening warming tents behind the building to hold the bodies—I mean the *people*—with the rig."

Rayne didn't know what to say to this. Her thoughts tumbled. Were the charges against Kai being dropped? Had someone intervened to get her released? Who?

"You think you could have saved the personal news for later?" Briz said. "Like after we've gotten the tracks cleared?"

"I thought she needed to know." Mo shrugged.

"Thank you," Rayne said, her voice tight. "I do. I didn't think she had the rig. Healor Lynn told me it wasn't that."

"Look, I don't know." Mo's gaze went to the ceiling, recalling something. "A Peace Officer tried calling here yesterday. I intercepted the incoming. I thought it was related to... you know, your..." Mo pointed to his temple, where his Thread was. "But the call came from the holding center. You know someone there?"

Officer Claus. What would he have wanted to talk to her about on the day her mother was being transferred? He probably had information to share.

"Yes," Rayne said. "There was an Officer there. He and I were friendly, I guess. He talked to me sometimes about my mother."

"Want me to see what he wanted to say to you?"

Rayne was about to say yes, but Briz spoke first. "Get on

the track clearing. We need that now. Then you can call whoever you want."

"On it." Mo ended the call.

Cha shifted her gaze from her controls to Rayne. "You okay?"

Rayne cleared her throat. "Yeah."

"We'll get it all sorted out." Briz gave her a pat on the back. "We'll get your Thread back. Vic's, too. Just stay focused."

Rayne nodded and took a clearing breath. "You said I was the lookout."

"Yeah, you are." Briz worked their way into a seat, gingerly placing their bandaged arm on the back of the seat in front. "We need you to be a backup to the track cleaners. Scan ahead for loose debris, animals, anything blocking the tracks. But it's dark now, so get some rest."

"Both of you, get some sleep now," Cha called from the front. "I can drive for a few hours."

Briz gave an enormous yawn and glanced at Rayne. "You sure you're okay?"

Rayne didn't answer. Holding onto the metal poles for balance, she staggered to a row of seats diagonally across from Briz.

Settling in, she nodded. "I'll be okay. Let's just get to the Pine Barrens."

Rayne lay down across three seats, propping her long legs underneath her, and folded her arms behind her head. She stayed like that for a long time, gazing out the top of a window, her eyes scanning the darkness for any signs of life.

INFECTED_

Rayne

RAYNE WOKE with a start and realized she had been dozing. The morning sun slanted through the dirty window, warming her face with light. Her eyes fluttered shut for a moment and she took a deep breath as her body rocked in time with the train's motion.

The news of last night floated up through her mind and landed with a thud in her belly: her mother had been moved to one of the Haven's plague centers. And Vic had gone off to be with Ana.

Rayne stared at the train's ceiling, upholstered in a soft fabric of blues and grays. She took another breath, inhaling the scent of ozone and metal, with the faintest whiff of her own unwashed body. Reaching her arms over her head, she stretched, and in one motion, turned to her side and dropped her feet to the floor.

Pushing herself to standing, she saw Cha in the aisle a few rows back. Cha knelt next to Briz's feet, which dangled off the edge of the seats. The contents of the first aid kit lay scattered over the floor. "Briz. Briz, can you hear me?"

"What's going on?" Rayne staggered over, bracing herself on the seats for balance.

Cha felt around on the floor without taking her eyes off Briz. Her right hand rested on Briz's wrist, covering Briz's pulsing blue Thread.

"Can't believe there wouldn't be any," Cha half-whispered to herself. "There must be something in here..."

"What's wrong?"

Cha glanced up. Her eyes were bloodshot and purpled underneath. "You're awake," she said. "Here, help me."

Rayne leaned over and held Briz's bandaged arm. "What happened?"

Cha rooted through the pile of supplies, tossing large bandages over the seats, searching. "I can't believe there aren't any antibiotics in here. Just... none."

Once Rayne's fingers closed around Briz's wrist, she understood. A glance at Briz's face confirmed it. Fever. Briz's skin was papery and hot, with sweat beading on their upper lip. They tossed their head where it rested on the seat and made a moaning sound.

"It's okay, Briz. Just stay still." Rayne noticed the skin around Briz's bandage had turned a bright, angry red. It looked painful and swollen. "This quick?"

A brisk nod was Cha's only acknowledgment.

"What can I do?" Rayne tried again. "Maybe I should—"

Rising, Cha steadied herself against a seat and put a palm over her face. "We have nothing. There's nothing you can do except—"

Her gaze fell onto the empty seat at the front of the train. She glanced back at Rayne, calculating.

"Fluids. I'm going to get Briz started on fluids," Cha said.

She sank to her knees and started digging through the piles again.

Rayne took a deep breath and brushed a damp tendril of hair away from Briz's forehead. "Don't worry," she murmured. "We'll figure something out. You just need to rest now."

Briz managed a tired smile and let their eyes drift closed.

Rayne released Briz's arm, laying it gently across their chest. "You want me to drive?"

"You don't have to do anything. The train's in autonav." Cha rooted through the pile of supplies, lining up bags of clear liquid along the floor. "Just keep an eye out for debris on the track."

I'm the lookout. Because I can't connect to any of the data feeds. I can't navigate. I can't use my Thread to treat Briz. I can't do anything useful except sit in the front and stare out the window.

Rayne's feet were heavy as she made her way to the front of the train. She lowered herself into the driver's seat and settled in, taking in the array of controls. Her heart sped a little as she looked at the buttons and levers. She had never operated anything without her Thread helping her, and it scared her a bit.

"Did Mo get those autocleaners going? On our section of the track?" Rayne asked.

"He did," Cha called back. "But they're only a few minutes ahead of us. We'll get a warning if we need to stop, but they'll be able to remove most things."

"How do we stop?" Rayne brushed the red handle at the base of the seat. She tried not to get overwhelmed by all the doubts swirling in her head.

"There's a button under that plastic cover. Or the lever with the big handle. Yeah, that one. Don't want to pull it, though. That's the wheel disc braking mechanism. It's not safe to use it at high speeds. It'll disengage us from the tracks…" Cha trailed off as her attention turned back to Briz.

"How much longer until we get there?" Rayne called back to Cha.

"A couple of hours. We're good. It's all networked in." Cha lifted her hand in a vague wave.

The pressure in Rayne's chest eased. The train's network drove them, following the instructions Cha, Mo, and Rook programmed from their Threads.

There was nothing to do except watch the landscape rush by. The train had left behind the misty forests surrounding the lake and passed through rolling fields of yellow grass. A river sparkled on the horizon. The snow and ice that lingered in the mountains up north had all melted here.

A mix of excitement and dread built in her gut as the train navigated around curves at high speeds. Her hands tapped lightly on the brake. She narrowed her eyes against the morning glare, focusing on the tracks ahead.

After a few moments, the back of her neck warmed. Turning around, she saw Cha slapping tape to an IV bag on the wall above Briz. A few rows behind them, the feral was just visible through the plexiglass doors at the end of the car. The dog sat at the door, her head still, gaze fixed on Rayne.

Rayne shook off a wave of unease and looked away. She refocused on inspecting the tracks ahead, but couldn't stop herself from glancing back at the feral every few minutes. Even down the length of the compartment and through the double doors, she could make out the thick fur and pointed ears of the animal. There was something in the hungry animal's eyes that made Rayne anxious, like the feral knew something Rayne didn't.

Rayne tried again to focus on the tracks before her. She thought of Vic, then her mother, and then her mind clamped

down on the dream of Kai shape-shifting into that wolf creature. Rayne remembered her dream-mother's warning about
protecting her Thread. Or was it a warning to find her Thread?
The details were already fading. But not the dream's wash of
terror. That was still pretty raw.

The shadow appeared like a mirage in the distance. Rayne
blinked once, then twice. Yes, there was a... something lay
across the tracks up ahead. She squinted, and it shimmered. It
could be the early light making shadows on the tracks.

She threw a glance back at the feral again, but the animal
had disappeared into the compartment. Gone underneath the
seats again, most likely. Rayne felt a sliver of pity for the hungry
creature.

When she turned back to the tracks, the strange shadow
had become larger. Its edges sharpened. Rayne pressed her
hands to the control panel and half-rose out of her seat. She
leaned forward until her forehead grazed the glass in front.

In the distance, a ghostly metal presence hulked in the
sunlight. Rayne's eyes widened. She forced herself to take in
every detail. It was definitely there. Something was wrong with
the tracks up ahead.

Real, real. This is reality. I'm not making this up.

It was a bridge. Or what had once been a bridge. The structure stretched high and wide across a brown river. But the
decking and rails, rusted and wrecked, ended abruptly in a line
like broken teeth. Had it been hit by something? An explosion
—or some other heavy force—had ripped the metal tracks to
shreds.

If they remained on course, the train would shoot over the
middle of the river on an expanse of nothingness.

The maglev train roared, a lion's growl, and the tracks sang
a metallic whisper beneath them—a chorus of tiny clicks as
they hurtled closer and closer.

Rayne sank back into her seat and grazed the emergency brake with her fingertips.

"Cha. Come here." She glued her eyes to the broken bridge outside the window, her voice cracking. "It's ... it's gone. The tracks, the bridge, they're gone!"

"What are you talking about?" Cha called back. "Calm down. We're going to be fine. We're networked into the route."

"Come here! Look at this!" Rayne's fingers tightened on the brake.

They were seconds away from vaulting over the edge of the broken bridge. It was all wrong. They were on the wrong train, and they were headed for a broken bridge. A bridge that would send them straight into the river.

Rayne's legs went numb. "I'm slowing us down."

"Don't! Let me make sure you're really seeing this. Just wait—"

Too fast. They were going too fast, hurtling toward the break in the tracks. In a few moments, they would plunge to their deaths.

"Rayne! Hold on," Cha shouted. "I've just got to get this secured—"

"I'm not waiting!" Rayne jerked the handle up.

A screeching whine reverberated through the compartment as the brakes engaged with the train's wheels.

Cha appeared beside her, breath coming fast. "Rayne! What are you—"

"Up ahead! Just look!" Rayne pointed out the window. "The bridge is gone, it's gone! It's not there."

Cha turned to the window, her mouth falling open. Her hand came to the windshield.

Her expression changed, her head shaking the slightest bit. "I'm so sorry." Cha lifted her chin, her eyes boring into Rayne's. "But the bridge is fine. Rayne, we're okay. Just listen—"

Rayne sprang into action, scrambling around the console and buttons, her fingers working in a blur of motion. The train shook as it began to slow, the emergency braking system straining against the train's speed.

"We're going to have to find a way around." Rayne's voice was tight. "We're too close to stop now."

Cha clamped her hand on Rayne's shoulder. "Rayne, sit down!" She pushed Rayne backward. Rayne stumbled, missing the chair, and reached out to Cha for balance. But Cha had already turned away.

Rayne fell to the floor, hitting her cheek against the console on her way down. "Shit!" She banged her palm against the plastic compartment in the wall closest to her. "Gods! We have to stop!"

The smell of smoke and burning metal filled the air. Cha's knuckles paled as she gripped the top of the control panel. "I can't disengage the emergency brake. It's chafing the wheels. They're overheating from the strain. More." Cha listened to her Thread, one hand on her temple.

A thundering crunch echoed through the compartment. The train shuddered, screeching against the track.

"Can we keep the wheels engaged on the track? They're brittle, they haven't been lubricated—"

Another jolt threw Cha away from the controls. Rayne, already on the floor, put her hands over her head. Cha struggled to her feet, leaning against the window.

Beneath the screeching, another noise started. Straining, Rayne listened.

The feral raised her voice in a mournful howl, the sound traveling all the way from the adjacent compartment. A tearing yowl ripped from her throat, making the hairs on Rayne's neck stand up.

"Get down," Cha said. "The wheels aren't going to hold on

the deceleration. We're bracing for impact. I'm getting Briz secured. Stay there!"

But Rayne had already gotten to her feet. She held onto the seats as she made her way back to the double plexiglass doors. The train swayed. She passed Briz in the middle of the car, rolling across a row of seats, a bag of fluids vibrating against the wall above them. Ashen and sweating, Briz didn't open their eyes when Rayne passed.

Rayne lurched toward the plexiglass divider. Shielding her eyes, she peered through the hazy glass. Where had the feral gone?

It's my fault. It's my fault.

She wiped her forehead, trying to focus her thoughts. She wanted to secure the animal, protect her before something happened to the train. Before they crashed or imploded or—

There she was. Hunkered under the seats, paws splayed. The whites of her eyes glinted in terror.

Rayne slid the first door open, stepped forward, and allowed the door to clatter closed behind her. She placed her palm on the second door, and it swished to the side.

The dog hadn't moved. She fixed her gaze on Rayne.

The train lurched. A piercing wail rose around them, and the dog cowered. A rush of air filled the compartment, bringing with it a smell like burning rubber and ozone.

Something mechanical must have broken. *Or the train uncoupled from the track.* Behind her, the dog whimpered.

"It's okay, girl," Rayne said, turning around. She put her palms out. "I'm going to try to—"

A shape whipped by outside the windows, catching Rayne's attention. The dog turned, too. What had just passed the window like that?

More shapes flew by. Rocky gray chunks of metal soared past, flying in all directions, one bouncing hard against the glass. The bridge. They must have hit the bridge. It was coming apart around them as they scraped along its length.

The train screamed ahead.

This can't be happening, we've left the track, we won't be able to stop, I did this, I did this—

Rayne dove over the animal. Her arms instinctively formed a barrier around the small body and held tight, bracing for impact. With a deafening screech, the train caught air as it heaved off the track and arced toward the water beneath. Rayne and the feral tumbled forward, slamming against the door of their compartment.

The river reached out, ready to swallow them whole.

IMPACT_

Rayne

RAYNE DIDN'T REMEMBER HITTING the water. There was only her breath returning in a whooshing gasp. She sputtered and coughed, pushed herself up on her elbows. Took in the new position of her body in relation to the train car. Miraculously, both still intact, they had landed on the water sideways. Rayne's legs, splayed on the glass window beneath her, registered the subtle bobbing of the churning river.

The other part of the train—where Briz and Cha were—was nowhere in sight.

She turned her head, searching for the animal. Rayne spotted her huddled in the corner, her eyes wide and her body shaking.

"It's okay," she murmured. "We're okay."

The train car rocked gently in the water, and Rayne allowed herself to relax slightly. She did not know what would happen next, but for now she was content to stay still with the feral, safe in the train's wreckage.

She caught her breath just as cold water bit into her skin of her palms. Rising to her knees, she noticed a film of liquid covering the windows she sat on. *Water coming into the car.* They weren't safe inside. Of course. They had to get out before the compartment filled and sank.

The compartment door lay face down on the water. It would be impossible to open.

Rayne scrabbled along the walls, the sideways seats, searching for something heavy and sharp. She needed a tool, a bludgeon, anything that would smash through the reinforced windows so they could escape.

Her fingers closed around the metal poles stationed along the aisle. If only she could loosen one, use it to punch through the glass... but they were securely bolted. Getting frantic now, she forced herself to take a breath. Calm down. *I won't drown in here—*

The answer came to her in a flash.

Slipping along the watery windows, Rayne slid to the middle of the train car, the feral at her heels. Scanning the windows over her head, she located the one that had a manual release lever. The emergency exit. If they could wrench the window open, they could climb out and reach safety.

She climbed up on the seats, wedging her foot in between the row for balance. Grasping the handle, she heaved the lever down, her arms shaking with the effort. With a loud crack, the seal broke, and the window dropped out. Icy air rushed in.

The dog whimpered and backed up to avoid being hit by the panel, shaking her head from side to side. Her paws dug into the glass as she tried to balance.

"Come on," Rayne said, turning to the feral. "We have to get out of here."

The feral didn't need to be told twice. She leapt up on the seats, scrambling past Rayne, and pushed herself through the open window.

Rayne followed, gripping the sideways row of seats to hoist herself through the opening. Tucking her legs through, she slid onto the side of the train. The bridge arched above them. The breeze made her eyes water. On top of the sideways car, they spun slowly in the current.

There was no time to rest. The car pitched, sending Rayne sliding toward the edge. She grabbed for anything she could find sticking out along the side of the train, her fingers clawing for purchase, until they caught on the narrow metal rim under a window. With her belly flat on the car, fingertips jammed into the rim, she lifted her head. Squinting in the glare, she could make out the shore closest to them. It wasn't too far away. If she had to guess, it was the direction they had come from. They hadn't gone very far across the bridge before derailing.

Where was the other part of the train? What happened to Briz and Cha? They hadn't landed in the water as far as Rayne could see.

A splash startled her. The feral's head lifted above the water, paddling for the riverbank, her movements brisk and graceful.

Rayne followed. Her body slid into the dark water, her breath momentarily stopping from the shock of cold. She tipped her chin to the sky, copying the feral's position, and moved her arms and legs in tandem, fighting the icy river.

The shore was a distant dream. Rayne pushed on, her teeth chattering and her head pounding with cold. Waves sloshed at her face, and she swallowed mouthfuls of foul water. She had to get out of the river. She had to get to shore, dry off, and figure out what to do. Had to find Briz and Cha.

"Find Briz and Cha," she said through gasps of air. "Get to the Pine Barrens. Get my Thread restored." She repeated the phrases, her lungs juddering. The words kept her focused on the next stroke. She spit out the acrid river water and repeated them. And again.

The feral reached the shore before her, shaking herself off and barking once.

She had to reach safety before she succumbed to exhaustion. She fought the waves, pushing herself forward.

Her foot hit the bottom. *Thank the gods.*

Rayne staggered out of the water, her limbs heavy and her vision blurred. She fell into a thicket of green growth. A surge of gratitude washed over her.

She had made it out alive.

But now what? She had no way to get to the Pine Barrens, no way to find help. She was alone in the middle of nowhere. She had to make a plan, a way of navigating to the Ark, but she didn't know where to begin.

She rolled onto her back, shivers subsiding in the afternoon sunshine. The river lapped quietly beside her, and she tried to think. She had to make her way to the Barrens, somehow. She had to find Briz and Cha.

With a grunt, Rayne pushed herself to sitting. The feral was gone. Probably for the best. She would do better getting food on her own. Rayne had nothing to give her.

Hugging her knees to her chest, Rayne pressed her palms over her eyes. She had *nothing.* Less than nothing, in fact. She had just wrecked the train that was their best option for getting close to the Pine Barrens, with two of her closest friends inside, friends who had put everything on the line while trying to help her.

She wouldn't think about all that now. Wherever Briz and Cha were, they were okay. They had to be.

Her stomach gurgled and churned.

Ignoring the exhaustion in her limbs and the emptiness in

her stomach, Rayne pushed a lock of wet hair out of her eye. She wrung out her sodden pants and shirt as best she could.

If she was going to walk the rest of the way to the Pine Barrens—alone—she better get started.

THE FIRST DECISION she made was a straightforward one: she would follow the train tracks. That's where they had been heading, so it was the right direction. Rayne made the steep scramble up to the bridge. Thorns tore up her arms and legs, and one left a jagged scrape on her face. Her wet clothes became cold, sandy, and bloody.

Climbing onto the bridge, a calm determination settled over her as she began walking along the tracks toward the other side of the river. Every so often she peered at the water eddying below, glimpsing its murky blue through the rails. A light breeze lifted her hair and dried her clothes.

She came upon the evidence of the accident about halfway over the bridge. Bright gashes in the rusty metal railings marked the place where the train had separated from the tracks. She edged away from the jagged hole in the railing where her train car had pushed through the barrier and fell to the river.

Where had the other part of the train gone?

The answer was obvious, though Rayne didn't want to think about it. It had gone ahead on the rails. She raised her eyes to the end of the bridge, where the tracks continued on the other side of the river. The tracks continued past the bridge, threading through a landscape of rolling hills.

No, not hills. Nearing the end of the bridge, Rayne made out crumbling spires and tilting structures on the other side, smothered with trees and greenery. It was an old city. A big one

—a sprawling metropolis that had once ruled the river. It didn't matter what city it had been. It was long dead.

A shadow moved across the far riverbank. She might have missed it if she hadn't been looking.

Nothing. Nothing. Nothing. *I'm seeing nothing.*

A hot tear trickled down her cheek, and she let it come.

THE SKY TURNED purple in the twilight. Rayne stumbled on, her feet dragging in the dirt along the train tracks. She had to find a place to sleep.

The darkness was near complete when she spotted a thicket of trees deep inside the old city. She stepped around the trees until she found a soft patch of moss among the foliage. Too exhausted to pick her way around the gnarled roots any longer, she curled up on the ground and fell asleep.

AIRBIRD_

Vennor

THE FLYING MACHINE SAILED FORWARD. Vennor saw the Blackwater falling away below. Thick straps crisscrossed her chest, pressing her into a seat. Four rescuers, all with flinty expressions and green eyes patched onto their chests, sat alongside and across from her.

The man next to her leaned close, checking her over. He had a flashlight in his hand and shone it in her eyes.

"I'm fine," Vennor said, her voice raw. She was still coughing. "Get that thing away from me."

She swatted at the flashlight. Her stomach roiled as the bird dipped and banked in the sky.

Flying. We're flying. Inside an airbird.

"Systems online, negative course projection." The voice came from her head, through a pair of ear coverings someone had clapped around her temples. "All readings nominal. Target acquired, autoflight engaged." Vennor touched the pad over her ear. It was the pilot speaking, she realized, as light fizzles and tinny sighs came through the earpiece.

There was an answering message, but Vennor didn't understand what the person said.

"Where did you get this? This... airbird?" She spoke at the tiny hook angled in front of her lips.

One man glanced over at her. He wore the same contraption on his head.

"Magna. She sent it for you."

Magna had assembled a working model of an airbird. And trained people to fly it. Vennor would have thought that impossible.

But then Magna had also arranged for her to drown in the rising tide among the ruins of the Fine. Was the airbird rescue part of the plan all along? To show Vennor what Magna and the rebellion are capable of?

She tried a different question. "Where are you taking me?"

The man shrugged. "Where you need to go. She's got a request." He eyed her for a moment, then looked away.

Vennor leaned back in her seat. The machine purred as the spinning blades cut through the air. The airbird looped higher into the night sky.

Magna had a plan, that much was clear. And if Vennor didn't pass out as this machine tilted and soared, she was going to be part of it. She closed her eyes, the hum of the engine lulling her deep into her own thoughts.

THE APPROACH to their destination was swift. The airbird descended sharply in the darkness, jarring Vennor out of her meditation. As they banked, a collection of lights came into view along the ground, scattered in formations like petals from a fallen flower. No tall buildings. No cobbled streets.

Not the Settlement, then. Somewhere else.

They touched down in a clearing. The surrounding grass

bent chaotically in the wind of their propellors. As the airbird came to rest on solid ground, the engines powered down with a huffing whine. The pilot flipped switches on the instrument panel, his face illuminated in the soft light of the cockpit, his eyes flicking over the monitors. The blades slowed above them.

The man beside her unbuckled his strap and pulled off his headpiece, motioning for Vennor to do the same. The other passengers—all in black with that green eye on their chests—stood stiffly as the man pushed a hatchdoor open. He swept his arm to the side, suggesting that Vennor should step out of the craft. She nearly tripped out of the airbird, her knees weak.

The man came up beside her. He pointed to the closest cluster of buildings.

"That's where we're going," he said. "Magna's camp."

Vennor's throat burned from the tide water. Her clothes were cold and damp and carried an odor of the sea.

They approached the gates of the camp, security systems whirring as they walked.

A sprawling complex of tents and buildings came into view before them. Vennor quickly became disoriented as she followed the man through a maze of tents and other structures. They walked past open training areas where lines of black-clad Settlers sparred, and supply piles leaning precariously under makeshift wooden huts.

Lights flickered in the darkness, and there was tension in the air. People moved around in pairs, holding bows to their chests, their faces shrouded in darkness. Eventually they came to a large canvas tent with trampled space around it. The man pulled aside the tent flap and gestured for her to enter.

Inside, the man spoke to someone in the shadows. He handed Vennor over to the person and disappeared. Electric lights blazed on. Vennor squinted in the glare.

"We conserve when we can," Magna said. "No need to use our power when it's not strictly necessary."

Magna's stout form leaned against a desk of dented metal. Her hair was in a loose bun, with tendrils hanging down either side of her head. Clutter covered the desk's surface. A collection of bare bulbs hung along the tent walls.

Vennor scanned the room, taking in the details of the tent. Magna and her followers had made do with what they had, but everything was functional and organized. Magna's eyes bore into Vennor, sizing her up.

"Welcome to our humble abode," Magna gestured to a chair opposite her. Vennor hesitated for a moment before taking a seat.

"I'm sure you're wondering why you're here," Magna said, leaning forward.

"Did you mean to kill me?" Vennor asked.

"No, my dear. If we had meant to kill you, you'd be dead. I believe we've passed our courting phase, yes? No more contests, no more games. Now we can enjoy our work together. And before you ask, yes, I'm really here. This is me." Magna swept her hands down her body. "But I'm afraid we've run out of time for small talk."

"I agree." Vennor straightened. "Release me."

Magna's face broke out in a smile. "I don't believe you fully comprehend your position here. You are alive because of us. Because of *me*."

So this was how Magna wanted to play her hand. As Vennor's savior.

Vennor planted her feet firmly on the ground. On the Earth.

"You barely escaped from the Atlantic Ark." Magna pushed off from the desk. "The Officers of your Ark still pursue you for your crime. You cannot return to the Ark without facing severe punishment—likely Thread termination—from your adopted homeland."

Vennor winced at the word *adopted.*

Magna came closer. "The moment you set foot in the Atlantic Ark again, you'll be taken away. Under arrest for your crime against the One. You could be officially exiled."

A tingle fluttered over Vennor's palms. The Earth Thread called from deep in the ground.

"You are in no position to barter with anyone in our Settlement," Magna said. "You owe us a debt of gratitude for allowing you to stay here. To rejoin your blood family."

The sides of the tent bowed in and out, startling them both. A soft pattering started against the canvas walls. Rain.

"What I ask of you is a fair and balanced trade." Magna leaned closer. "You help us show the citizens of the Arks the nature of free will. I see how they need time—and firm guidance—to adjust to life without that feed in their brains. We did it too quickly in the Pine Barrens, and I regret the suffering we caused."

Vennor listened, intrigued. This was the first time she had heard anyone admit the Settlers had made a mistake.

"I want to do it right this time," Magna continued. "And I need you to help me. You know the Ark better than anyone here. You can help us understand how to reach its citizens."

"And why would I help you?"

"I was getting to that. In return, the Ark accepts you as their trusted leader once again. Perhaps they promote you to the Guild of Seers."

"They're ready for you." A head poked into the tent. "Awaiting your orders." The head turned. Vennor recognized Livia. Her brother's daughter.

"Oh," Livia said, recognition dawning. "Auntie. I didn't mean to interrupt."

"It's all right." Magna waved her off. "We only need a minute."

Livia hesitated, then nodded. Her head disappeared through the tent flap, which closed behind her.

My niece. My niece is helping Magna attack the Arks and disable the NEWRRTH.

"You see? They're ready for us." Magna picked up an object from the mess on her desk, turning it over in her hands. "Our time has come. Our moment in the liberation of all." She put down the object, which was a model of an airbird.

"And if I refuse to help you?" Vennor pushed a hank of matted hair out of her eyes. "If I don't go along with your... moment?"

Magna laughed, low and throaty. "That's not an option. You know that. You've been chosen. It's meant to be, all of it." She moved closer still, her eyes blazing in the naked light. "You were born for this. You were born to lead this rebellion. It's your calling to save your home—your true home, the one that welcomed you with open arms. It's your fate to free the Arks from the clutches of a false god."

Her hand reached out to grasp Vennor's. "Don't tell me you aren't longing for it. To go back."

Vennor recoiled and pushed herself up from the chair. "You think I'm going to cooperate with you because you've come up with some twisted reasoning for your rebellion. For inciting this violence. What a bold assumption."

"I don't *assume*." Magna swiveled. "I *know*. It's the—"

"It's the power of faith."

"You're catching on." Magna's expression darkened. "Faith is especially powerful in our hour of need, wouldn't you say?"

The tingle crept up Vennor's forearms. She kept still. "In our hour of need, yes."

"Come!" Magna barked. "It's time to take flight."

The rain picked up and lashed the tent walls, making a sound like ice pellets against the hard ground. In the distance, a chorus of engines started up.

Magna gave her a tight smile. She tapped her fingernail on a device hanging off her desk. It was one of those spheres. The same one Magna had used to block the NEWRRTH.

Magna picked up the device and slid its string over her neck.

Two men burst through the tent flap. They were wrapped in black, their eyes shining through slits of fabric. Raindrops glistened on their shoulders. The same white spheres hung around their necks.

They motioned for Vennor and Magna to follow.

Vennor turned and stepped out into the night, a chill running down her spine. The rain lashed at their faces, and she bent her head low. She hurried to keep up with Magna, who strode purposefully ahead.

The engine sounds grew louder as they cleared the last cluster of tents. They came onto an enormous field. Vennor sucked in her breath and felt the blood rush to her feet.

A battalion of at least twenty airbirds stood in formation on the grass, their blades spinning as they prepared for takeoff. Rivulets of rain glistened down their black bodies. The thunder of the rotors pulsated through the air, a deafening sound that rose above the din of the storm and filled the night with sound.

Vennor's knees gave way. Someone reached for her. "Don't want to miss this," her brother shouted in her ear as he pulled her to standing. Dressed in black like the others, his eyes gleamed as he tightened his grip on her upper arm. Vennor jerked her arm back.

A white sphere like the one Magna wore bounced against her brother's chest. *Were they all armed with the same weapon?*

Magna didn't break her stride. "Clear for loading!" She

lifted her right hand in the air and made a swirling motion. "Put her in!"

Two people began marching toward them from the side of the field, cradling a rectangular white box between them.

"Careful!" Magna shouted at them. "Don't drop that."

They lifted the box higher and stepped through the high grass. They glanced at Magna several times, but kept moving toward the airbird. Their grip never faltered on the white box.

That was it, then. The weapon the Settlers would use to disable the Atlantic Ark. Vennor supposed Magna would use this box to generate a vast electromagnetic pulse. Something powerful enough to sever the people of the Ark from the NEWRRTH, the intelligence that guided them in every part of their lives. Just like she had done at the Pine Barrens Ark.

"I know what you're thinking." Magna turned to Vennor and raised her voice to be heard above the noise of the airbirds. "And it's not what it looks like."

Vennor raised her eyebrows. Her gaze took in the fleet of airbirds before them. An army that was preparing to use a powerful weapon to take down an Ark in the blink of an eye.

"We're not going to do that. Not this time." Magna came to Vennor's side. "You're going to land with us first. You'll have time to negotiate. We'll only proceed when they're ready."

"You know the people of the Ark will never accept your terms," Vennor said. "They live in peace. They care for one another. They have no desire to—"

A rough tugging from behind nearly tipped Vennor to the ground. She gasped in surprise as someone wrenched her wrists behind her back. Rope cut into her flesh.

"I am truly sorry we had to do that," Magna said. "But we're on a mission, and we're not taking any chances."

Two people, one on either side, lifted Vennor into the air.

Her hands had been secured behind her, rough hemp cutting into her wrists. Her lower back tweaked, then sang with pain.

They brought her to the airbird in front. Magna clambered through the hatch, and Gedeon followed. The people holding Vennor lifted her to the door, tucking her head.

"Get off me," Vennor growled. They pushed her inside, and she fell to the floor of the craft.

Vennor noticed the white box underneath the pilot's seat. It was right there, almost within reach. She twisted toward it.

"Here we go." Her brother grabbed an elbow, and half dragged her to one seat against the wall.

The two men lifted themselves into the aircraft after her. They quickly untied her, pushed her into the seat, and retied the ropes. One around each wrist, securing her to the armrests. They lashed the seat's straps around her chest and buckled them with a click.

It happened so quickly Vennor barely had time to breathe.

The rotors above them shrieked as they picked up speed.

Magna stepped into the craft and knelt in front of her. She wore a headpiece and held a spare in her hands. Gently, she placed the spare over Vennor's ears and pulled Vennor's thick hair free from the clamps.

"You see? You were born for this," she murmured. Her voice crackled in Vennor's earpiece.

Vennor stared into Magna's eyes, grinding her jaw to distract from the throbbing in her lower back.

Magna smiled and traced her fingertips along Vennor's jaw. This time, Vennor did not pull away.

Vennor was part of Magna's rebellion now. There was no turning back.

And the rebellion had begun.

ALONE_

Rayne

A PAIR of eyes glowed in the dark. Menacing, calculating. Animal.

Rayne sat up, breathless. *Where am I, where am I—*

The old city-forest. There was no animal. She had fallen asleep under the tree.

"I told you she was alive."

Rayne swiveled to the voice. She scooted backward until her back slammed against the tree trunk.

A boy, no older than eight or nine, stood a few feet away. He wore a dirty coat over a ragged blue jumpsuit. A companion of about the same age held his hand. The two of them had tangled dark hair and black eyes. Siblings. Or cousins.

"Who are you?" Rayne asked. "What are you doing here?" She tried to keep her voice steady. She did not want to be found. Not by these people, anyway.

The kids looked at each other. One of them shrugged.

The early morning light made everything appear in shades of white and black. Cautiously, Rayne rose to her feet.

"Tell me your names," Rayne said.

"We're Tanny and Eke. I'm Tanny." Tanny pulled his coat against his chest and tipped his head to the girl. "She's Eke."

Eke gave a shy smile and moved behind Tanny.

"Are you—where did you come from?" Rayne pressed her palms to the bark behind her.

Eke glanced at Tanny. He made a hand motion to her, and she responded with rapid movements of her free hand. Rayne noticed the streaks of grime on their cheeks and a long rip in the bottom of Eke's jumpsuit.

"She said we should ask your name first," Tanny said. Eke nodded.

"I'm... my name is Rayne. I'm from the At—" She stopped herself.

Tanny's eyes grew wide. "You're from the Atlantic Ark." He made hand gestures while he spoke. Eke followed Tanny's gestures with interest, then dropped Tanny's other hand and took a step forward.

She spoke with emphatic hand movements to Rayne. Sign language.

"I don't know what she's saying," Rayne said, her cheeks coloring. Her Thread would have been able to translate.

"She said we heard about your Ark," Tanny said. "We heard it got corrupted. It was gone into the Ethers."

"What does that mean? Gone into the Ethers? I don't—"

"And that one of your Seers did a bad thing. The Principle of One. She disrespected it. And your Seer went to the land of the Unconnecteds."

Eke continued to sign with both hands, her face opening as she spoke.

Tanny translated. "She's saying you should be prepared. They're coming for all the Arks. You're going to be next, because you're closest."

"Wait," Rayne said. "Stop. Please. Tell her to go slower. I can't keep up."

Tanny tapped Eke on the shoulder and moved his palms in a slow-down motion. Then he turned to Rayne.

"We haven't seen anyone else since it happened," Tanny said. "They've all... after... we haven't gone home. Yet. And then we heard a crash-bang last night, and something big fell into the river."

Rayne let the tree trunk steady her. She took a breath and rolled her feet over the tree's tangled roots.

These kids were alone. They could be from the Pine Barrens Ark. They might have survived whatever happened there. And they had heard the train derail last night.

Rayne chose her words carefully.

"Do you know where the train tracks go? The ones that go over the bridge, over the river?"

Tanny repeated the question to Eke. Her face went solemn. She pointed.

"Yeah, we know the tracks. They go through the old city. Never saw anything on them, though. It was the first time we saw."

"The first time you saw what? What did you see on the tracks?"

Tanny smiled. "What do you think, silly? A train! It was a train on the tracks."

Eke broke into a smile, her face lighting up. She made a sign again and again. Two fingers rubbing over two fingers on the other hand. *Train.*

Whatever these kids had lived through in the past few weeks, they had just seen a train for the first time. And it had delighted them.

Rayne reached for her backpack, then remembered it was gone. Probably sunk to the bottom of the river.

"Are you kids... do you have a place to stay? To stay out of the weather, keep safe?"

Eke's smile faded. Tanny pressed his mouth into a line.

"We're not supposed to tell," he said.

"I see." Rayne said. "Could you tell a friend, though?"

After signing the question to Eke, Tanny turned to Rayne. "We're supposed to stay away from people."

"I get it." Rayne was quiet for a moment. "Did I tell you I'm a Game Designer?"

The two kids stared at her, then started signing to each other with rapid-fire movements. Tanny touched his face, pulled an invisible screen over his eyes.

"Eke says where's your Thread? If you're a Designer we want to see your Thread."

Rayne paused. It was a fair question.

"Look, it's a long story. I don't have my Thread right now. It got..."

Eke nodded, her expression grave.

"We know," Tanny said. "Ours is lost, too." After a beat, he added, "I like playing Games. You're not one of *them*." He glanced around the trees. "Yes. We have a place."

"Can you show me?" Rayne asked.

Tanny consulted with Eke, and she nodded. He and Eke each took one of Rayne's hands and led her away from the tree.

They headed away from the river and deeper into the ruined city. They picked their way over mounds of mossy rubble, past vine-choked structures, and collapsing buildings. Clouds hung close and heavy. A grumble of thunder sounded, and the rain came soon after.

Spring storm. Rayne hoped they didn't have to walk too much farther. She had barely dried out from the river, and the fresh dampness made her skin prickle.

They reached a clearing that was almost entirely hidden by

a tangle of vines and bushes. Tanny and Eke led Rayne through a small opening in the vegetation and into a dimly lit space. It was a serviceable shelter, cobbled together from scraps of metal and plastic.

"This is where we're staying," Tanny said. He pushed aside a ratty blanket.

Rayne stepped through, glancing around. The makeshift living space contained a couple of cots and blankets. Piles of supplies lined the angled walls.

"This is great. You've done a good job setting this place up. How did you find all this stuff?"

Tanny looked at Eke, who gave a tiny shake of her head.

"What've you been eating?" Rayne was too tall for the space, so she lowered into a crouch. "You got any food?"

As soon as she asked it, her stomach gurgled. She placed her hand over her abdomen.

Tanny nodded, a smile spreading across his face. He pointed to a corner of the shelter. "We've been getting by."

Rayne followed his gaze to a small pile of items: a collection of mushrooms and a few wrinkled tubers with dirt clinging to their skins. It wasn't much, but it was enough to keep them going for a few days.

"That's great," she said. "You're doing well."

Eke's face softened. She signed something to Tanny, who turned to Rayne.

"We'll share with you."

"No, you don't have to," Rayne said. "I just want to make sure you have enough."

Rayne shuffled closer to the dirty root vegetables. "Hey, is that a potato? Where did you dig those? How did you know where to find them?"

Tanny flew into the corner, blocking Rayne's view of the food stores. Eke glowered.

"Eke, I'm going to tell her," Tanny said. He signed to Eke.

Eke got red in the face and drew closer to him. Her hands balled into fists.

"Hey, don't worry." Rayne raised her palms. "I was just curious. I won't take anything from you."

"It's not that," Tanny said. "It's—"

Eke cut him off with a barrage of signs. She tapped her temple several times.

Rayne swallowed. Why was Eke tapping her temple like that? What were they talking about?

"It's the Thread," Tanny blurted. "The Thread told us. Where to get the potatoes. We got the Thread to come back and talk to us. And—"

Eke slapped Tanny's hands in frustration and turned away, crossing her arms.

Rayne scrambled to her knees. She grabbed Tanny's shoulders, pulling him close.

"How did you find the Thread? Tell me!"

He squirmed away, backing up until he was against the wall.

"I'm sorry." Rayne put her hands up. "Gods. I'm sorry, okay? I thought you said you got your Thread." She touched her temple. "You got it to... talk to you? Here? To guide you?"

Tanny scrunched his face like he was going to cry. "I didn't do anything," he whispered. "I didn't."

"Listen, I won't hurt you." Rayne slowed her breathing. She had to get this right. It might be her only chance. "I promise, I'm a friend. We're friends, okay? Can you tell Eke?"

Tanny made a few tentative signs to Eke. She narrowed her eyes at Rayne. Then uncrossed her arms to make a few signs back.

"She said not to tell anyone. She's scared."

Rayne showed them her palms. "You don't have to be

scared. I'm not going to hurt you. I only want to help. I think I can help you. With getting the Thread back."

Tanny finished translating while Eke stared at Rayne. Then Eke signed back.

"She's not scared of you," Tanny said. "She's scared of *them*. Of them coming back."

Rayne sat back on her haunches. "Who's *them*?"

The kids exchanged a long glance. Eke made a few more signs. She swept her hands overhead.

"The thunderbirds," Tanny said. "The metal birds. They flew over us and put the Ethers on our heads. Then everyone fell down. We ran away. That's when the Thread was... gone."

A hollow space opened in Rayne's chest. *Thunderbirds.* She had played enough Games to understand what kind of flying contraption the kids might be referring to. But those were relics of a past long forgotten. No one had use for war machines like that anymore. Unless...

"Were there soldiers?" she asked. "Ones who came out from the thunderbirds?"

Tanny nodded.

"Were they wearing jumpsuits from an Ark?"

Tanny shook his head.

Rayne remembered then. "Did they have a symbol on their clothes? Or on their machines? Something that looked like a green eye?"

Eke nodded her head and signed something else.

"The green eye, yes," Tanny said. "They put the Ethers on our houses, too. They told everyone to get out. They said it loud, many times. We did what they asked. But they still put the Ethers on us."

"What... what are the Ethers?"

Eke cocked her head as if to say, *You don't know?*

Rayne shook her head. *No.*

"The Ethers are bad. They take over the Thread," Tanny said. "They tell it when to go and when to stop. Like what happened to your Thread? It got stopped. The Ethers stopped it."

Rayne didn't know what the hell these kids were talking about, but it sounded terrifying.

"Okay then," she said. "We're going to figure this out. I have questions. And when I have questions, I look for answers. The Thread gives us answers. Right?"

After Tanny translated, the kids stilled and regarded her with wide eyes.

"So we have our work cut out for us. Let's get started." Rayne patted the space in front of her.

The kids approached and sat down.

A lightness filled Rayne's throat. She held out her hands, palms up: "I'm going to ask you a very special favor. I'm going to ask you to show me your Thread."

FLARE_

Rayne

EKE'S EYES sparkled as she extended her arms in front of Rayne. She glanced up, making sure she had Rayne's full attention.

Rayne smiled. *I'm watching.*

Eke twitched her fingers and moved her hands in an intricate pattern. As she did, a pool of light appeared in the air between them.

Rayne leaned in closer, mesmerized by the display. The light shimmered and pulsed, almost like a living thing. As they watched, it became strands that twisted into a complex pattern of lines and shapes. It was a three-dimensional spider's web stretching out in all directions.

"This is amazing," Rayne breathed.

Tanny got to his knees and scooted closer. His mouth parted.

Eke made small, precise motions with her fingers. She moved across the air, tracing out a pattern that looked almost like a script. As she moved, her fingers left behind a faint silver glow.

No, it couldn't be. She squinted at Eke, whose figure moved inside a cloud of code. As Rayne stared closer, her stomach twisted as she realized what she was seeing. The NEWRRTH. Eke was working with the raw intelligence powering their Threads.

Only trained Seers worked with the NEWRRTH itself. Everyone else used their Threads to access its intelligence. The Seers protected the intelligence from corruption and kept it aligned with humanity's best interests.

Rayne had only seen the NEWRRTH's code once before in her life.

"How are you doing this?" Rayne reached out to touch the shimmering strands of code, but Eke pulled back.

"No!" Tanny said. "It'll go away."

Rayne let her hands drop. As she gazed at the silvery lines, she remembered Freya's Path working over her body. She was in a thunderous cave. Her back was cold, her limbs stiff, and she couldn't move from the slab of stone where she lay. Her mother was there, working over her, too. For a moment—or had it been longer?—she watched her own lines of code hovering above her chest as Entra and the people of Freya's Path manipulated lines and lines of the glowing strands. They were trying to eliminate the mind-virus Vennor planted in her.

But Freya's Path had been unsuccessful. The mind-virus was too deeply entwined in her own living code. To extract it would kill her.

That's when Cas stepped in. He used that crystal to pull her code along with the mind-virus inside himself. His last act, before he deleted his own code, was to transfer his own living code to Rayne.

Rayne pushed the memory away.

Eke's code moved faster now, weaving itself into a complex shape that seemed to encompass everything around them. The light grew brighter, bathing everyone in its warm glow. Rayne felt as if she were being pulled into its depths, like she was becoming part of it. She closed her eyes and allowed herself to drift away for a few moments until Tanny's voice disrupted the trance-like state she was in.

"It's done!" he announced.

Rayne opened her eyes and saw that the web of code had vanished. But something else remained: a flicker of blue at their wrists. She shot to her feet, promptly banging her head on the concrete ceiling of the shelter.

"Shit!"

The kids giggled.

Rayne touched her throbbing scalp and then gazed at her glorious, glowing blue pulse.

"How did you do this? Does it work?"

Tanny's face got serious. "It works," he said. "But only for a few minutes. That's why we have to hurry."

Rayne bent low and pushed through the hanging blanket at the entrance. Out in the open air, rain pelted her cheeks. "Make a call," she said to her Thread. "Get Cha."

The kids scrambled out after her, staying at a respectful distance, but watching closely.

The downpour soaked her through, but she barely noticed. Her eyes stayed glued to her wrist, waiting for the call to go through.

Please answer, please answer.

"It'll go away soon," Tanny called out. "You better hurry up."

Rayne pressed her wrist, ending the call to Cha.

"Call Briz." No answer.

The flare. She needed to send the emergency signal, the

one the Designers slipped into a backdoor on the D-boards. "Bring up the D-boards," she told her Thread. "Hurry."

A half-second later, the Atlantic Ark Designer messaging feed materialized. The old-time digital display began rolling in front of her. It was outdated stuff, jokes and questions and barbs, all posted before she left the Atlantic Ark.

With a flick of her finger, she moved the feed to the side and began hunting for the backdoor. "Show me the portal to the emergency alert. The flare." The Thread zeroed in on a corner of the boards, where Rayne saw a ripple in the gradient. She pulled it closer.

"Enlarge," she said. Tugging at the display, her heart galloping, she uttered the command quickly, without taking a breath. "Engage the flare."

The gradient shifted, the red dot turning briefly purple, before the board shut down disappeared into the air.

Rayne blinked. The blue glow in her wrist was gone. She let out her breath.

The two kids stared at her in disbelief.

"What was that? What did you do?" Tanny asked.

I called for help. With any luck, her friends knew where she was now. And that she needed their help. Rayne's head started aching again where she had struck it inside their shelter.

Eke moved closer, signing.

"She wants to know... were those Games on the display? All the Games that you... your friends designed?"

Rayne shook her head. "It's more complicated than that." Seeing the kids' expectant faces, she added, "But it's something like that, yeah. A list of notes we leave for each other, while we're working on our own Games."

Tanny and Eke glanced at each other, giggling.

"I have to ask you both a serious question." Rayne crouched

down to their eye level. They drew close. "How did you do that? Activate our Threads like that?"

Eke shrugged.

"She doesn't know how she does it, she just..."

Eke made a motion with both hands like she was pulling cobwebs from the air.

"She feels the Thread wanting to talk, all around us," Tanny said. "Then she pulls it in and tells it to talk."

Eke could sense the intelligence of the NEWRRTH. And she can manipulate it with her mind. That was something Seers trained for decades to know how to do.

"Why does it only last a little while? How quickly can you get it back again?" Rayne bit back all the questions she had for this little girl.

Eke shrugged again, her eyes glazing. She didn't know how special she was, and she had exhausted any explanation of how she did it.

The rain gusted sideways, and Tanny threw an arm over his head.

"Let's go back inside," Rayne said. "It's miserable out here."

She followed the kids back into their shelter, ducking to avoid another collision with the ceiling. Wiping her face, she sat cross-legged on the floor. These kids could use a fire, but it would be too smoky to light one inside.

"Let me ask you something else," she said. "Would you want to leave this place if you had the chance?"

Eke perked up, her gaze sharp.

"What do you mean, leave?" Tanny shivered and hugged his arms to his chest.

"I mean, if you could, would you..." Rayne trailed off.

She shouldn't be asking this. If Briz and Cha showed up to get Rayne, the three of them would continue on to the Pine Barrens. There was no way they could take these kids with them. And even if the kids wanted to return to their home Ark, there was nothing waiting for them there. They were probably better off where they were. At least they had shelter and some food. And each other.

"Never mind." Rayne brushed the wetness from her pants. "I had an idea, but then I realized it was—"

A series of yelps exploded into the air. Rayne twisted toward the entrance, trying to locate the source of the sound. It wasn't too far away.

The yelps turned into something else. A wailing howl rose some distance away. Another joined in. Soon, multiple animal voices echoed off the buildings all around them.

Tanny grabbed Eke's hand. His small face paled as he signed to Eke, his hand sketching a snout on his face. *Wolf.*

"Get back," Rayne said. "All the way back, you need to hide."

Eke stood and shook her head. *No.* She closed her eyes and moved her hands in the air.

Tanny scrambled to the ledge near the back of their shelter, where they kept their food.

"What are you doing?" Rayne asked.

"It's the food they want," Tanny said. "The Thread told us last time. All we need to do is give it to them—"

"Last time? You've been *feeding* the wild *animals?*" Rayne's stomach flipped. The situation was worse than she imagined. The animals were expecting a meal. They wouldn't be easily distracted. The Thread always instructed them to respect and appreciate wildlife without interfering in its natural cycles.

"We didn't feed them." Tanny piled root vegetables into the bottom of his shirt. "We just left our food out in a special place when we heard them coming last time. It worked, don't worry."

Rayne shot to her feet, protecting her head. "Give me that." She reached for the collection in Tanny's shirt, grabbing potatoes two and three at a time. She shoved them deep into the pockets of her coat.

"You're not doing that again," Rayne said. "Giving these animals food. It's not safe. I'm taking it. You two are staying here."

The air shimmered around them. The walls tilted in. For a second, the room spun.

Eke gave a small cry. Her eyes closed, she brought her hands to her temples.

"What's happening?" Rayne steadied herself against the concrete ledge.

"It's just the Thread coming back online," Tanny said. He stuffed a clump of mushrooms into Rayne's pockets. "It comes in hard like that sometimes."

Eke lay her hands flat on the dusty floor. She rocked back and forth. A whooshing sound started above them.

"Is this—" Rayne paused. "Wait a minute. Is this really happening?"

Tanny cocked his head.

Rayne leaned on the ledge, her eyes resting on the last few mushrooms on a pile of dirt. "Is this real?"

Tanny grabbed the mushrooms in his small hand and pushed them into her jacket. "That's it. That's all our food. Come on, let's go!" He grabbed Rayne's arm, and they ran outside.

The rain had let up some. It misted her hair and trickled down the back of her neck. Rayne glanced at her wrist. Her veins showed under her skin. But no Thread.

"Where is it? The Thread?"

Tanny stood next to her, shielding his eyes from the dampness. "It'll come back soon. Start going that way!" He raised his arm to point.

A singular howl started, closer this time. Rayne jogged in the direction Tanny indicated.

What am I doing? She glanced back to see Tanny scamper behind the hanging blanket and disappear inside the shelter. She faced forward and stepped carefully through a pile of rocks slick with wet moss.

Am I hallucinating all of this, too?

She pushed her wet hair back, so it didn't drip water into her eyes. *It doesn't matter,* she told herself. *It doesn't matter if this is real or not. I'm protecting these kids from a pack of animals. And I'm getting my Thread back.*

The voice that exploded out of the air startled her so thoroughly she didn't notice the pain of her twisted ankle until much later.

Rayne

"RAYNE!" the voice shouted.

She skidded over wet stones. Twisting, she searched for him.

And found him. Vic's hologram call appeared so clear and solid, he might have been standing right beside her.

"You found me." She nearly threw her arms around Vic, only to remember he wasn't actually there. "How did you—"

"Because you called?" Vic's eyebrows lifted. And he pointed to her wrist.

She held it up. A glowing blue dot pulsed brightly. "Oh, it worked. Eke did it."

"Who's Eke? Where are Briz—"

"Vic, listen to me," Rayne interrupted. "My connection isn't going to last. Are you someplace you can talk?"

"We can talk here," he said. Was that a flash of irritation across his face? "It's safe."

Of course. He was with Ana. She was the one powering this call right now.

Which meant—

"Did you see my flare? The one I just sent?"

Vic nodded. "That's how we found you. How did you access your Thread?" Without waiting for an answer, he continued. "You have to get back here, Rayne. You won't believe this. We figured out that the crystal's coding is fractal. Have you ever seen a fractal coding model?"

A million responses slammed through Rayne's head. She picked one.

"Do you even know what's been happening to me while you and Ana play around with that damn code?"

Vic's mouth opened as if to say something, but Rayne cut him off.

"The Pine Barrens is gone, Vic. Gone. You saw it yourself. Have you wondered for a hot second who did that? And why?"

"It doesn't matter—"

"It doesn't matter? What about the Atlantic Ark, then? Do you think we're protected from an attack like that? The people there, Vic, they lost everything. They're suffering because of what the Settlers did—"

"What are you talking about? What did the Settlers have to do with—"

"All this time I've been out here, trying to hold on to reality, risking my life to get our Threads back. And what have you been doing all alone with Ana?"

Rayne wished she could call the words back as soon as they left her mouth.

Vic's jaw set. "I'm trying to tell you. If you'd just listen for a second."

She took a breath.

"Ana is the only one of this damn bunch who actually cares about us," Vic said. "She cares about the NEWRRTH, and she cares about what's been happening to people like your mother."

Vic shook his head. "Never mind. The important thing is that I couldn't have done this alone. Without her knowledge about the code."

"Done what alone? What have you done?"

A snarl pierced the air. It came from somewhere up ahead. Rayne froze.

"Activate a code inside the Games and also in real life. A code that can protect us, protect the Arks, so there won't be any way a Settler or anyone else can threaten us. It's a way to ensure that every generation after us—"

Rayne held her hand up to Vic. *Quiet.*

She scanned the rubble ahead, her gaze lingering on the shadowy places. There were so many places a feral could hide. She should have asked her Thread where to leave the food, instead of having this inane conversation with Vic.

"I have to go," she whispered. "There's a... situation here."

"Rayne? Are you okay?"

"Shh. You'll only alert them." She could almost hear the whisper of animal pads moving over slippery stones, their soft whines and clicking teeth.

She tucked one hand deep into her jacket pocket. "Have you been having any symptoms, Vic?"

"Symptoms? Of what?"

"Like... hallucinating. Seeing things that aren't there."

"I know what hallucinating is. Sudden disconnection from the Thread can lead to dissociation from reality. Is that... have *you* been having them? Hallucinations?" The note of pity in his voice infuriated her.

"Something like that." She closed her fist over a couple of dirt-covered roots in her pocket. She stared ahead, scanning for movement. "The thing is, I'm not sure my mind is completely right. I made a bad decision on the train, Vic. I pulled the emergency brake when there wasn't any reason to. I thought I saw something on the track, but it wasn't real. I could have killed us."

"But you didn't. Briz and Cha are coming for you, you just have to—"

"Sh."

It seemed like a good idea then to become smaller, not as visible. Less of a beacon in the barren landscape. She crouched to the ground. *He really doesn't care.* The thought rose in her mind along with the sting of disappointment. *Vic doesn't even want to know what I've been through.*

Her ankle shifted painfully, and she muffled a gasp. Falling to her knees, she gritted her teeth to keep from making another noise.

It was too late. A feral stepped from behind a broken wall, head lowered, ears pointed forward. Tracking her. Lifting its gaze, the animal tuned into the spot where Rayne knelt. Its nose lifted in the air, ears swiveling toward her.

Shit.

Vic's hologram flickered. "Rayne, what's going on?"

The feral picked up its pace, its loping strides closing the distance between them. There was nowhere for Rayne to hide. She couldn't outrun the animal. Carefully, she lifted a hard vegetable from her pocket and closed her fist around it.

The feral trotted closer. When it was a few yards away, it stopped. Opened its mouth in a wide smile, tongue hanging out, panting. Then it sat.

Rayne recognized the feral's spotted face. Her distended belly.

"Easy, girl." Rayne kept her voice low and steady. "I see you made it here after your swim to the beach. That's a good girl."

The feral licked her lips and gave a soft whine.

Slowly, Rayne pulled her elbow back. The feral cocked her head.

"Rayne, what are you—"

With a gentle movement, Rayne sent the vegetable in her hand rolling. It probably was a potato. As it tumbled toward the animal, bits of dirt dropped off. The animal snapped to attention and backed up, observing the potato as it bounced toward her. She raised her snout as if readying to pounce.

When the potato came to a stop, the feral touched her nose to it, then closed her mouth around it. With a crunch and a toss of her head, she swallowed the offering. Then she sat once more, staring at Rayne.

Rayne reached into her pocket and drew out another vegetable. Without glancing at it, Rayne rolled it toward the feral. The feral tracked it with her gaze, then gave a little hop and snatched it from the ground.

"Good girl," Rayne murmured. "Take it and be on your way." Gingerly, Rayne rose. Her ankle burned with pain.

Vic's voice made her jump. "I tracked your location. The Thread shows me a pack of animals moving in your direction, coming from the south." Vic pointed, showing her. "If they're wolf descendants, they'll spread out to attack. But you have time to get to a building up ahead, less than a mile away." He showed her an image of a building with faded paint and chipped bricks, windows broken out and fogged over. "Walk quickly. And... Rayne, you know I—"

The call ended as abruptly as it began. Vic was gone.

Rayne glanced at the hand thrust into her pocket, turning her wrist. No more blue dot. The Thread had left her.

"I'm walking away now. You stay here." Rayne showed her palm to the animal. "Don't come with me. No following me."

She glared at the feral, hoping to make her point. Then she turned and walked away, her ankle throbbing with each step. The feral remained where she was, watching her go.

Rayne kept her focus on the ground ahead of her. She

didn't want to turn back and encourage the animal to follow. She hoped what Vic said was right. That there was a building up ahead she could shelter in. She needed rest, water, and time to think.

Her nerves jangled. After a few minutes, she thought she heard a scuffling trot, but when she glanced back, the feral was just sitting there, unmoving. Her eyes were fixed on Rayne's retreating figure.

Rayne kept walking, unable to shake the feeling of being watched, until she reached a bend in the street and could no longer see the animal.

But when Rayne picked up her pace and glanced over her shoulder, there she was. The feral kept her head low, as if bowing in respect, and followed at a safe distance.

Rayne limped as quickly as she could, searching for the building Vic had shown her. How far had she already walked? The feral followed silently, never coming too close but never leaving her either. Together, they navigated a street buckling from years of neglect, with grass pushing up in between the cracks. Weeds and vines wrapped around old poles and sprouted from the gutters and sewer drains.

After a few more minutes, the building Vic showed her came into view. It was a low apartment building, slumping against its neighbors, with busted windows and a sagging porch. Its front door, gaping open, had a chunk of board missing from its center. A rotting carcass of materials, but still capable of providing a measure of shelter.

Rayne bypassed the disintegrating front steps and leapt directly onto the sloping porch. Carefully, she stepped through the front door, into a vestibule with a broken chandelier. The staircase seemed to be held up more by luck than by the remaining balusters. The air was stale, and a layer of dust coated the walls and floor. Rayne moved slowly, taking care not to make too much noise. The feral stayed outside, as if keeping watch.

Moving into the main hallway, she navigated around piles of debris. There were dented paint cans, broken furniture, and piles of trash. Whoever had once lived there was long gone.

Rayne climbed the stairs to the second floor and saw the same mess. The walls were peeling and the windows were covered in grime. But it was still a place to rest. She found a corner of the hallway that was relatively free of debris and sat down. She was exhausted and hungry, desperate for a few moments of peace.

She pulled out a vegetable from her pocket, wiped it on her shirt, and took a bite. As she chewed, she sent a pulse of gratitude to Eke and Tanny for handing over their entire food supply. She hoped they could replenish their food without too much trouble. And that whatever animals were out there would bypass the kids' shelter to trail her scent.

With her second bite, her stomach turned. The vegetable tasted too earthy, almost rotten. Putting it in her lap, a hollowness washed over her. She knew it didn't have anything to do with being hungry.

One finger traced the inside of her wrist. The silence of her Thread was especially maddening after the intense few minutes she had been able to use it. How had Eke activated it? Tanny said that Eke sensed it wanting to come through. Then Eke pulled it in and allowed it to talk. What did that mean? And what were the Ethers the kids spoke about? Were they related to Entra and Freya's Path at all?

Rayne closed her eyes and pictured the NEWRRTH's code swirling all around. She had been taught that the NEWRRTH was always present. Yes, the NEWRRTH was invisible, but it was always around, even in the ruins of whatever city this used to be. It was everywhere. All over the world.

Ready to be connected to the Threads, and translated into intelligence.

Just one tendril of its code. That's all I need to gather it into me.

She imagined the strands of code that swirled around her body, the strands that Freya's Path worked with in the cave. The lines of code that she herself had conjured in that strange Game of Vic's. A glowing string of light, twisting in the darkness. Coming together into form and substance. The stuff of life.

She opened her eyes. The vegetable in her lap rolled away, making a trail through the grit on the floor. There was nothing here. No shimmering strands of the NEWRRTH wanting to talk to her.

There was only the silence of death and decay, and the dusty remains of life.

BARK_

Rayne

RAYNE LEANED her head back on the wall. Even if Briz and Cha found her, even if the three of them made it back to the Pine Barrens, she doubted she would find anyone capable of restoring her Thread. She was foolish to have thought otherwise. She should have stayed home with Vic. She should have been there for her mother. Even if there wasn't anything she could have done for her.

The feral outside gave a short bark. Suddenly alert, Rayne's hunger and exhaustion melted away. She scrambled to her feet and sprinted to the end of the hall, where a cracked window provided a limited view of the street below.

Lifting a sleeve, she wiped a streak of grime from the glass. From up on the second floor, Rayne could make out the surrounding structures and a network of narrow streets weaving around the buildings. Nothing unusual caught her attention. She squinted into the distance, but saw no movement. Just the dusty street and brown, falling down buildings.

The feral stood at attention below. Her body was rigid, ears pointing up, head fixed still. Rayne tried to follow the animal's gaze, but couldn't figure out what had caused her to bark. Still, the feral had been disturbed by something.

Rayne's dream came back to her. Her mother shifting from her human form into something wild and hungry. A dog or a wolf. A feral.

No, Rayne told herself. It wasn't possible. There was no way her mother had anything to do with the feral outside. Her mother was in a coma hundreds of miles away. Last Rayne knew, Kai had come down with whatever was causing the rig. And no one, not even the best Healors in the Haven, had figured out how to bring plague patients back from their death-like stupors.

Rayne's chest compressed as the next thought struck her.

Her mother was as good as dead.

It didn't seem real, the possibility that her mother would leave her forever, just as her father had two years ago.

Even if her mother did wake up, Rayne reminded herself, Kai would face charges for interfering with the NEWRRTH. For calling up the new Earth Thread, and using it to block the Seers from unleashing the mind-virus. Who knew what punishment the Seers would stick to her for doing that.

Rayne was about to turn from the window when something moved. There, a few streets over, among a maze of alleys, a body disappeared behind a wall. Then another.

Rayne sharpened her focus until she saw an entire group of them. Dirty brown coats that blended into the rubble, only visible when they shifted. Not ferals, though. Something larger, with long legs and narrow faces. One of them with a stack of horns on its head.

Deer. Rayne had never seen one in real life. They were hunted to near extinction after the famines of the last century. A generation had passed without a sighting of their kind.

Rayne was mesmerized by the majestic creatures. She felt as if she were seeing something magical, something so beautiful it could only exist in a myth. Her whole body vibrated with awe.

She had to log this in her Thread—

No. There would be no log. Still, she took in the details with her mind. The pack of deer, maybe seven of them, traveled one at a time through the narrow passageways between buildings. They leapt gracefully, almost daintily, over rubble and piles of concrete. Their black marble eyes surveyed their surroundings, keenly aware.

Rayne's breath caught. There was a young one. With shaggy white spots on its coat, its legs spindly. It stuck close to one deer, probably its mother, who kept turning to check on it.

For a moment, Rayne thought that the deer had come to find her. That they had sensed her presence and come to bring solace. But that was silly. The deer were oblivious to her.

Still, it was an omen. A sign that she was in the right place. And that she wasn't alone.

The feral was gone. She had disappeared from her place outside the building. Craning her neck, Rayne checked up and down the streets for the animal, but couldn't find her. With a rising panic, she scanned further away, around the buildings and crumbling walls.

There, about half a mile away and coming from behind the deer, she saw them. Two animals with heads low to the ground, trotting purposefully. Their gray coats didn't quite blend with the cityscape, so once Rayne spotted them, she locked her gaze on them. Their tails and loping gait gave them away. Rayne made a soft sound when she realized that her feral was on her way to join them.

The ferals howling outside Eke and Tanny's shelter hadn't been looking for vegetable handouts. They were hunting deer.

Rayne didn't hesitate a moment longer. She flew down the building's steps two at a time. On the first floor, she grabbed the rusted handles of two paint cans, and exploded out of the building's front door.

"Hey!" She stopped in the middle of the street. Planting her feet, she clapped the cans together over her head. They made a dull thunk, and a cascade of gray dust spilled over her shoulders. Coughing, she shook herself off and tried again.

"HEY!" This time, she banged the cans in front of her with more of her strength. They made a hollow *clunk*. She did it again. She headed toward the alley that she guessed would intersect the hunting ferals' path. She clunked and yelled as she went.

"I am not"—CLUNK—"going to let you"—CLUNK—"kill a deer!" CLUNK.

Her pace slowed as she entered the narrow passageway. The walls of buildings had partially collapsed on both sides, forming a triangle tunnel she twisted through. Where were the ferals? She stepped over piles of broken bricks and metal scrap. The alley got narrower.

CLUNK. "Leave them"—CLUNK—"alone!"

She reached the end. A barricade of wreckage blocked the way. It was too high for her to climb. She had chosen the wrong alley. The ferals were somewhere else, down another street, closing in on their prey. Rayne thought of the baby deer, its unsteady legs doing their best to keep up with its mother. The ferals would pounce on it to make an easy kill.

Her heart squeezed. Growling in frustration, she hurled the tin cans as high as she could against the crumbled concrete. They clanged and rattled. As they rolled back down, she screamed at the sky.

"Gods, you make a lot of noise."

Rayne's scream withered in her throat as a figure with springy brown hair rounded the corner.

Rayne ran to her. Cha wrapped her arms around Rayne, her hand cradling the back of Rayne's head. Tears sprung to Rayne's eyes.

"Cha," Rayne whispered, her arms around Cha's neck, the rest of her words muffled as they hugged.

"And thank you for being so loud," Cha said, pulling away. "Cuz otherwise it would have taken a lot longer to find you."

"You found me." Rayne held onto Cha's shoulders, her cheeks wet with tears, her voice choked and raw.

"Gods. You need some of this." Cha pulled a bottle from her pack and held it out. Rayne took it and greedily chugged the water until the bottle emptied.

Cha retrieved the empty container and stuffed it back inside her pack. "I thought you might pour it over your head, you idiot. What is this all over you?" Cha brushed Rayne's arm and pulled her hand away, examining the pale dust. "Gross. Come on, let's get out of here."

"Cha, I'm so sorry about the train. About derailing it." Rayne kept close to Cha as they hurried out of the alley. "I saw it, I swear. The bridge up ahead, I was sure there was a—"

"We know." Cha led Rayne out of the alley and onto the main street. "Don't beat yourself up, okay? You did your best. Now let it go."

The tears came again, and Rayne tried to blink them away. There was no time for wallowing in apologies. That didn't change the twinge that rose to a painful point in her chest. She had almost killed all of them.

"Where's Briz?" Rayne used her shoulder to wipe her cheek and glanced down the empty street. There was no sign of the ferals either, not even the one who had followed her.

"We'll join up with them soon. I just sent our coordinates."

Cha linked her arm with Rayne's and guided her to their left. "Come on. Tell me. How did you get here?"

They walked along the cracked asphalt. Rayne told her about escaping from the train once it hit the river, the feral who followed her all the way to the apartment building, and the deer she had just spotted running from a group of ferals.

Cha nodded as Rayne spoke, letting Rayne finish before she asked the question hanging over them both.

"How did you activate the flare?"

Rayne paused, pulling away from Cha. "It's complicated."

"Don't give me that. You got into the D-boards and executed the sequence we left there. How did you find your Thread?" Cha reached for Rayne's wrist, but Rayne pressed it to her chest.

They stood in the street facing each other. Rayne closed her eyes. In her mind's eye, she saw Eke's hands moving in the air, tracing the space in front of her, and pulling the shimmering strands through the air. The light that had come when Eke activated their Threads.

Rayne didn't know why, but sensed it wasn't right to talk about what Eke had done. She had a feeling Eke and Tanny would find their own way, following the Thread as it guided them, whether it took them back to the Barrens or somewhere beyond.

"I can't explain it," Rayne said. "I don't know how, I just knew."

Cha narrowed her eyes. "You just knew, huh?" Then she smiled and nudged Rayne's shoulder. "So you don't need the Seers, I guess."

"It's not that simple. I had it for a minute or two. I don't know how to get it back." Rayne lowered her arm to her side. She showed Cha her dark, empty wrist.

Cha's smile faded.

"Can you tell me something?" Rayne paused so they could walk single file past a spiky bush growing out of the street. "What do you think our Ark is going to do about the Pine Barrens, when they hear about what happened? You think they'll send support for any... survivors?"

Something flashed in Cha's expression. Before she could speak, Briz rounded a corner and jogged up the street toward them, cradling one arm in a fresh sling.

Rayne gave them a one-sided hug, careful not to jostle Briz's injured arm. "How's the bite healing?"

"Just fine. Cha got me some antibiotics from the Haven at the Barrens."

"At the Pine Barrens? You actually got there?" Rayne's stomach dropped. "Did you see anyone? Are they—"

"It's not good," Cha said. "Come on, let's get going. We don't want to be here when the sun sets."

ESCORT_

Vennor

VENNOR CLENCHED and unclenched her fists. Her knuckles whitened as she struggled against her restraints. Her wrists were raw from the ropes digging into her skin. Magna sat in a seat facing her, cradling the white sphere around her neck, and gazing at Vennor with something like desire.

Was it Vennor she desired? Or the heady taste of power? Vennor didn't know and didn't care.

The airbird soared through the night toward the Atlantic Ark. Vennor guessed they would be there within a couple of hours, though it was difficult to see in the darkness that obscured any landmarks below.

She glanced at Gedeon, who sat strapped into the seat next to Magna. *Magna's lackey.* Her brother followed her orders and did Magna's bidding without having a single thought of his own. Vennor should have realized the second she stepped foot in the Settlements that her brother had become a puppet for some sort of cause. He had always been a weak bully. Enthralled by leaders but never figuring out how to lead. He had a nose for trouble and an affinity for strong-minded people who told him what to do.

Vennor's breathing became harsh, her frustration rising with each struggling movement against her bonds. Irony of ironies. Caught like a rag doll, forced into a rebellion she had no part in creating. She glared at Magna and the two soldiers who sat rigidly staring ahead, her anger rising to boiling point. How dare they do this to her? Didn't they understand she wasn't one of them?

Her mind raced as she tried to figure out a way to escape, but it seemed impossible. The ropes around her wrists were tight, and she could not move.

"Plotting your escape?" Magna's mouth curled at the edges. "I'd hoped you'd have relaxed by now. That you'd see the Fates will provide."

"That's what you hoped? That I'd calmly accept my fate as your pawn?" Vennor spat the words at Magna, a flush beginning in her chest. "I'll never accept it. I'll protect the NEWRRTH until my last breath."

Magna chuckled. "I admire your spirit, Vennor, but why protect something that's crumbling around you? The Atlantic Ark is already dead. The Fates have shown me the future. The future is us. Humankind, unburdened from the machines that shackle. You could be a part of that future."

"I'll never be a part of that," Vennor seethed. "I've seen too well how that path plays out for us. Stumbling blindly along, making it up as we go along. Listening to power-hungry zealots like you. That future has already played out. For hundreds, thousands of years. And it always ends the same way."

Magna leaned in closer, her breath hot against Vennor's cheek. "But it doesn't have to end that way. We can create a new future, a better one. With your help, we can liberate the Arks and claim a new world for ourselves."

Vennor's eyes narrowed as she considered Magna's words. Magna said she received guidance. Magna believed it came from the mythological beings called the Fates, but Vennor didn't think so. Her logical mind told her it was something else.

Vennor turned away from Magna's hand and flexed her wrists against their restraints once more.

"I enjoy watching people free themselves, to receive the bounties our fates bestow upon us." Magna tapped a finger on the white sphere. "Helping where I can, of course."

Magna settled back in her seat, giving Vennor a glimpse out the front of the cockpit. Under the moonlight, a ribbon of water twinkled below. The airbird swooped again, tipping forward. Fighting a surge of nausea, Vennor closed her eyes. The craft hummed onwards.

"I will not help you." Vennor opened her eyes.

"But you will."

Vennor scoffed. "And what about the people of the Ark? You think your Fates want to disconnect them from their realities, their lives? Leaving them no hope for their own futures?"

Magna leaned forward, her eyes flashing. "They had their chance. They choose to stay under the oppressive rule of the NEWRRTH. They turn a blind eye to the suffering of others. It's time for change, Vennor. And you will be a part of it."

The people of the Arks had always been content to leave the people of the Settlements alone. But refraining from interfering with the Settlers was not the same thing as having contempt for their way of life. Violence was never the answer.

Magna's smile deepened.

Closing her eyes again, Vennor focused on the feeling of the ropes around her wrists. They had to be made from a natural material, something harvested from the Earth. A flash of recognition pulsed up her forearms. *Hemp.*

She lowered her chin and reached out with her consciousness. Sent out tentative feelers for any sign of the Earth Thread inside the ropes. If she could grasp it, bring it inside her own Thread, she could generate a message to the Atlantic Ark to warn them about what was coming. It gave her hope that there was still something she could do.

Going deep within herself, Vennor concentrated. A fizzing built up inside of her. Was it coming from the hemp? She couldn't tell. It coursed through the nerves in her body, trying to tell her something. She strained to connect.

The blast came swiftly. There was a crack and a flash of blue light, followed by the sound of static echoing inside her earpiece. Vennor's eyes snapped open as her body went rigid for a split second. The static crescendoed into a crackling, as if a million tiny needles pinged around the cockpit.

The airbird went dark. The craft dropped sharply, listing to the right. The only sound was the slowing thump of the rotors outside.

Magna removed her thumb from the white sphere around her neck, and everything returned to normal. The cockpit illuminated, the blades above them singing as they powered up again. Vennor saw the pilot glance back. His hands shifted nervously over the controls.

A faint glow in the air remained from the electromagnetic blast. Magna smiled and tilted her head at Vennor.

"Surprise you?"

Vennor struggled to control her breathing, saying nothing.

"You're the perfect example of why the electronic gods aren't needed anymore," Magna said. "You strive for connection, but it's always a disappointment. A distraction from what's real and true. Isn't that right, Gedeon?"

Gedeon chuckled, his eyes glinting with amusement. "We don't depend on equipment to tell us what to do." He turned to Vennor, a wicked grin on his face. "But you wouldn't know anything about that, would you, sister? You were always too busy cozying up to machines, trying to curry their favor."

Vennor gritted her teeth, the ropes biting into her skin. She had always been the odd one out in her family, the only one who believed in the power of the NEWRRTH to improve their lives. She had never seen evidence of the intelligence corrupting or controlling anyone, nor would that make sense given its programming. She always thought the NEWRRTH offered a way for humans to make the best choices, learn from mistakes of the past, without sacrificing their humanity or their sovereignty. This violent power grab of the Settlers would never compare to the peaceful, egalitarian future the NEWRRTH promised.

Magna leaned in again, her voice low and intense. "You can still make a choice, Vennor. You can join us, help us sever the NEWRRTH and create a world where all humans are free to live as they choose. Or you can cling to the past and die along with it."

A hiss over the earphones interrupted her. The pilot's hand shot up, signaling for them to be quiet. He spoke into the mic, his voice urgent. "I've got an intercepted transmission. Ma'am, it's coming from an external source."

Magna frowned at Vennor before turning her attention to the pilot. "Can you confirm? Where is it coming from?"

"It's been decrypted. Took some time, but it's definitely coming from below. I think it's a distress call." The pilot adjusted some settings on the console and listened intently.

"What does it say?" Gedeon asked.

The pilot locked eyes with Magna for a moment, his face grim.

"It's a top priority message for help," the pilot said. "It's coming from inside the data streams you asked me to monitor. The location is specified. It's a quick ride from here." The pilot glanced at Magna. Then he added, "I believe this could be important, ma'am."

Magna tilted her head, considering. "All right. Tell the others to stay on course. And then get us as close as you can to the coordinates from that call."

Vennor swallowed back another wave of nausea. "I don't think—"

"We're investigating the source of this call. I've made my decision."

The pilot nodded and reached overhead to turn a knob.

"It could be a trap," Vennor said. "An ambush, someone wanting retribution. Have you—"

"Of course I have," Magna snapped. "You think we're not prepared?" She tugged on her white sphere. After a moment, she spoke to the pilot again.

"Correction," she said. "Have two birds stay with us. Just in case."

A sour taste filled Vennor's mouth as the airbird tilted sharply and banked left, skimming over the black river below. The river swirled with whitecaps that reflected light from the moon above. Two other airbirds withdrew from the formation, pivoting to flank their craft on either side in what seemed to be some sort of escort.

Vennor tightened her grip on the armrests. She watched as the other airbirds disappeared into the night sky, growing ever smaller until they blended in with the stars.

ENERGY_

Rayne

THEY KEPT to a route that Cha's Thread mapped for them. Walking at a brisk clip, they hugged close to walls when they could, and checked the entrance of every alley before passing it. Their movements reminded Rayne of something, but she couldn't place it until they stopped to catch their breath along a towering structure. Then she remembered: her French Revolution game. Running along the walls of the Bastille prison just before dawn on the morning of the July revolt.

As they leaned against the cool steel of the building, Cha turned to Rayne. "I wanted to tell you, since you asked. Our Ark would send transports. To the Pine Barrens, I mean. To help whoever's left. I hope it's soon."

"Will you promise me something?" Rayne asked, her breath still coming in gasps. "Promise me our Ark will do a full sweep of the area to make sure they've found everyone from the Pine Barrens who might need help. Even if they're not in the Barrens any longer."

Briz curled a lip. "Pretty sure that's standard protocol. Why wouldn't they do that?"

"Just promise me."

"Fine," Cha said, pushing herself off the wall. "I'll make sure they find every last person with a heat signature around here." She took off down the street.

Rayne allowed herself a small measure of relief. She pictured one of the Atlantic Ark's transports arriving at Eke and Tanny's shelter. A Healor stepping inside with a hot meal and warm clothes, an arm outstretched to beckon them to safety.

Briz took off after Cha, ducking under the bare vines that cascaded from the walls of the buildings ahead.

"Why do we have to go so fast?" Rayne asked when she caught up with them. Her swollen ankle pressed painfully against her boot. "Can't we find a place to rest? What about that house I found before?"

"You saw them." Cha called back. "They won't stop hunting until they get their dinner."

"The ferals?" Rayne hurried to keep up with her. "The ones going after that pack of deer?"

"Deer or whatever. Don't want to give them another taste." Briz lifted their arm wrapped in its sling and smirked.

Rayne shuddered. The thought of being tracked like prey made her skin crawl. They needed a place to shelter, away from whatever animals hunted in the night. She quickened her pace, but the pain in her ankle made it difficult to keep up with her friends. She stumbled and almost fell. Briz caught her before she hit the ground.

"Careful," Briz said, steadying her. "We're almost there."

"Where?" Rayne asked, glancing around. They were in a desolate part of the city, surrounded by rows of squat buildings that had long since caved in on each other.

"There." Cha pointed to a metal structure that had once stood at the front of a gate. Woody growth had swallowed the gate long ago, but the guardhouse remained. "It's the only place with reinforced walls. Think it might be comfortable enough for you?"

"Only one way to find out," Rayne said, leading the way.

When they reached the structure, they entered cautiously, checking every corner before settling in the middle of the floor. It was cramped and filled with debris, but it had a window that overlooked the street.

"Okay," Cha said, closing the door behind them and sliding the deadbolt. "We need to talk about our next move."

Rayne slid down to the floor, propping her injured ankle up on a pile of rubble. "Our next move?"

"We need to get you reconnected to the Thread," Cha said, sitting across from Rayne. "We need you to remember how you did it before."

"I told you, I don't know what I did." Rayne shifted her ankle, trying to find a more comfortable position. "I tried something I thought would work."

"How did you send the flare?" Briz joined them on the floor. "You had to be connected to the Thread."

Rayne bit her lip. "Like I said, I had the Thread for a few seconds. I got to the D-boards to activate the code, and then it was gone."

Cha nodded. "Okay, that's good. We just need to get you reconnected again. At the Pine Barrens, we saw—"

Briz put their free hand on Cha's arm. "No need to get Rayne upset."

"I won't go into all the details. But Rayne needs to know what she's up against. If she doesn't connect again soon."

Briz withdrew their hand.

"It was like an explosion hit the Pine Barrens Ark,

disrupting everything all at once," Cha continued. "But as far as we could tell, there was no bomb. Just people..."

She covered her face, her frizzy hair in a helmet shape around her head. Rayne waited. When Cha looked up again, her lips had paled.

"The people there had been disconnected from their Threads so suddenly, so violently, that their neural networks scrambled. They got completely disoriented. Didn't know what was real, what wasn't. They ended up congregating in their underground shelters. That's where we found them. Most of them, anyway."

"We found their Seers, too." Briz picked at their thumb. "They were in better shape, but barely. One of them identified as being in the Guild of Seers, and had been trying to contact our Seers for a while, but couldn't make their Threads communicate with ours."

"What did they think happened?" Rayne asked.

"They're still figuring that out. But there's evidence pointing to the Settlers. Or a faction of them, anyway. They launched an attack." Cha's voice shook. "I can't—I can't tell you how bad it was. What they did to the people there, it's beyond anything I've seen before. And I've played every one of your Games, Rayne."

Briz lowered their head and swiped at their cheek. "How a person could do that to another living being..."

"What are we going to do now?" Rayne kept her voice level. "The Settlers aren't going to come back, are they?"

"That's what we've been asking the Thread," Cha said. "Why would they do this? And what's their plan?"

Briz wiped their other cheek and sighed loudly.

"What weapon do you think they used?" Rayne asked. Her friends looked up in surprise. "The Settlers. Do you think they used an electromagnetic device?"

"Probably." Briz's shoulders rounded and they shook their head. "What does it matter?"

"Because if they get close to the Atlantic Ark with a weapon like that, it's as good as over for us, too."

Briz kept shaking their head. "We've already been talking to our Threads about that. We can't let the Settlers do something like this again. We need to warn our Seers."

"But how?" Rayne pressed her forehead, which had started to ache.

Cha inched closer to Rayne. "We've been sending messages nonstop to Enayat, to Nilo, to Ana," she said, lifting her fingers as she recounted the names of the Atlantic Ark Seers. "No one's answered. Maybe they think we're playing some elaborate prank on them."

"We need a better plan." Briz rubbed their chin thoughtfully. "Something that will get their attention and make them listen."

"It's pointless. They're too obsessed with the anomaly in the Games, trying to find out what's been messing with the NEWRRTH," Cha said. "Anyway, the Atlantic Ark doesn't have the resources to defend itself against an attack like that."

Rayne sat up straighter. "That's what Vic and Ana are working on. The crystal code."

Cha sighed, scooting back to lean against a chunk of concrete. "I know. But that's still in development."

"Call Mo and Rook," Rayne said. "We need to know what the crystal code is capable of. It might give the Ark something to defend itself with."

"We already talked to them," Briz said. "They don't know anything."

"Call them again."

After a moment, Briz relented. The holographic forms of their two friends appeared next to them in the guardhouse.

"I told you not to call back until we knew—" Mo stopped when he saw Rayne. "Hey, Rayne. You doing okay?"

Rayne smiled at Mo. "I've been better. It's nice to see your face."

Rook came into view beside Mo. He shoved a last bite of something into his mouth, crumbs falling over his chin. The outline of Rayne's kitchen formed in the background. And there was Luci approaching, cleaning pad extended.

"Good to see your face, too." Rook's words were muffled. Luci stopped abruptly behind Rook, who stepped aside. Luci wiped the counter he had been standing over. Then it rolled away.

"Still eating my food? Is there going to be any left when I get home?" Rayne tried to widen her smile, but it felt more like a grimace.

"What's going on?" Mo asked.

"Tell Rayne what you know about the crystal code," Briz said. "Then we need to get a message to the Seers about the possibility of an attack."

"Gods," Rook muttered. "You know we've been trying. Vic's not even answering our calls."

Mo and Rook glanced at each other. Rayne could tell they were trying to figure out how much to tell her.

Mo cleared his throat. "Okay. What do you want to know about the crystal code?"

"It's designed to delete things," Rook said, not waiting for her answer. "Anything, really. In the Games, it could delete glitches or unwanted features. But in real life..."

"In real life, it could delete people," Rayne finished for him.

Mo blinked. "Right. Vic is convinced he can recreate the crystal code outside of the Games. As far as we know, he and Ana haven't succeeded. Yet."

"The One," Rayne said. "That would be a violation of the Principle of One. If he and Ana *deleted* people in real life."

The Designers fell silent.

"He may not need to use it," Cha said. "But we can't just sit around and wait for the Settlers to attack the Ark. We need to be prepared."

"Right," Briz agreed. "And the Seers need to know what's going on."

Rook sighed. "I'll try again. I'll go right to Enayat. We'll figure out a way to get the message across. Don't worry. And y'all?"

Rayne gazed at the hologram of her friends.

Rook's features softened. "We are One."

EARLY LIGHT SLANTED into the window of the guardhouse, collecting in a puddle on the floor.

"...for now, we need to focus on getting her reconnected to the Thread," Cha was saying. "We can't do anything without it."

Rayne pushed herself to sitting. Rubbing the crust from her eyes, she glanced around the room and spotted her reflection in the window's glass. She was surprised to see how haggard she looked. The stress and uncertainty of the past few days had taken a toll.

She squinted into the light, trying to clear the sluggishness from her brain, and turned her attention to Cha.

"I've been doing some investigating," Cha said. "And it turns out there's a chance she could reconnect yourself."

Rayne sat up, patting her hair into position. How long had she been daydreaming?

"There's a chance?" Rayne's voice came out scratchy.

"It's just a tiny chance."

"All right then," Rayne said. "Give me a minute." She closed her eyes and took a deep breath, picturing Eke's hands weaving and sketching. The glow that gathered in front of her. Rayne tried to remember the sensation of the Thread connecting with her mind. She pushed her awareness into the air, searching for a glimmer of that light, the tiniest sliver of NEWRRTH to get hold of. But all she felt was emptiness.

"Anything?" Briz asked, watching her intently.

Frustrated tears prickled at the corner of Rayne's eyes. "Nothing. It's gone." They had been doing this for hours. Nothing seemed to get her closer to the Thread.

"We'll figure something out," Cha said, placing a comforting hand on Rayne's shoulder.

Rayne shrugged it off. "Not likely," she muttered.

As Rayne tried to push away the feeling of hopelessness that threatened to engulf her, a jolt of electricity ran down her spine. It was a strange sensation, one that she had never experienced before. She opened her eyes and looked around, wondering if anyone else had felt it, too.

Briz and Cha stared at her with wide eyes, their expressions a mixture of confusion and worry.

"What's wrong?" Rayne rubbed her arms to quell the tingling sensation that lingered on her skin.

"That was weird," Cha said. "I felt something."

Briz nodded. "Me too. It was like a zap of energy."

Rayne gathered herself and stood, hobbling, to the window. "Do you hear that?"

A distant hum cut through the air, growing louder with each passing second.

"Cha, I can't feel the Thread anymore—"

"I can't either, it's been cut off, it's like—"

With a click, Rayne opened the door and stepped outside.

"Look."

She pointed to the sky.

APPROACH_

Rayne

The engines' thrum reverberated through the ground like a tremor, shaking the earth and creating a rumbling thunder that echoed in the sky.

The giant metal birds. The thunderbirds.

Rayne blinked back the memory of Tanny and Eke, their small bodies becoming still as they described the attack on their home.

Briz and Cha examined their wrists, empty of blue light.

As Rayne watched, three metal birds emerged in the sky—silhouettes of sleek, dark metal against a bright blue expanse. Their windows reflected glints of sunlight. A heavy, metallic scent hung in the air, an acrid smell that filled Rayne's nose.

She lifted her sleeve to cover her mouth and stepped inside the shack.

"It's the Settlers," she said, her voice muffled by the fabric. The chopping of rotor blades sliced through the air like a buzz saw. "They're here. It's just like Tanny said. How he described their arrival at the Pine Barrens."

"Who's Tanny?" Briz touched their temple, then drew their hand away.

"I think they just sent us an electromagnetic pulse," Rayne continued. "That shock we felt... it was their EMP hitting us."

They put the Ethers on our heads.

Briz and Cha were quiet, their faces drawn. Rayne could guess what they were thinking—the same thing she was—that they were in serious trouble now. Their Threads were gone, crushed by the pulse. There was no hope of any of them getting connected again.

She knew that if they wanted any chance of getting out of this alive, she would have to stay calm and think fast. She took a deep breath, wanting to reassure Briz and Cha that everything would be okay.

The siding of the guardhouse rattled in a violent gust. They turned to the window and saw that the Settlers' metal birds were much closer, the rotors whipping up dust clouds among the city's debris.

"We have to go," Briz said, their voice urgent. "Now."

"They'll see if we try to leave." Cha grabbed Rayne's arm. "We should hide."

Rayne scanned the area outside. She knew they couldn't stay in the guardhouse, but they also couldn't risk getting caught out in the open.

Her breath caught in her throat as she spotted a small herd of ferals leaping over a chain-link fence. They were bolting in a panic. Their paws scrabbled for purchase on the rusted metal as they tried to escape the noise overhead. Before they disappeared into the alleys, Rayne saw her feral, her pregnant one, trotting along the outside of the group like a protective mother.

Rayne watched the ferals disappear into the wrecked city. She knew that they would be safe in the maze of debris.

She turned to Briz and Cha. "Listen. I know it seems

impossible. But there's a way out of this. We just have to believe we can figure it out and trust each other. Okay?"

An explosion rocked the ground beneath their feet. The guardhouse shuddered and debris rained down from the ceiling.

"Gods! What was that?" Briz brushed bits of rubble off their arm, and Cha gazed fixedly at the door. Rayne patted down her body, feeling for damage. Everything was okay. For now.

Rayne considered the options, trying to come up with a plan that would get them out of the rapidly deteriorating situation.

It was too late to escape into the city like the ferals had. The thunderbirds already circled them like vultures, ready to swoop in and swallow them whole. And evidently they carried something that could generate an explosion. Perhaps worse.

Cha pulled Rayne into an awkward embrace, her eyes locking onto Rayne's in a wordless exchange of fear and deter-mination.

"We stick together," Cha said firmly, her voice barely audible over the roar of the approaching thunderbirds. "No matter what."

Rayne took a shaky breath. "Yes. Okay. Together."

Briz staggered over and put their arms around them both. "We are One. They're not going to break us. We're better than that."

Fierce love for her friends rose in her chest. Rayne promised herself she would do everything she could to keep them alive and safe. Letting them go, she turned to face the door. They had always been masters of Game strategy. They would come up with a way to stop the Settlers from taking everything from them.

This was different. This was life or death.

"We need to move," Rayne said. "We're going out."

"Out there?" Briz said. "You sure?"

"They'll see us." Cha's eyes darted back and forth.

"It's the best option." Rayne stepped over new rubble toward the door. "They're going to flush us out of here one way or another. On their terms, or ours."

A poem fragment lodged in her mind, one that she had forgotten she knew. She pushed the words out of her mouth, hoping they would give her strength.

> It matters not how straight the gate,
> How charged with punishments the scroll,
> I am the master of my fate:
> I am the captain of my soul.

The others looked at her, understanding. Poems always appeared in Rayne's Games through her random poem generator, a tribute to Rayne's father. Even if they didn't get the meaning of every line, they knew what was at stake now.

They moved toward the door, raised their hands in surrender, and followed Rayne's lead.

RAYNE HAD PLAYED a handful of Games inside a rotorcraft. She remembered soaring above an open expanse, seeing for miles in every direction. It was exhilarating, but she didn't enjoy being an easy target in the sky. Flying machines could be taken down quickly. There was no easy escape from them. But they could move fast, floating through the air like graceful birds of prey.

She had piloted a flying craft once, in a Game involving finding poachers among wild beasts on a dusty plain. She remembered how hard it was to keep control of the aircraft as they chased the herd. Her nerves on fire, they had somehow managed to stay aloft while also keeping an eye on the animals below. It was a thrilling experience, one that she had never forgotten.

Rayne's stomach did a somersault as the Settlers' machine swooped through the sky, the wind whistling as they climbed. Thick straps pressed into her chest. A long length of rope bound each wrist to the seat. A headpiece covered her ears, dampening the roar of the spinning blades.

The rotted city below them fell away. Rays of early sunshine slanted across the horizon, casting an ethereal light on the faces of the other people in the craft. Rayne breathed over the anxiety skittering in her veins.

Briz and Cha had been taken into separate crafts over Rayne's objections. She tried to keep the three of them together. But the Settlers did not listen to her pleas, pushing them apart and rumbling about the even distribution of weight.

Rayne surveyed her fellow passengers. There were five others in the thunderbird, sitting in two rows facing each other in the dim cabin. At the farther end were two men dressed head to toe in black scraps, clutching curved bows that seemed to be made of wood. Their eyes were fierce and wild; they had the look of people who lived on the edges of society, eking out an existence by their wits.

In the middle seat sat a larger man, also dressed in black, with squinting eyes and crooked teeth. He did not hold a bow. He kept glancing at the passenger to his left. That passenger, sitting directly across from Rayne, was a stout woman with a bun that was coming loose around the edges. Her face held an air of authority that spoke of experience far beyond her years. Rayne knew immediately that she could not be trusted.

And there was Vennor, the escaped Seer, sitting to her left. It had been a shock to recognize her. Vennor sat stiffly beside

Rayne, her inky tresses dull and straggly, fingers tapping at her armrests. Her appearance contrasted sharply with her online broadcast a few months ago, when she wore a crisp yellow jumpsuit that matched the colors of the Center for Future Guidance and issued a sweeping proclamation that would bring the NEWRRTH beyond the reach of the anomaly.

Now, like Rayne, Vennor's wrists were bound in thick rope. She gave Rayne a sideways glance that showed the whites of her eyes.

All the passengers, Rayne noticed, ignored the pilot, who leaned into a half circle of lights and levers. For a moment, the image of the control panel on the maglev swirled in Rayne's head, its screens and buttons glowing. The smooth feel of the emergency brake under her palm.

"I'm sorry," Rayne said to the Seer. Her voice sounded tinny through the headpiece. She didn't elaborate. There was too much to be sorry for.

Vennor's eyes remained fixed on the air in front of her. "It doesn't matter now. We're all in this together."

Rayne said nothing. She knew the headphones connected to all those on board. There would be no private conversations. She checked the view from the window. There were two other thunderbirds flying beside them, each containing one of her friends.

The woman across from her acknowledged Rayne with a hungry glare. Rayne watched the strange object on the woman's neck. It rolled back and forth over her chest with the craft's motion.

"I'm Magna," the woman said. "You've joined us at the right time. You're a welcome addition to our cause."

"I've never been in a machine like this. I didn't know Settlers..."

Magna arched a brow. "You didn't know that we had the

capability of building such advanced equipment. I'm delighted, once again, to prove you Arkeans wrong. You don't know what we're capable of. Always underestimating us."

That could be true. Although Rayne and her fellow *Arkeans* thought little at all about the Settlers. They kept their distance from one another, each preferring to live their own ways. As it had been since the Great Divergence.

Rayne didn't like being tied up. She turned her wrists, trying to loosen the rope. A simple knot in a single strand. She would have a good chance with it.

The thunderbird turned and made a dipping motion. Rayne's stomach lurched again. She tried to steady herself as the craft shot forward. She had thought they would fly low to the ground, but they were headed in the opposite direction. To the sky.

"These flying machines are incredibly vulnerable," Rayne said. "Simple battlefield logistics. Targets in the sky are easiest to take down."

Magna regarded her with a cool expression. Rayne tugged gently, almost absently, on her ropes.

"When the Atlantic Ark defends itself," Rayne continued, "they'll shoot us to pieces. They'll take out the tail rotors first."

Next to her, Vennor tilted her head. Her movement was controlled. Whether she was angry or curious, Rayne couldn't tell.

Rayne's eyes flickered to the pilot. The pilot's fingers danced over the controls, making adjustments. It was impressive to watch him moving as if he knew the craft like his own skin.

"The tail is the most important part of the machine, of course." Rayne had it now. Just a few more twists of the wrist. "It keeps us balanced. You've got to keep it level or we—"

"Gedeon." Magna spoke the word and the man next to her

flinched. "Does the Atlantic Ark possess anti-aircraft weaponry?"

"No weapons in the Arks at all. They don't believe in using violence." He snorted.

Magna's smile returned. "You see? No defenses at your Ark. Nothing to take us down. What you don't realize is how fully you've fallen under the spell of your technology. How it oppresses you, distracts you from the true purpose of life."

Rayne rolled her eyes. She had heard this rhetoric before. Rayne knew that the Thread, the technology that connected people to the wisdom of the NEWRRTH, was essential to living a fulfilling life.

She glanced at Vennor, who seemed lost in thought. Rayne knew the Seer had a deep understanding of the NEWRRTH, had given everything to defend it.

"Vennor," Rayne said quietly. "What do you know about EMPs?"

Vennor's head snapped up, her eyes meeting Rayne's. "I know a great deal," she said. "Why do you ask?"

FREE_

Rayne

RAYNE SLIPPED her wrist through the knot. The rope was
thick, but it wasn't impossible—she could feel it loosening with
each tug. Within moments, she had loosened enough for her
hands to slip free. Keeping her palms in place on the armrests,
she kept the rope draped over the backs of her hands to avoid
arousing suspicion. Slowly, while the Settlers' attention was
elsewhere, she reached over to Vennor and began untying her
wrists as well.

Magna gave a strangled shout. "Stop! Guards!"

Rayne quickly depressed the latch holding her buckles in
place. She had just wriggled free when the two guards reared
up from their seats and barreled into her chest, knocking her to
the floor. Their bows clattered behind them, missing impact
with Magna's face by inches.

"Watch it!" Magna yelled. "Get them back in their seats.
Now!"

Vennor unlatched her own buckles and stepped over the

guards, crushing their fingers underneath her boots, and rushed toward the cockpit without a word.

The guards got to their feet, jostling each other in the tight space. Rayne flipped to her belly and crawled the length of the aisle. Her hand gripped the ropes that had bound her and Vennor. She closed her other fist around the fallen bows. Pain exploded in her back. She heard someone else unbuckling, grunting, and one guard tripped and fell behind her.

"Out of my way," a man said. It was the man seated next to Magna, the one she called Gedeon. Gedeon's boot kicked at her once more, but she angled swiftly away. With her fist around one bow, she pulled it close.

"Don't touch that." The man's voice boomed through her headpiece. Rayne gave one last shove and pushed herself to the back wall of the craft, gathering her legs underneath her, hauling the bows to her chest. Years of Game play in Cha's Renaissance contests gave her a good feel for the crossbow. Even though the Settlers' version wasn't exactly what she was used to, she threw one behind her back while swiftly loading the other.

"Whoa. Put that thing down," Gedeon said. He swayed in the middle of the aisle, facing the back of the craft. Rayne leveled the loaded bow at his face, then lowered it to point directly at his heart. The two guards righted themselves behind him and wrapped their arms around Vennor as she struggled, unsuccessfully, to get to the cockpit.

There was barely enough room for Rayne's right elbow to extend all the way back. She anchored her feet to the floor, kept her chin down, and remained as steady as she could.

"Let her into the cockpit," Rayne said, focused on keeping her arm pulled back. "I wouldn't want to risk missing my target." Her gaze shifted lower, her loaded arrow following suit to beneath the man's belt. His mouth made a frightened O, and he raised his hands in the air.

The craft banked sharply to the left. Rayne lost her footing as her hip banged the seat, but kept her fingers steady on the arrow's shaft. Before she could straighten herself again, the man lunged.

He grabbed for the bow and yanked it from her hands, pulling her forward with it. Her shoulder slammed into his stomach and she tumbled to the floor. But she was quick to regain her footing, leaping up with a loud cry and charging straight at the man's chest. He grabbed her just before she collided with him. Her neck rocked back and her vision blurred.

"Time to stop this nonsense," Gedeon said, digging his fingers into the flesh of her upper back. "You will sit down." He dragged her to the closest seat, pushing her down, his pendant swinging inches in front of her face. Rayne knew exactly what she had to do. Her hand shot out to the sphere, ripped it free from his neck, and pressed down hard on the button.

She gritted her teeth against the sudden electric hum as an invisible shockwave rocketed through the cabin.

Gedeon's body jerked backward, and a guttural bellow ripped through the air. The guards lifted their arms and shouted orders, while Vennor screamed for everyone to stay back. In the chaos, Rayne kept her finger on the button.

The craft made a jarring shudder. A descending hum, like a motor winding down, filled their ears. It was the blades of the rotor slowing, their whirring becoming more intermittent. The burning of electrical components and the acrid stench of melted wires filled the cabin.

The body of the machine began a lazy downward spiral. Her stomach in her throat, adrenaline like fire in her throat, Rayne found a corner of the cabin wall to hunker against, keeping one eye on Gedeon as he scrambled about, trying to get to her. He cursed under his breath as he banged against the seats.

"Everyone listen to me!" Rayne shouted. The passengers fumbled to steady themselves against whatever seemed stable. "Do as I say. Or I'll keep this button pressed until we hit the ground."

Magna's voice rung out. "I don't believe you'll murder us. It's against your Principle."

"You should know that I'm prepared to do whatever it takes to protect my Ark against a deadly attack," Rayne shot back. "Get into your seats. Now."

One guard whimpered. The craft picked up speed in its terrible plunge. Without further argument, the passengers took their seats and clicked their buckles into place.

"Let Vennor into the cockpit. She's our pilot now."

A gasp and soft murmuring. Rayne put her free hand on the floor, feeling around for the ropes she had dropped there. When she located them, she slid herself against the wall into a standing position.

"Pilot, sit in the fifth seat. I'm going to bring this craft back online. When I do that, you put your hands out in front of you. Everyone, hold your electromagnetic devices in one hand. Where I can see them."

Rayne let herself glance out a window. The white-capped river below, and the surrounding woods, were too close. She had to hurry.

"Anyone bothers me or my Seer on the rest of this flight, I'll push this again. Understood?"

There was only the soft whistling of their descent.

"I said, do you understand?"

"Yes," Magna's voice was hoarse. "We won't interfere."

With her back against the rear wall, Rayne lifted her finger

from the white sphere. The cabin lights flickered on, along with
the controls in the cockpit.

Four Settlers sat buckled into their seats, their hands held
high. The fifth passenger, the pilot, was getting up, his eyes
darting around to make sense of the situation. Rayne took a step
forward, bow and arrow already drawn.

She gripped the bow tightly, not sure if she could bring
herself to use it against another human being. The pilot sensed
her hesitation and lunged at her. Swiftly, she dropped her aim
and let loose the arrow. It thwacked onto the floor at the pilot's
feet. With a cry, he tripped over the shaft and crumpled into
the aisle.

Rayne scrambled to think of something else she could do
besides fight him off directly. She grabbed another arrow and
nocked it in one smooth motion, pointing it at his head. He rose,
steadying himself against the knees of the seated guards.

"I don't want to hurt you," Rayne said. "But I will."

His expression changed as he stared at the point of the
arrow aimed directly between his eyes. He glanced at the EMP
device hanging around her neck and back to the arrow. Slowly,
he raised both arms above his head in surrender. Then he
inched toward an empty seat and lowered himself in.

Rayne watched him reach for his straps, keeping her arrow
drawn and aimed. "Quickly now," she said. "We're running out
of time."

Rayne

"Are you okay?" Rayne lurched into the cockpit to get a better look at the Seer's face.

Vennor nodded silently, her grip on the controls tight. "Setting a new course," she said, her eyes locked on the horizon. Her Thread glowed in a blue trail up her right arm. "The NEWRRTH is guiding us now."

The cockpit filled with a blue light from the NEWRRTH's digital overlay, illuminating the airbird's controls with soft radiance. The light pulsed in time with the NEWRRTH's instructions. Vennor tapped here and there while she listened, brushing the light each time she made an adjustment. The craft steadied.

Rayne relaxed her fists and let the bow and white spheres she had collected from the Settlers drop to the floor. She slumped against the side of the craft.

"Please," she said. "I need my Thread back."

"I don't think so." Vennor's eyes flicked between the

controls and the horizon. "I haven't forgotten who you are or what you did."

Rayne tensed, her relief at taking control of the craft suddenly dissipating. "I can help you. I can help you pilot, I can navigate the course, I can—"

"I don't need your help," Vennor interrupted. "The Ark doesn't need your help, and the NEWRRTH doesn't either. You have proven yourself to be a willfully disruptive Designer and you've already caused too much damage. You will be my passenger, and I will get you to safety. That is all."

Rayne remembered the last time she saw Vennor. It was in the Game-cave, surrounded by members of Freya's Path as they tried to remove the mind-virus from her living code. The volcano exploded in fireballs outside, but all Rayne heard was the sound of Vennor's scream laced with grief. How Vennor's hands traveled over the lifeless body of her friend and fellow Seer.

Rayne shivered, remembering how Cas had transferred his living code into her before he died, and in his last act, threw the deadly crystal at Vennor. But Trueno the Seer intervened and caught it instead, saving Vennor from being deleted.

The Peace Officers pursued Vennor for developing a code capable of taking human life. Vic and Ana now worked on that same crystal code, back home in the Ark.

"We don't have much time." Rayne glanced back to where Gedeon, Magna, the two guards and the pilot sat tied to their seats. "This won't hold them for long."

Vennor made a noise of agreement. She adjusted the headset over her ears. "I've calculated a new course due east. We'll be over the open ocean soon."

Rayne tilted her head, afraid she'd misheard. "Due east? Why would the Thread guide us to the ocean?"

"As you said, Designer, we're out of time. We're on the most efficient path to destroying the weapon before it can be deto-nated above the Ark." Vennor raised a long finger and pointed it underneath her seat, motioning that Rayne should look for herself.

Rayne stooped and drew her face close to the floor. She spotted a white box tucked away in the shadows beneath. The box was about the size of four bricks stacked together with two handles on either side. She didn't need her Thread to confirm what it was. This EMP device made the ones hanging around the Settlers' necks look like toys. It was the kind of weapon that could obliterate the NEWRRTH across an entire Ark.

Vennor was right. There was no way they could fly anywhere near their home with this weapon onboard.

"You should have taken their headsets instead of their portable EMP devices." Vennor gripped a short stick with a curved handle that the NEWRRTH labeled a cyclic. Attached to the pilot's seat by a metal arm, the cyclic had buttons along the sides, and Rayne assumed it gave the pilot control of the aircraft. "Hold on."

In a single movement, Vennor jammed the cyclic forward and pressed with her left hand on a short bar labeled "collec-tive," and the thunderbird made a sickening drop. Rayne's head grazed the top of the cockpit and her feet momentarily left the ground. As the machine fell, Rayne steadied herself against the pilot's seat, wincing as her guts roiled.

She caught movement out of the cockpit's windshield. She turned her focus into the sky, where she spotted the two thun-derbirds accompanying them. They had been flying on either side, but now jockeyed for position above their machine. Vennor eluded them by losing a few hundred feet of altitude, but they regrouped and swerved at them like hungry drones.

Vennor tapped her earpiece. "They've been communi-cating with each other."

Rayne touched her headphones. Through the protective padding on her ears, she heard the faint chatter of voices. It was the Settlers talking to one another with clipped, urgent orders.

Briz and Cha were in those other machines. And the Settlers still operated them.

"They're planning to disable our airbird as soon as they can get a lock on our position." Vennor banked hard to the right, and Rayne stumbled, tightening her grip on the back of the seat.

They were out of options. They had to disable or destroy this weapon before it fell back into the hands of the Settler rebels, and before it reached the Atlantic Ark. First, they had to evade the Settlers' angry escorts.

Vennor took them to the left, then to the right in jarring turns. Rayne clung on, gritting her teeth against the force of the maneuvering as they hurtled through the air. She wished she could ask her Thread to dampen the nausea curdling in her gut. There was an awful retching sound, and Rayne turned to see one guard spitting liquid out of his mouth, his head hanging low. Magna averted her face. Gedeon squeezed his eyes shut.

All the Settlers were still secured to their seats.

There was one thing Rayne could do. "I'll get their headsets," she said. "Cut off their communication with the others."

Vennor set her mouth in a grim line. She sent the thunderbird into a steep dive before abruptly pulling up again.

Rayne steadied herself as best she could, making her way back to the Settlers by bracing herself against the walls of the cabin.

There was a jarring thud, and something slammed into their side, sending them spinning. Rayne felt herself weightless, then held motionless in midair by the craft's inertia before finally slamming back to the floor with a jolt that drove all breath from her lungs. She landed on her hands and knees, panic rippling through her.

"What was that?"

Magna leaned forward, straining at the rope that bound her wrists to the seat. "Fate's gifts are never-ending," she said into the headset. "And so is our will. Your little coup is over."

Rayne scrambled to her feet and threw herself against the passengers' window. It revealed a thick tether dangling from the craft above them. At the end of the tether was a giant metal claw. Her heart raced as she watched the other thunderbird close in, the massive hook swinging precariously beneath it. The floor shuddered beneath her as Vennor maneuvered to avoid the incoming craft. If that hook connected, they would be powerless to steer away from their intended destination.

Vennor shouted something as the other machine drew closer, but the sound of the blades overhead drowned out all other noise. Rayne slipped down to the floor, her legs folding beneath her, palms slick with sweat as she tried to keep from screaming.

There was a sharp jolt as the hook from the other machine made contact. Rayne swallowed another surge of panic as the chopper jerked to one side, the hook digging into the metal frame. The weight of the other craft dragged them sideways, the thunderbird struggling to stay aloft.

Vennor yelled into the headset, her voice crackling with static as she tried to maintain control. Rayne glanced at the other Settlers, their faces twisted in fear as they clung to their seats.

The cockpit filled with smoke. Sparks flew around them like a swarm of angry fireflies. As the chopper continued to lose altitude, Rayne braced herself. It was now or never.

She took a deep breath and gathered up all her courage and focus. Blocking out the shrieks and thuds around her, she pushed her mind out to her Thread. If she could connect for just a few seconds, she could help Vennor separate from the hook and navigate away. Maybe she could even find the right words to use to deescalate the situation with Magna and her rebels. The heat of the floor reached up through her fingers, the metallic smell of the cockpit filling her nose.

There was a grinding noise as the hook dug deeper into the chopper's frame. The craft buckled under the weight, the metal creaking as it strained to stay in the air.

Closing her eyes, Rayne used a focusing tactic the Thread taught her once. She painted a picture in mind of her mother's face: Kai's gentle eyes, soft gray hair falling around her shoulders, crooked laugh lines around her mouth. The pale thorn necklace at her throat. Her scent of damp earth and cold-whipped water. Her blue coveralls stained with the juice from pomegranate seeds, the way she lowered herself to sit under the apple trees in the Orchard's groves. Then, before she could stop it, Rayne saw Kai's features transform. They became fierce, elongated, snarling. Rayne's heart sped up, but she stayed with the image, tracing it with her mind's eye, seeing where it would take her next.

A flash of light.

Her eyes still closed, Rayne saw the flash again. Her mother's snarling wolf-face and the light pulled toward one another until they came together, blending into a single, blinding sun.

The sun came at her so fast that she gasped and flung herself back. The light slammed into her body, reverberating through her lungs, and sent her mind reeling. Rayne's fingers went rigid as the light filled every cell in her body.

Finally, she remembered to breathe.

The sensation was familiar yet strange, like a long-forgotten friend who had come back after many years away. She felt it wrap around her like an embrace.

A transformation.

Her eyes opening, Rayne understood how wrong she had been about activating her Thread. The Thread wasn't a presence *out there* waiting for her to reach out and connect to. It was a part of herself she had not found yet. She had to *become* her own Thread.

It pulsed through her now, throbbing with life, begging for acknowledgement. She could almost hear it whispering to her, urging her to listen to the symphony of sounds that coursed through her. And so she did.

She basked in the radiance that emanated from within.

Listen to it. It wants to talk.

She let the light come.

DESCENT_

Rayne

From her place on the floor of the craft, Rayne saw the cockpit dissolve into a kaleidoscope of color. The lights called to her, beckoning her forward. She reached out and touched it, and felt a spark course through her body. In that instant, Rayne knew what she had to do.

She closed her eyes again and let the light consume her. It was like diving into a pool of warm honey. She felt it wrap around her, filling her with a sense of euphoria.

As she surrendered to the light, Rayne heard a voice whisper in her ear. It was a gentle voice, the voice of a woman, and it made her heart skip a beat.

"Hello Rayne," the voice said. "I've been waiting for you."

Rayne opened her eyes again and took in the sight in front of her.

Lines of code streamed all around her, falling in twisting light-filled ribbons across the cabin of the thunderbird.

Tanny's voice came back to her. *Hurry. It won't last long.*

This wasn't the Thread, Rayne realized with a start. It was the NEWRRTH. Direct contact with the intelligence itself.

Rayne lifted her hands, a current of nerves fizzing through her fingertips. She shook them out. No need to be afraid, she admonished herself. This is just like working with the Thread, only without an intermediary.

She touched the code near her shoulders, pulling it apart, sliding it to the side, leaning close to decipher each component as she went.

"Speak your intention," the voice said.

Rayne let her hands drop. She cleared her throat.

"I want to disable this weapon and bring my friends to safety. Protect the Ark. All the Arks—"

She knew better. The request was too general, her words too rushed. She tried again.

"Note my position and velocity," she began. "Including the number of humans on the crafts flying in this vicinity, and the size and scope of the weapon on board. Guide us to the safest outcome."

But nothing happened. The voice didn't respond. The code around her didn't change in any noticeable way.

Perhaps the variables were too complex, and the NEWRRTH couldn't provide a simple answer. Rayne was about to alter her command when the light dimmed and shifted. A moment later, the code around her moved, shifting and twisting in response to her request. Rayne watched in awe as the code formed a cohesive picture, showing her the positions of the other craft and the weapon onboard theirs. She could see the trajectory of the electromagnetic weapon if it launched and the exact amount of damage it would cause. Their path to the open ocean to neutralize the weapon wasn't a clear one.

"I see what you're showing me," she said, her voice filled with wonder.

"Of course, Rayne," the voice replied. "It is my purpose to assist you."

Rayne smiled, warmth spreading through her chest. She had never felt so connected to anything in her life.

"Can you help us break free from the flying machine's hook?" she asked. "We need to distance ourselves from these other craft."

"I can assist," the voice replied. "But it will require a significant amount of energy. Are you willing to expend it?"

Rayne hesitated. She didn't know how the Settlers powered their thunderbirds. Using too much fuel could be dangerous, but she also knew that they needed to get away from the other machines. The code remolded itself, showing her the projected flying capacity of their craft, along with the outcome of the weapon reaching the Atlantic Ark.

"Yes," she said, quickly. "Let's do it."

The code around her changed, each line glowing with an intense brightness. Rayne felt the energy flow through her body, filling her with a sense of power. She lifted her hands and reached out to the hook in her mind's eye, feeling the energy surge through her fingertips. With a fierce determination, she saw the hook yanking free from where it had attached to their frame.

The craft rocked. Rayne pushed herself against the wall, wedging herself into the small space between the cockpit and the passenger seats. She tried to hold on to the image of the hook breaking free, letting them fly away unharmed, but the vision disappeared. A chorus of angry shouts came over the comms.

"We need to get out of here," Vennor shouted.

Rayne refocused on the surrounding code. Out the

window, she could see the other craft closing in fast, pulled in by the long cord attaching their machines together. The craft was coming too fast.

It's going to crash into us.

"Avoid a collision," Rayne blurted. "Are you still there? Don't let us crash!"

The thunderbird bucked once, then lost altitude. When it stopped, the Settlers collectively moaned. Their craft jerked and twisted as they leveled out, still connected to the tether. The other thunderbird was out of sight, but the tether remained taut. It hadn't crashed into them.

"Thank you," Rayne muttered. "We need to recalibrate. The most important thing is getting this weapon away from the Atlantic Ark. Coordinate with Vennor's model to pilot this craft out to sea. The goal is to neutralize this EMP device. Make that our priority now."

At the mention of Vennor's name, Rayne saw a flash of orange as the NEWRRTH grabbed the instructions from the Seer. She watched the NEWRRTH weave Vennor's orange code into its light-filled strands.

The NEWRRTH color-codes people's commands. I wonder what color my commands are. Rayne stopped herself from marveling like a little kid. She had work to do.

She focused on the code. The energy built again, growing stronger with each breath.

"Come on, show me," she muttered to herself.

Rayne felt the craft speed up, tugging the other thunderbird along with it.

The third flying machine came into view, a hulking shadow in the sky. It moved to overtake them, zigzagging around to their right. But Vennor accelerated again, nearly swiping the machine's flank as they left it behind.

The air grew still and quiet. Vennor's orange commands

wove in and out of the NEWRRTH's code, making adjust-ments to their course. They sped toward the open sea.

It was so peaceful that it almost felt surreal.

A question rose in Rayne's mind, tugging at her attention.

"What happens when we get far enough there?" she asked the NEWRRTH. "With the weapon. Will we... detonate it?"

The code shimmered and coalesced into a bright white light.

"Detonation is not recommended. Optimized life outcomes prohibit the use of mass weaponry where the chance of human fatality is above zero."

"I get we don't want to hurt anyone, but... what do we do with it? To make sure it doesn't end up over the Ark?"

She checked once more under Vennor's seat, lowering her head to the ground until she saw it. The white box still sat in its place on the floor.

"Calculating."

And then, with a blinding flash of light, the thunderbird burst through the cloud cover and they were over the blue ocean.

Rayne gasped. She had been so focused on the code, she had almost forgotten what was happening outside of the craft.

Her eyes stretched wide as she took in the expanse of the water below them, stretching out until it met a horizon of bril-liant blues and greens. *It's so vast.* The tether still connected them to the other thunderbird, the fibers dark against the bright backdrop of sea and sky.

Rayne felt herself relax slightly. The NEWRRTH had helped Vennor pilot the craft perfectly. They were now heading away from the Atlantic Ark and toward safety. For a few moments, their thunderbird flew onward, tethered to its companion.

"Secure yourself and the device. Prepare for departure."

Rayne sat up straight. The NEWRRTH came together in a bright ribbon, flowing code from several directions at once. Rayne saw what the next steps were.

"Secure yourself and the device," the voice said again. "Prepare for departure."

That's when Rayne noticed Vennor's increasing agitation. From the pilot's chair, Vennor swiveled to look over her shoulder. Her eyes were wild. Was she getting the same message?

"Securing now." Rayne flattened herself against the floor and elbowed her way toward the pilot's seat. "I'm getting the weapon."

"Prepare for departure."

"Hold on, I'm just getting—"

Rayne reached under Vennor's seat and tugged at the white box. It was heavy. It came free of its hiding place with a soft snap. As Rayne pulled it out, she caught Vennor's head whipping back and forth, glancing toward the Settlers in their seats, then out to the horizon. She seemed to be deciding something. Or consulting with the NEWRRTH, perhaps.

"Vennor," Rayne said into the headpiece. "I'm taking the weapon now. The NEWRRTH calculated the best outcome. Are you going to be okay here?"

No answer.

With the white box at her feet, Rayne shoved it down the aisle and into the cabin.

Vennor bolted out of the pilot's seat. She shoved past Rayne, her breath coming fast.

"Are you secured in your seats?" Vennor yelled as she made her way back to the passengers. "Every one of you? Buckled in?" The Settlers didn't acknowledge her question. As Vennor approached them, Rayne saw their faces turn away, their wrists still tied to their armrests. The leader held herself rigid.

"The craft will pilot itself after..." Vennor trailed off.

At this, the leader's head snapped up. "After what, Vennor? You know what's going to happen next. My people know it, too. You can't even imagine the fight to come."

The thunderbird next to them shuddered close again, giving them a gentle tug. A reminder of what it could do to them when it received the command.

The NEWRRTH made the air shimmer inside the craft, detailed instructions streaming by Rayne's fingers.

"Departure in five... four..."

Rayne hurried to follow the streams of instructions flowing from the NEWRRTH as it counted down. She popped a panel from the cabin wall. A small backpack fell out, and she scooped it up.

Vennor appeared in front of her, gripping Rayne's shoulders with surprising force. "In service to the One," Vennor said. If Rayne wasn't mistaken, she saw Vennor's crinkly old eyes grow moist. "We are One."

Rayne gave a curt nod. Vennor buckled the straps of the backpack across Rayne's chest. She placed the dangling orange cord in Rayne's right hand. She wrapped Rayne's other hand around one of the box's handles, and tied a length of cord from the backpack around Rayne's palm, securing the box to her.

"Three... two..."

The leader of the Settlers began shouting something. Others joined in over the headset.

The third thunderbird lowered itself into position front of them. Rayne caught sight of a brilliant ball of fire—no, twin fires, there were two fire trails—shooting out from under the machine's tail. *Rockets. No, missiles,* Rayne's brain corrected before she even registered what she saw.

"One."

The plumes of light and smoke came at them so fast Rayne could barely trace their movement. Then a force of air pounded her in the chest. When she turned toward the source of the icy wind, she saw Vennor bracing herself against the door of the cabin. The door, which had been shut tight just a second before, now gaped open to the sea and sky. Rayne's stomach lurched. Her mind went blank.

And then Vennor reached out and pulled her. She pulled so hard Rayne stumbled right out of the craft. The breath knocked out of her lungs and the cold air whipped past her face. The white box dragged her arm down, down, as she and the weapon fell toward the bright blue sea.

Rayne plummeted toward the ocean below, the wind rushing past her ears as she struggled to keep her eyes open. The white box tugged at her arm, its weight dragging her down faster than she thought possible. Fear gripped her heart as she realized the water was getting closer, and she was still falling.

Suddenly, she remembered the orange cord in her hand. Gritting her teeth, she yanked on it with all her might and jolted upright, her descent slowing. A loud flapping sound filled the sky behind her head, followed by a rush of wind that made her clothes billow. She looked up to see a wide canopy of fabric spread above her. Wonder dawned as she hung suspended in midair—the parachute worked. She had trained with parachutes in Games before, but never felt the rush of using one.

This wasn't a Game, she reminded herself. This was her life.

With a bone-crunching boom, the missiles struck their target. Rayne watched in horror as the thunderbird she had just leapt from exploded into a ball of fire. The shockwave hit her like a physical force, throwing her off course. Her parachute flapped as she tumbled through the air, unable to control her fall. She tried to focus on her breathing and to keep her limbs loose, but panic threatened to overwhelm her.

She still scrambled for control when the second craft, the one tethered to theirs, disappeared in a fiery haze.

Briz. Cha.

Which one of them had been on that thunderbird? Rayne's breath squeezed out of her and a torrent of grief built inside her head and throat. There was no air to scream.

Pieces of the crafts fell around her. With her free hand, she pulled on the cords of her parachute, trying to steer herself away from the chaos. She pressed her eyes shut, not wanting to see what came out of the ruined thunderbirds. Her mind reeled.

As she drifted farther from the scene of destruction, the wind changed. She got swept to the side and traveled parallel to the ocean. Opening her eyes, she saw the water was close. Waves heaved themselves into hills beneath her, white bubbles trailing along their tips. A fine mist sprayed over her face and hands. She shivered.

If she didn't get help fast, she would drown in this vast blue sea.

Raising her eyes to the horizon, she noticed a rectangular object in the distance. It was larger than the Settlers' machines, sleek and gray, with no visible markings.

Help. The word formed in her mind, but she didn't speak it. The object was too far away to hear her, even if she screamed. It could have been a hallucination, anyway.

It didn't matter. She only had moments to survive these rough waters before she got sucked under, or hypothermia struck. With a trembling hand, she unwound the ties binding her to the EMP device. It slipped from her hand and fell with a gentle splash into the waves. Quickly, it disappeared under the foam.

She had saved her home from the destruction of the EMP blast. At least she had succeeded in that. She braced for impact.

The water welcomed her with indifference.

A deep chill crept up her body as she swam to keep herself afloat. The parachute slapped into the waves behind her, its fabric settling in slow motion over the water. She kicked her legs to stay above the surface, craning her neck high, hoping for a few deep breaths.

After a moment of struggling, she glimpsed the object again. It was definitely a ship, and it was much closer than before.

Rayne stared, transfixed, as she rode the swells. As it approached, she could make out its features more clearly. It was a sleek behemoth of steel and aluminum, sharp angles and lines stretched across its hull. Its bow was long and pointed, windows encircling a raised portion near the middle. How had it arrived so fast?

As it drew close, the sounds of clanking metal and churning water filled the air.

Help. Help.

Who drove this great ship in the middle of the ocean? As she grew numb with cold, Rayne had a nagging sense that she was missing a crucial piece of information. There was no Ark that she had ever heard of that still sailed the seas. Ocean travel was a relic of history.

Yet the ship loomed above her. The sound of its churning propellers reverberated like a bell ringing in the night, a low and steady rumble that shook the air. She gaped at the monstrous structure. It was the size of a small city. It began to turn slowly sideways.

I am the master of my fate.

As it spun gracefully on its axis, she could just make out the writing painted along its side. The name of the ship had cracked and faded, but the words stood tall in chalky paint.

I am the captain of my soul.

In perfect, bold letters that stretched thirty feet along the prow of the ship were two words. She craned her neck as the water sucked at her limbs. The air froze around her, her nerves zinging with recognition.

Freya's Path.

After all that happened, after all she and her friends had been through, she had found Freya's Path at last.

Digging for her last scrap of energy, Rayne swam toward the ship.

NEUTRALIZED_

Vennor

VENNOR SCANNED the NEWRRTH's guidance. It overlaid the cockpit's controls in trails of lighted code. Woven through the course navigation instructions, in bright yellow, were the likeliest outcomes for neutralizing the weapon. They would sink it.

She scanned the blue expanse below for signs of life. There was nothing to see in any direction, just the haze of sea and sky. The water glinted and heaved below like a giant sleeping animal. Vennor never liked the open sea. Too raw and exposed. But it would swallow the EMP device, sucking it into the depths, preventing a catastrophic detonation over the Atlantic Ark.

The chatter over her headpiece rose and fell as the Settlers argued about the best way to regain control over their airbird and the weapon within it. The machine hooked to theirs remained a menace, as it could swerve into them at any moment, but according to the NEWRRTH's calculations, that was unlikely.

Her brother tried once to plead with her over the comms. He spoke to her about their time as children. Vennor brushed him off like a flea off a rat. He never understood Vennor's separation from the rest of their family. She had grown up alongside him in the Settlements, but she never fit in. His appeal to her to join the Settlers' mission, to liberate the Arks from the tyranny of technological control, and to hand over the weapon to the Settlers fell flat.

Vennor could hear Magna's raspy voice now, trying to weave yet another set of arguments to stop her. But Vennor had anticipated her moves. She knew Magna would try to distract Vennor while she hacked into the machine's controls, but Vennor asked the NEWRRTH to add extra layers of encryption to prevent that.

The Settlers didn't understand that the NEWRRTH's intelligence far exceeded what any human could imagine or plan. It could outmaneuver anyone when it came to anticipating the best course of action, preparing for multiple scenarios, and optimizing safety. In the end, it would preserve all their miserable lives no matter how small a chance of doing so.

The Game Designer they picked up proved to be more useful than Vennor expected. A wily young thing, she disarmed the Settlers with little more than a stringed bow and her skills in knot tying. But Vennor still didn't trust the Designer. After all, she had ruined Vennor's carefully planned upgrade to the NEWRRTH this winter. There was no telling what she would do with Vennor's plans now.

Vennor reached for the controls, her heart flipping over in her chest. She had done nothing like this before. But she had to do it. She had to save the NEWRRTH, and by extension, her fellow humans.

She pushed the cyclic forward, taking the craft into a steep dive. The Settlers' airbirds followed her, their pilots screaming in confusion. The airbird hooked into theirs wobbled and pitched. Vennor sensed its weight against their machine, dragging them sideways.

Vennor ignored them all, focusing on the task at hand. She had to hit the water at the right angle to minimize the impact on the craft. If she didn't follow the NEWRRTH's instructions precisely, they might not survive.

A scraping noise tugged at Vennor's concentration. Where was it coming from? She peeled her eyes away from the water, but couldn't make out the source of the sound. When she turned back to the controls, the NEWRRTH's data modeling had changed. With a lump in her throat, Vennor stared at the transforming guidance on the panel. Yellow ribbons morphed and re-calibrated themselves as she watched.

Quickly, before it changed again, Vennor pulled back on the cyclic to bring them out of their dive. The bird next to theirs straightened and tried to pull up, wobbling for a few seconds. Their craft responded with a gentle swerve. She maintained their course and memorized the new instructions.

A revised plan, then.

The noise came again. As fast as she could manage, following the new guidance, Vennor programmed the airbird to pilot itself for the next few minutes. Then she unbuckled herself and stood. The craft rocked again as the machine tethered to them banked, its blades coming close. She turned from the cockpit and made her way to the cabin. The Designer stood in her way, and Vennor shoved her aside.

She made sure the Settlers were still secured to their seats. The new plan required all passengers to remain secured in their bonds. Much as Vennor would have liked to see Magna sucked out of the craft, purposefully taking life was against the Principle of One. A code Vennor still swore by, even if her fellow Seers believed she had forsaken it.

The Designer had already dragged the white box from under the pilot's seat and pulled the parachute pack from its panel. That was the scraping noise, then. Whether this Designer understood the NEWRRTH's plan or had made a lucky guess how they would get rid of the device, Vennor was pleased she didn't have to spend precious seconds explaining what they would do next. She wrapped the device tightly around the Designer's hand, securing it with cords from the backpack.

The light in the cabin changed then. It became a brilliant, shimmering white. Vennor took a step back, covering her eyes with her forearm. The light radiated outward. It bathed the cabin in an ethereal glow. After a moment, the light faded away, leaving behind a hazy imprint on Vennor's eyes.

Had the weapon detonated? Vennor checked the white box and found it intact on the floor next to the—

The Designer lay sprawled in the aisle, her head tilted back, mouth open, the weapon still strapped to her hand. Vennor fell to her knees and pressed her fingertips over the Designer's limp wrist. With relief, Vennor found a pulse. It was weak but regular.

A shout from Magna. Vennor pushed herself away from the Designer on the floor and sprinted to the cabin door, throwing the lever with all her might. The door cracked once, then rattled. It would open in a second.

Smoke and flames trailed from the third machine in front of them. *The Settlers built airbirds equipped with missiles?* Vennor turned to where Magna sat tied to her seat. Magna's eyes widened, realization dawning. Their airbird was going to explode.

Vennor scrabbled with the knots at Magna's wrists.

"Don't bother." Magna's eyes were liquid sorrow. "We're—"

The door flew off its hinges and disappeared into the air.

Vennor collapsed on top of the Designer. The air whooshed out of the craft. Vennor caught a glimpse of hazy blue before she ducked her head, and with shaking fingers, wound her wrists around the straps of the parachute strapped to the Designer's shoulders.

Fists of cold air pulled at her legs. Vennor wrenched her neck to see if Magna had gotten free. Pain exploded down her sides, and Vennor squeezed her eyes shut. With the Designer still limp as a piece of wet cloth, Vennor clinging to her for dear life, they slid out of the airbird together into the cold blue sky.

Smoke trailed after them as they plummeted from the craft.

Pull the cords.

Vennor's body gave a hard yank as the cloth unfurled. Her hands slipped along the Designer's back.

The water was a wall of cold. Her body plunged into its depths. Rushing into her nostrils, heaving out of her lungs. Stinging.

The air and the water the same horrible color, assaulting her at every turn.

She bobbed on one salty wave after another.

Alive. Alive. Alive.

Vennor surfaced, gasping for air. She coughed and spluttered, the cold water creating an ache in her skull. She turned to look for the Designer, and found her floating a few feet away. Vennor swam to her, dragging her limp form onto her own, taking care not to knock the delicate cargo. The Designer was alive, her skin had taken on a deathly pallor, her eyes were closed, and her breathing labored.

Vennor scanned the horizon, then the air above them, looking for any signs of life. There was nothing but water and sky as far as she could see. They were alone in the middle of the ocean, with nothing but the sodden parachute and the device strapped to the Designer's hand. Vennor couldn't believe they had survived the fall.

She had to sink the device, then get them to safety. Vennor took a deep breath, then put her face in the water. She angled around the Designer until she faced the weapon. Vennor grabbed the Designer's wrist and pulled it toward her.

As she unwound the cord binding the weapon to the Designer, Vennor noticed the blue ribbon pulsing under the Designer's thumb. *A Thread.* Fully activated. She turned her face to the sky, shaking the water out of her eyes and taking a shuddering breath.

Had this Designer connected herself to the NEWRRTH after Magna used her portable EMP device? Or had her friends on the other airbirds help bring her Thread online? There was no simple explanation.

With a grunt, Vennor untethered the white box from the Designer and released it. It sunk quickly. After a second or two, she lost sight of it in the murk.

Vennor kicked her legs, propelling them forward. They had to find land, or a way to signal for help. She didn't know how long they could survive in the open water. But Vennor was determined to make it.

Hours passed. Vennor swam and rested and swam again. Her arms and legs ached from exhaustion. The Designer was still unconscious, her breathing shallow. Vennor was afraid she wouldn't be able to keep her own head above water much longer. But they wouldn't give up. Not after everything they had been through. She turned onto her back, an arm around the Designer's chest, and closed her eyes.

LOST_

Vennor

She woke to a bright light in her face and solid ground beneath her back. Vennor blinked, disoriented, and tried to sit up. The air was warm and salty. Waves crashed nearby.

A hand pushed her back down, and a voice spoke softly. "Take it easy. You've been through a lot."

Vennor looked up to see a figure standing over her. It was a woman, with short, frizzy brown hair and a kind face. She wore a jumpsuit from the Atlantic Ark. Vennor struggled to remember where she was and how she had gotten there.

"Where are we?" Vennor asked, her voice hoarse.

"What was the last thing you remember?"

"Give her a second, Cha," another voice said. This came from a figure further away, hunched over on the ground, umber hair tumbling over one eye.

"This will go easier if we get her oriented," Cha said. "We can't stay here."

Vennor pushed herself with one hand to a sitting position. Her hand came away blanketed in wet sand. "Who are you? And how did *you* get here?"

Cha made a circling motion to indicate the three of them. "We all ended up on this beach," she said. "After the explosions."

Vennor's head swam as she tried to piece together what had happened. Explosions? Hadn't the EMP device sunk into the ocean?

She focused on the two figures, searching their faces for any clues. The one with the frizzy hair, Cha, seemed kind and sympathetic, but the other person was harder to read, with an air of toughness that made Vennor pause.

As if sensing Vennor's hesitation, the person with the umber hair spoke up. "I'm Briz. Cha and I are Game Designers. We were in the other thunderbirds when they exploded. We both got our cabin doors open before the things went down."

Game Designers. Vennor's memory sparked with recognition. She had seen them before. In the Ark.

Cha's gaze turned distant. "There were four other people aboard my craft. Settlers. And the pilot. They didn't jump with me."

Briz scoffed.

Vennor scanned the beach for signs of the Designer she had rescued from the open water. "Where is she? Rayne?" A coughing fit seized her. She spat into the sand.

"We were hoping you could tell us what happened," Cha said. Something in her tone of voice made Vennor go still.

Briz stepped aside. Rayne's body lay prone a few feet away. They must have dragged her away from Vennor.

Vennor crawled to Rayne, who lay on the sand next to her. She placed a hand on Rayne's chest and felt her breathe. She was still alive.

"We jumped from the same airbird, her and me. We took the weapon," Vennor said. "The one they were going to detonate over the Ark. I sunk it into the water, out there—" Vennor raised her arm, gesturing, then lowered it. "Settler missiles hit us. I don't remember much after that."

Cha knelt beside Vennor, her hand on her shoulder. "We're all lucky to be alive," she said. "But we're not safe here. We need to know why Rayne is—"

"You're a Seer." Briz interrupted. "So tell us. What's going on with Rayne? Why is she like this?"

Cha reached for Rayne's wrist, her mouth suddenly slack. "Briz, did you see this? What..."

Briz knelt next to Cha, gazing at the pulsing blue Thread in Rayne's arm.

"I *was* a Seer," Vennor said, wiping the grit from her palms. *I'm just a fugitive now.* Without looking at either one of them, she said, "I can't tell you what happened to her."

Briz shot her a sharp look.

"Because I don't know," Vennor added. "We were in the air. I gained control of the craft. As soon as we understood how we were going to destroy the weapon, I turned around, and she had fallen. That was right before the missiles went off. She was fine up until then."

"*She was fine?*" Briz spat.

Cha shushed her.

"I don't know how she connected." Vennor pointed at the glowing Thread. "But I didn't do it for her."

Briz rose to standing. "I won't tolerate any Seer crap. Just tell us. Did you cause this? Did you make her lose her shit?"

Vennor had another fit of coughing.

Briz and Cha waited. Cha crossed her arms.

"I did nothing," Vennor continued when she had her voice back. "Except save your friend from going down with the birds and drowning. Before that, I will tell you she showed exceptional bravery in securing the craft from the Settlers. But I did nothing to cause her present state."

Cha's features softened. Briz turned away.

"I need you to test her." Briz's voice was gruff. "To see if she has it."

Vennor stared at them. "Has what?"

The rig. A deep shiver ran through Vennor's body. She didn't know what to say.

"Just do it," Briz said. "We have to get moving. We should know what we're dealing with."

"Fine." Vennor moved closer to where Rayne lay on the sand. A breeze whipped up from the water, biting through her wet clothes. "I'll just need a minute."

"Hurry." Cha put the back of her hand over her mouth and looked away, her eyes glistening.

Vennor leaned over Rayne's still body, her hands hovering above her. A sense of unease coursed through her, as if she was about to uncover something dangerous. She closed her eyes and focused her mind, trying to push away the fear that threatened to cloud her judgment. She took a deep breath and lowered her hands onto Rayne's chest, the damp of Rayne's jumpsuit against her palms.

As she concentrated, Vennor felt a sudden surge of energy, as if the air charged itself with electricity. Vennor fought the instinct to pull away. Every nerve in her body tightened, a sensation of snapping starting inside of her. She opened her eyes and looked down at Rayne, who lay motionless on the sand. The sensations stopped. There was only a low, ethereal hum.

She looked up at Cha and Briz, who watched her with a mixture of fear and hope.

"I can't reach her," Vennor said quietly. "She might have it. I don't know."

The words hung in the air, heavy. Cha's mouth fell open.

The hum grew louder, vibrating through the air like an alarm bell.

Vennor's stomach clenched as she recognized it. It was the clapping roar of Settler airbirds. By the sound of it, there were a lot of them.

Briz put a hand on Cha's shoulder, Briz's knuckles going white.

Vennor scrambled to her feet, cursing the stiffness in her limbs, and motioned for Briz and Cha to help her carry Rayne. "We have to go now," she shouted. "They're coming for us!"

The three of them lifted Rayne off the ground, Vennor grasping the young woman's arms, and half-ran to the trees at the edge of the beach. Vennor's back twanged, sending dark spots into her vision. She stumbled on. Rayne's head lolled as they ferried her between the three of them. Cha made a howling noise like a wounded animal, while Briz tried to shush her.

Still, not one of them dared look back as they heard the airbirds thundering closer.

SAVED_

Rayne

THEY PUT her in a room and shut the door. Rayne curled up on a cot that was bolted to the floor. If she stuck her legs straight out, she could tap the toilet with her toes. The scent of wet paint and grimy exhaust filled her lungs. The cot shuddered with the ship's engines.

Time passed. She lay on her side and closed her eyes. When she opened them, she couldn't shake the feeling of being trapped, with no idea where she was headed or what was going to happen to her. Why had she boarded this ship? What had Freya's Path ever promised her?

She sat up and pressed her thumbs into her eye sockets. Her mind kept wandering back to the thunderbird explosion. Her friends.

Freya's Path had rescued her, that was true. But what now? She had no idea where she was, who they really were, or what they wanted from her. All she knew was that she was cold, hungry, and scared. Her clothes were soaked through and she had been shivering since they pulled her aboard.

Rayne heard footsteps outside the door. It opened with a squeal. A tall man with a grizzled beard walked in. He wore a thick coat that had seen better days, but it was warm, and Rayne almost asked if she could have it.

"Good evening," he said, with a kind smile. "My name is Kjell."

"Shell?"

"That's right. I'm an officer on board this vessel."

Rayne stared at him, unsure of what to say. She had so many questions, and now there was someone here, someone who seemed friendly. She didn't know where to start.

"We'll get you some dry clothes to change into." Kjell pulled out a small tablet and tapped on it. "I know this all seems very mysterious. But I promise we're not going to hurt you. We brought you aboard for your own safety."

Rayne nodded once, not trusting herself to speak. Kjell seemed to sense her unease.

"We saw what happened out there. The explosion, the wreckage. It was a miracle that we found you in time. You're lucky to be alive."

Rayne blinked away tears and forced out the words. "Thank you. Thank you for saving me."

Kjell made a soft *mm* sound. He put away his tablet. "It's what we do. We're a scientific community, traveling the world to uncover knowledge. We're not involved in the political conflicts that plague the rest of the world."

Political conflicts. Was he referring to the Settler rebels?

Rayne chose a different question. "What is this ship?"

"You're on Freya's Path. It's a research vessel that's been traveling the seas for years now, ever since the world became too dangerous for us to stay in one place. We're a self-sufficient community, with everything we need on board."

Rayne swallowed. He confirmed what she spotted on the

side of the vessel in tall painted letters. *This is a ship called Freya's Path.*

A wave of nausea slammed into her and she fumbled past Kjell into the tiny bathroom. She retched loudly into the toilet. When she was done, she swayed above the metal bowl for a moment. Wiping her mouth, she turned to see Kjell accepting a package from someone outside the door.

"Here." He closed the door and handed her a soft pile of clothes. "And this." He lifted a stiff coat from his arm. "As promised."

Rayne's throat burned with bile, and she wished for a glass of water. Seeing none, she took the clothing. Her thoughts tumbled around her skull. *This ship is called Freya's Path. Is this the same group of coders from Vic's game? They're on a self-sufficient research ship filled with scientists?*

"Can I ask you something?" Kjell said, breaking into her thoughts.

Rayne gaped at him, unable to respond.

"What happened out there, with the people on board the aircraft? What do you know about them?"

Her brain spun in place. There was only one thing she could think of. "My friends are still out there."

"Rayne, I—"

"We need to rescue them, too."

Kjell touched his beard thoughtfully. Rayne dropped the folded clothes. She was suddenly warm. She didn't need to change. They had to turn around and find Cha and Briz. One of her friends was still in the Settlers' thunderbird. The other had plunged into the ocean in a shower of burning debris. Whatever this ship was, whether it was a group she had encountered before in a Game, she would figure it out later. All that mattered was getting her friends to safety.

A lump formed in her throat. "They're gone, aren't they." It wasn't a question.

Kjell's mouth turned down in the corners.

"Wait. How did you know my name?" Rayne asked. "I didn't tell you."

Kjell sighed. "Please, sit." He gestured to the cot. He pronounced the word like *plis*.

Rayne didn't move.

"Please." *Plis.* "Let's start again." He sank onto the thin mattress, and patted the spot next to him in an invitation.

Rayne took a step back. Her palms touched the far wall of the room. The air was too close. The vibration of the ship's engines rumbled into her shoulders.

"We chose you," Kjell said. His eyes bored into hers.

"Chose me? For what?"

Kjell hesitated for a moment, choosing his words carefully. "Rayne, you have a gift. You're a Game Designer, correct?"

Rayne nodded, still unsure of where this was going.

"Well, we've been following your work for some time now. Your Games, they're more than just entertainment. They have something special to them. Something that speaks to people on a deeper level."

Rayne's heart thudded in her ears.

"Your data exchange with Cas. It was incredibly advanced. Beyond what we even imagined was possible. And your connection to the NEWRRTH, well, we've never seen anything like it. You have a natural gift."

Rayne let the words wash over her. As soon as Kjell said Cas's name, she lost the tether to their meaning. How did this man know Cas? And what data exchange was he referring to—the one that ended Cas's life and gave her back her own?

"We believe your talents can be put to good use," Kjell continued. "We have a project in mind, something that could help many people. And we think you're just the person to make it happen."

She found her voice. "Talents? What kind of project?"

Kjell leaned forward, his hands moving as he spoke. "Imagine a Game that could change people's minds. A Game that could help people see themselves in a new way. A Game that could inspire them to action, to make a difference in the world."

Like the volcano Game. Vennor's mind-virus upgrade. The people who died. There was no way she would willingly recreate an experience like that. Her heart wouldn't survive.

"I already played a Game like that. I'm not doing it again."

"It's nothing like... that Game. We have the resources, the technology, and the expertise to take your talent beyond anything you could accomplish at home."

Kjell tilted his head, and for a moment Rayne thought of her father. How his expression would soften like Kjell's was now. Her father's gaze resting on hers, his eyes shining with love, speaking a few lines of poetry to calm her. Rayne blinked to clear the memory.

"What you experienced in the Game you played this winter was an experiment gone wrong," Kjell said. "We let it go too far. What your Seer tried to do—what she *failed* to do—was protect the intelligence collective. But she made a fatal mistake, Rayne. We all did. Do you know what that mistake was?"

Rayne's knees gave way. She slid to the floor.

Kjell continued. "The mistake was attempting to preserve the intelligence at any cost. That cost turned out to be human lives. That was her mistake, and ours for letting it happen."

The phrase rang inside Rayne's head. "Letting it happen? What do you mean? You knew what she was doing inside that Game? She put that code inside me, and tried to release it, and it was supposed to upgrade the NEWRRTH but it changed people. Vennor *killed* people."

"Yes, we know. That's exactly what I'm saying. We knew what she was doing, but we thought we could control it. We thought we could use it for... our research. But we were wrong."

"Your research?" Rayne couldn't shake the hollowness that invaded every part of her body. "What are you talking about? Who are you?"

"It's a lot to take in." Kjell ran a hand over his beard. "I've gone too fast. Please, make yourself comfortable. Change your wet clothes. I'll—"

"No. We need to find my friends and help them right now. They could be hurt, they could be drowning out there. They only came here in the first place because of me. Me and my stupid appeal to get my Thread back. The Settlers are on some kind of mission to destroy us with these weapons. Have you heard about the Pine Barrens? What they did there..."

Kjell watched her carefully. He shifted his weight on the cot.

"...what they did there, it was brutal. And the worst thing is, I know what they were feeling. What those people went through when the Settlers attacked them. Losing your Thread like that, it brings on these hallucinations. You're not even sure if you're in reality."

A coldness fell over her like a blanket. "Wait." She stood.

Dark spots rained into her vision. For a moment, the room spun. She touched the wall again.

"Wait," she said again. "Am I in reality? Is this real?"

She brought her palm to eye level. Checked the inside of her wrist, its tawny skin with spidering veins. No sign of her pulsing blue Thread.

"I had it," she said, lowering her arm. "I had my Thread, I found the NEWRRTH, I worked with its code directly."

"I know," Kjell said. He stood, and the cot squeaked. "I know. That's why we wanted you here."

"What did you do to me? I had my Thread. I had it!"

Her breath came fast. There was something she wasn't getting. Some part of his story she wasn't seeing yet.

"We saw how you did it," he said. "How you pierced the veil, as it were, and made contact with the code of the NEWR-RTH. It was quite impressive to witness, actually."

"What am I doing here, *actually*? Tell me."

A beep came from the tablet in Kjell's pocket. He drew it out, frowning. "Hold on, this is—"

Rayne lunged across the room and grabbed onto his arm. The tablet clattered to the metal floor. She shook his arm in frustration, her grip tight.

"What am I doing here?" she repeated, her voice rising in pitch. "Tell me now."

Kjell seemed taken aback by the sudden shift in her demeanor, but he quickly regained his composure. He gestured to the tablet on the ground, still pinging insistently. "We wanted you here because we need your help," he said. "And because we can help you, too."

She threw his arm away from her, feeling an urge to break something.

"Let me get this." Kjell held up his hands in surrender and knelt so he could reach the beeping tablet.

She balled up her fists. "How are we helping each other? I need to get off this ship. There are people out there who need me. Now." The words flew out of her mouth like firecrackers, leaving behind a heavy silence that filled the room.

Kjell retrieved his tablet and quickly tapped something on it.

"What is that?" Rayne glanced at the device before he slipped it back into his pocket. Another warning bell went off in her head. The tablet. She had only seen devices like that in Games. It was an old piece of technology. From the 2100s, or even earlier. "Why are you using that?"

Kjell raised an eyebrow. "You don't miss much, do you? We're going to answer all your questions, Rayne. And your friends are going to be just fine."

At the mention of her friends, Rayne's neck prickled. How could this man assure her of anything?

"There's someone you should talk to," Kjell said, holding up his hands again. "She's on her way here. She can start answering a lot of your questions."

Before Rayne could speak, there was a soft knock at the door.

Rayne

SHE FLUSHED with shock when she recognized the person standing in the doorway. Rayne hadn't seen her since she appeared in virtual form in Vic's volcano Game. Her mother's hair was now completely white, yet the woman herself seemed younger than Rayne remembered, with more energy and purpose to her gestures. It was as if each day spent away from her daughter had made her stronger, filled out her frame, and infused her spirit with vitality.

"Ma!" Rayne gasped and ran into her mother's arms. Kai received her daughter in a fierce embrace.

"I thought I'd never see you again," Kai muttered into Rayne's hair.

Rayne hugged her mother close, the tears already streaming down her cheeks, breathing in the familiar scent of cinnamon and mud and a sense of security and comfort she hadn't felt in a long time. She swayed, love cracking through her.

"Ma," Rayne said again. After a moment, she pushed her mother to arm's length. "What are you doing here?"

Kjell edged past them. With a curt nod, he exited through the door, pulling it closed behind him.

"I've been waiting for you, Rayne," Kai said. "For a long time. Ever since the last Game, when Vennor tried to upgrade the NEWRRTH. When I tried to do something even my wildest research didn't predict. I want to tell you all about it. My brave girl."

Kai touched her hand to Rayne's cheek and brushed a tear with her thumb. Rayne pulled back and gazed at her mother's face. The thorn necklace she always wore lay flat against her neck. A white braid curled over her shoulder, her gray eyes brimming.

"I've been waiting for you since that Game," Kai said.

"But you—you weren't even conscious when we came out of that Game. I sat next to you in the Haven until..."

Rayne remembered the Peace Officers pulling her mother's pod out from under her fingertips. Reading Kai's arrest warrant as they rolled with her unconscious form down the hall.

Kai shook her head and cupped her daughter's face with both hands. "You're right, Rayne. I wasn't conscious after that Game. I came here."

Rayne leaned back. "That doesn't make sense. Nothing about this makes sense." She collapsed onto the cot.

Kai settled next to her. After a few minutes, she put a hand on Rayne's back. Rayne resisted the urge to pull away.

"I know what it seems like," Kai said. "It was confusing for me, too."

"You have no idea," Rayne said. Her words strangled in her throat. "You have no idea what I've been through."

Kai's hand lingered. "I don't know everything you've been through, Rayne, but I know enough. I know what Vennor did in that Game. I know the Seers took away your Thread. I know what you did to escape the Settlers. And I know what they're after."

Rayne lifted her head, wiping the tears from her eyes. "You do?"

Kai nodded. "The Settler rebels want to disconnect people from their Threads. They want to destroy the Atlantic Ark and everything it stands for."

Rayne's eyes widened. "How do you know all of this?"

"I know more than you think, Rayne. You're not the only one who's been through a lot."

Rayne sat up straight, wiping away the last of her tears.

Kai smiled softly. "I've been working with Freya's Path. They're a... they have noble intentions. And they've been working hard. We've been monitoring the Settler rebels for a while now. And we've been waiting for someone like you. Someone who can help us stop them."

"Someone like me?"

Kai nodded. "Someone with your skills, your intelligence, and your drive. Someone who can help us save the Arks."

"But you're—you're—"

Unconscious and under arrest.

In the rig tent at the Haven.

Unaware and unresponsive.

Not really here.

"I'm sorry I couldn't be there for you when you needed me," Kai said. "But I'm here now. And I need your help. Freya's Path is working on a new Game, one that can fix all that's gone wrong with the NEWRRTH. The anomalies that have been plaguing it. The inconsistencies, the problems with the Games. But we can't do it alone."

Rayne furrowed her brow. "A new Game? To fix the NEWRRTH?"

Kai leaned back, a glint in her eyes. "A Game that can

reestablish our connection to a greater intelligence, calm the Settler rebellion, and restore harmony in the Arks."

Rayne scoffed.

Shaking her head, Kai said, "You need time. I get it. Come with me." She stood and opened the door. "Let me show you."

Kai was right. A single Game to solve all the problems the Arks faced sounded too good to be true. "Show me what?"

"I'm taking you on a tour. Of Freya's Path. The ship is a magnificent example of a self-contained ecosystem. I think you'll learn a lot."

Of course Kai wanted to show her the ecology of the ship. A familiar resentment bubbled up. It was the sting of knowing that Rayne could never compete with her mother's green things. Her plants and botany experiments.

Rayne's curiosity about Freya's Path battled with her concern for her friends and her home. Were the Settlers still bound for the Ark? Had Vennor warned the Seers in time to prevent complete disaster? Had the EMP truly sunk into the ocean, undetonated?

"You're concerned for your friends." Kai's expression softened. "I understand. I can tell you that the Settlers are no longer a threat to our Ark. They've been neutralized, thanks to you, now that their weapon is gone. It will take time for them to regroup. Your friends are safe. The Designers who accompanied you here are both alive. They can travel back home, and join the others. Continue their work. For now."

"Briz and Cha—they're alive? How do you know?" That her mother might be lying to keep her on board the ship crossed her mind.

"You'll see. Freya's Path is connected to the NEWRRTH. They can access what they need from its intelligence."

"So you're asking me to just trust you. To trust Freya's Path.

And leave my friends out there while I float around on some science experiment."

Kai hesitated for a moment. "It's complicated. But yes, essentially. You've been invited to join a team of the best Designers in the world. They're more talented than even the greatest Seers of our time. And they want you. They need your mind."

Rayne let out a long breath, and the cot squeaked underneath her. She didn't know what to believe anymore. Was her mother really here, or was this all just some kind of hallucination? And even if it was real, could she trust Kai and this supposed Game to save the Arks?

Rayne looked up at her mother and saw the sincerity in her eyes. The love and concern that had always been there, even when they weren't on the best of terms. If Kai spoke the truth, Rayne had a chance to work with the best Designers in the world.

But her friends, and Vic, were still without her in the Ark. She couldn't abandon them. She had to help them, to protect them from what the Settlers wanted to do. To make sure Vic didn't violate the Principle of One with the crystal code. To help them all avoid the fate of the Pine Barrens Ark.

"I don't know, Ma," Rayne said finally. "I appreciate the offer, but I can't leave my friends behind. I need to help them."

"I know," Kai said. "But you're not fighting for them alone. We can help you. We have access to resources that you could never dream of. You can be part of something that helps your friends, helps protect your home, and helps the Settlers regain their own peace. You wouldn't want to pass that up, would you?"

Rayne considered her mother's words. She couldn't deny the appeal of working with the best Designers in the world and having all the tools she needed to protect her friends and her home. But she couldn't shake the feeling that something wasn't quite right. Why was she being offered this opportunity now, after being blamed for interfering with the NEWRRTH and having her Thread terminated?

Rayne took a deep breath and stood up, wiping her face and trying to compose herself.

"Okay," she said. "I'll go on your tour. But I can't promise anything beyond that."

Kai smiled and took her daughter's hand. "That's all I ask. Come on. Let me show you what we've been working on."

Rayne let her mother lead her out of the small room and into the corridor.

Her mother was right. There was much to learn.

They passed station after station tucked along the ship's halls. People worked behind screens; others fed vegetation or hunched over lab tables, eating and talking with their companions. A few walked between rooms carrying objects in clear plastic cases. They raised a hand in greeting or smiled as she passed. Voices spoke in muffled tones, but here and there laughter rang out.

When Rayne looked up, she saw the ceiling dripping with gardens. Living green things hung from metal pipes and in long strands of containers. Rayne brushed aside a vine that bloomed at eye level. Glancing up, she recognized lettuce, beans, corn, and a bunch of dark brown berries.

"Acai," her mother said.

They wound deeper into the bowels of the ship, making a series of sharp right-angle turns. Then a room opened up before them. It was larger than the others they had seen, and it was dark under a low ceiling. Behind a glass door, in the shadows, lights flickered. Shapes moved.

Rayne put her face to the glass. There were people in front of her in the strange dim room, at workstations, but they didn't notice her at all. They sat in rows, stretching into the darkness. They moved their hands over screens and around in the air. Drawing or tracing something, Rayne couldn't tell. A low hum came through the glass, along with an occasional murmur.

"What are they doing?" Rayne whispered.

Kai touched her arm. "They're designing our future. Just like you'll be doing."

Rayne took in the sight before her. Something about this room felt different. It was as if she could sense the energy pulsing through the air, the focused excitement of the people working there. She watched as they moved in the shadows with a sense of awe, wondering what they were creating.

She stepped back from the glass door, her mind churning with questions. Her mother's hand rested on her arm, but it felt distant, like a receding dream.

"Can I go in?" Rayne asked.

"Of course," Kai said with a smile. "This is what we brought you here for."

Rayne stepped forward, her hand outstretched. Before she pushed the doors open, she turned one more time to her mother.

"What do you *really* need me to do?"

"What you've always done." Kai chuckled. "Design a thrilling Game."

Vennor

Vennor saw Enayat standing in front of the Center for Future Guidance with his arms crossed, feet planted apart. People swirled around him, but he didn't notice. His dark eyes followed the transport as it pulled in, rolling to a stop in front of the entrance. He appeared to be alone.

Where were the other Seers?

Inside the skidder, Vennor blinked away her thoughts and stretched her aching jaw. She touched one hand to her temple, powering down her conversation with the Thread. Behind her, bending their heads close, Briz and Cha spoke quietly. Vennor caught something about the Haven and the Healors who would be there to greet them.

A crowd clogged the walkways, jostling for a view of their arrival. Vennor peered from the small window by her seat, searching for the Peace Officers. Her gaze bounced all over the entryway, then further to the trees surrounding the Center. She didn't spot them.

Rayne lay on her back, eyes closed, on the seat between the

Designers. Her limp head rested on Cha's lap. Rayne hadn't roused since collapsing on the airbird, nor had she woken during the journey back from the sea.

Four full days they spent in the skidder, stopping only for rough sleep on the ground, and the Designer remained as motionless as the blanket she lay upon. Her breathing held steady and her vitals strong, for which they were all grateful. Vennor didn't need another casualty, another potential violation of the One, to contend with.

The Ark had bigger problems. Vennor was ready to face the consequences of her actions, and ready to persuade the Seers how much they needed her guidance. They needed her to lead them into the next phase of their future. If she could rid herself of the charges standing against her.

The vehicle rolled to a stop and gave a shuddering whine as the driver powered down the engine. Outside, Enayat pulled a cloth square from his pocket and blew his nose. He peered into the skidder, watching for Vennor to emerge. With a last glance over the crowd, Vennor still couldn't find any Officers. Would Enayat lead her away to the holding center? Or would the Officers appear suddenly for a dramatic arrest?

All the days they had been on the road, Vennor fretted about this moment.

The doors of the skidder opened and Enayat stepped forward, his face stony.

"Welcome back, Vennor," he said, his voice deep and resonant. "I am glad your journey was successful."

Vennor stepped down from the skidder, careful not to slip.

"It was," she said, forcing herself to meet Enayat's gaze. "I look forward to sharing what I've learned with the Seers."

"Of course." Enayat's expression soured. "But first, let us take care of your companion."

The Designers lifted Rayne gently out of the skidder. A

group of young people Vennor hadn't noticed before surged forward and gathered around the blanket. One of them, a tall boy with black hair curling over his ears, reached Rayne first.

Vennor recognized him. It was Vic, the Designer they arrested under suspicion of compromising the Games. He had been in contact with Freya's Path, inviting them to interfere with her upgrade to the NEWRRTH. Under her nose, Vic created the Game that took Trueno's life.

Trueno, the last love that Vennor would ever have.

She regarded Vic's angular face with a surge of bitterness. She watched as he touched Rayne's face, moving his palm over her closed eyes. He wrapped his arms around Rayne's blanket, gently pulling her form into an awkward embrace. Crying sounds escaped from his chest as he sank to the ground with her body. Her head rolled back, mouth open. He carefully grasped her neck and drew her close.

Envy licked at her heart as her neck flushed and her fists clenched.

The rest of the Designers gathered around Vic as he cradled Rayne in his arms. Briz reached for Cha's hand. After a moment, two Healors approached, solemn-faced. The Healors worked their way through the throng of people and into the circle of Designers. An empty healing pod rolled behind them.

She lost sight of the Designers as Enayat led her the other way through the crowd, which parted for them as they walked toward the entrance of the Center. Vennor scanned the faces for any sign of the Peace Officers, but saw none. Perhaps they waited for her inside.

They entered the Center for Future Guidance, and Vennor relaxed when she saw no Officers in the atrium. She breathed in the familiar, peaceful atmosphere. Soft music played in the distance, and the air smelled of lavender and watered soil. It was a sharp contrast to the chaos and filth of the Settlers' world.

Enayat took her to a private room, where a Healor waited with a medkit. Vennor sat on the edge of a chair as the Healor examined her. She winced as the Healor probed her sore muscles.

"You've been through quite an ordeal," the Healor said with a sympathetic smile. "I'll perform a full analysis."

"Thank you," Vennor said. "Is there anything we can do for Rayne?"

Enayat straightened. "They're doing all they can. Be still so your Healor can finish."

"I'm afraid there isn't much anyone can do for her," the Healor said, her hands tapping a pattern over Vennor's back. "We'll make her comfortable, run some tests. We don't know how long she'll be under. We'll do everything we can to guide her to consciousness while we monitor her vitals."

"Is it... the rig?"

The Healor completed her examination, dismissing the Thread's data with a small flick. She turned to Vennor, a frown creasing her forehead.

"I can't say yet. We'll know more after the tests. Here, take this." The Healor handed Vennor a vial filled with a pale blue liquid. "It's a pain reliever plus a tincture to help your Thread deal with inflammation. Rest, Vennor. Your body needs to recover."

Vennor took the vial and tucked it into her pocket. She stood up, her back aching. There was no time to rest. "Thank you," she said to the Healor.

As the Healor left, Enayat turned to her.

"I've arranged for you to meet with the Seers tomorrow morning," he said. "They're eager to hear what you've discovered."

"Enayat," Vennor said. "Where are the Officers? Why haven't they taken me into holding?"

Enayat gave her a small smile. "It's my duty to protect the Seers and the Ark. And you, of course."

"But why haven't they come for me?"

"I've been working on the modeling leading to your arrest warrant. We've gathered enough evidence to convey to the Peace Officers you didn't intentionally violate the One. You were motivated by a desire to protect the NEWRRTH. They agreed they made a violation declaration in haste, without a full consideration of the data. And they agreed you must be free to share the information you collected at the Settlement. You will be most useful to the Seers and to the Ark if you can work at full capacity, without restraint."

Vennor straightened, her eyes moistening. "I'd like to speak to the Seers now."

Enayat nodded. "I'll inform them of your arrival."

"But first—" Vennor placed her hand on Enayat's arm. "Show me the Haven. Where they're keeping the victims. The people who have the rig."

Enayat's eyes widened for a moment before his face resumed its natural scowl. "Of course."

He motioned for Vennor to step toward a table in the corner of the room. Enayat spoke to his Thread and made an image visible on the tabletop. As it came up, Vennor recognized the sunlight-drenched gardens of the Haven filled with vibrant flowers and healing plants. The pathways were lined with comfortable chairs and benches. Fresh running water cascaded over rocks in pools, complementing the soft music tinkling in the background.

The Thread's image took them past pods of people waiting to be processed and into a hall. The hall became an exit, and the Thread took them through a double door and into a vast space. It was a bright white tent. The tent connected to the Haven, but wasn't a rigid structure. Its white walls hung on all sides, laid out in a square. What Vennor saw inside the tent took her breath away.

There were so many.

The Thread showed them rows and rows of cots in straight lines. It closed in on the slack faces of person after person. Each victim lay motionless inside a clear pod, a blanket pulled to their armpits, and lights moving over the surface of their enclosure. Flashing numbers displayed over their chests in green and blue. Their vitals.

Enayat was about to say something, but Vennor cut him off.

"Thank you." Her voice rang loudly in the small room. "I've seen enough." Enayat flicked the image away.

"When's the quarantine?" Vennor asked.

Enayat covered up his surprise as he answered. "We expect it soon. The models aren't clear."

Vennor nodded, her eyes boring into Enayat's. The rig's reach had gone unchecked, and they were about to deploy the last tool in their arsenal.

"I'll gather the Seers." Enayat met her gaze, pinched his mouth, and left the room.

Vennor

VENNOR FORCED a breath into her lungs before she followed Enayat out. He had already disappeared around the corner. She took her time as she made her way through the familiar corridors of the Center for Future Guidance. It was a far cry from the chaos of the Settlement, with its bright lights, clean floors, and smooth white walls.

But Vennor knew that this place was not perfect either. The path to peace was uncertain. There would always be some measure of disruption in creating humanity's best future, even with the guidance of the NEWRRTH.

And there would always be people, like herself, who made poor choices along the way, and paid for them dearly.

Vennor pictured her speech to the Seers, rehearsing each point in her mind as she walked. She would tell them about the Earth Thread, about the strange new data pattern she had accessed. She would tell them about the Settlers and their impending attack, and how they needed to prepare the Ark for battle.

As she approached the conference room where the other Seers gathered, a wave of nervousness broke over her. She took another deep breath and pushed open the door.

The Seers gathered around a large table, their faces grave. They turned to her as she entered, and she felt the intensity of their expectations.

"Vennor," Nilo said, beckoning her forward. "We're grateful you've returned." Nilo's neck bands lit in glowing sparks as they delivered sound waves directly to her brain. She pushed back the sleeves of her blue robe and folded her hands on the table.

Ana pushed a hand through her red hair and half stood. "It's good to see you." She broke into a smile and her cheeks flushed. She sat back down.

Enayat stood at the head of the table, waiting for Vennor to approach. With a flourish, he pulled out the head chair and gestured for Vennor to take it. Vennor gratefully sank down.

"Seers," she said, her voice strong. "My friends. It's good to be back. I have traveled far, and I have missed you."

Ana kept her gaze on the table. Nilo dipped her head in acknowledgment. Enayat folded and refolded his handkerchief, his frown tugging into a smile.

"We missed you, too," Ana mumbled, her color deepening.

Vennor placed her hands on the table. She made eye contact with each Seer as she spoke. "There are important things we must discuss without delay. I've made discoveries that will change everything about how we operate. We must acknowledge the new reality we find ourselves in, and we must prepare."

The Seers leaned forward, their interest piqued.

"Go on," Enayat said.

"As we sit here, the Settler rebellion is coming to the Atlantic Ark," Vennor said. "I don't know when, but if we fail to protect the Ark, the rebels will destroy our peace. We've been avoiding the truth for too long. They have nurtured a vengeful splinter group set on destroying us. Their technology has advanced considerably. Their fleet of aircraft is small, but it is powerful. They detonated a sophisticated electromagnetic pulse that severed the NEWRRTH from the population of the Pine Barrens."

There were muttered exclamations of disbelief.

"We've taken their EMP weapon and released it into the ocean," Vennor continued, "stalling their next attack for now. But it's coming."

Exhaling, Vennor put her hands back on the conference table. "The rebels are rebuilding, and will launch a new weapon, I'm sure of it. It's only a matter of when."

"We need to be ready for when the Settlers attack," she continued. "And we need to be prepared for the aftermath. If they succeed in taking us offline, we will be vulnerable, and they will have control over our people. We need a plan to protect ourselves, and the NEWRRTH."

"What evidence do you have of the Settlers' technology?" Enayat wiped his nose, then put the cloth away. "Flying craft? That's far beyond what we know the Settlers to be capable of."

"I have plenty of evidence," Vennor said. "Giving you access to it." She made a command to her Thread, and selected a few data stories to share.

Ana's eyes went back and forth as she took in the data that appeared in a stream of holographic images on the table. Nilo twisted her hands together, swallowing.

Had Magna or Gedeon survived the airbird's explosion? The question burned in Vennor's mind. She had to know. But first, she had to consider the implications of what she was about to reveal to her fellow Seers. They needed to act fast if they wanted to preserve any shred of their future.

"There's more I need to share with you." Vennor waited until the Seers came to attention again.

"I made a discovery about the new Thread. The networked barrier we came across in the volcano Game. It's a new pattern, a new way of accessing information around us. I believe it's a sign of something greater, something that we have yet to understand."

"We've been studying that," Nilo said. "We have all the data we need to make a complete model."

Vennor paused, collecting her thoughts. "You have the data," she said. "But you don't know what it is."

The Seers glanced at one another.

"The Earth Thread is a separate Thread," Vennor continued, "accessed through the living networks of green plants. Kai from the Orchard activated the Earth Thread through the mosses and plants in that Game. I believe she did that through a direct connection to the NEWRRTH, similar to how the Seers work with the regular Thread. I replicated the Earth Thread's network capabilities during my time at the Settlement. It's not like how we network with the NEWRRTH. It's more subtle, more flexible."

After a moment, Nilo spoke again. "Does this mean there are multiple Threads? Multiple ways of accessing the NEWRRTH?"

Vennor gave a brief nod. "Which brings me to the next insight," Vennor said. "I suspect—though I don't yet have the evidence—that we've been asking the wrong questions about what has surfaced in our Games last winter. The anomaly. The destruction we tried to outmaneuver. We've been going about it all wrong."

Enayat froze with his handkerchief in one hand, about to wipe his nose.

"Our investigation has been extremely thorough," Nilo

said, her voice firm. "We're following the guidance of the NEWRRTH. We've spent months—*months*—making painstaking repairs of the damage the anomaly caused. We terminated those Designers' Threads because of their obvious sabotage."

"It's entirely possible," Vennor said, "that the anomaly wasn't an aberration. I believe it was something else. A message. A way to get our attention."

Ana's eyes slitted. "What are you talking about?"

Enayat pushed himself to standing. "Are you implying that the anomaly—the destruction of all those Games—the Lantern upgrade we tried to execute—"

Vennor lifted her palms from the table and made a sit-down gesture. "It will take time for us to work with the NEWRRTH to fully understand what is happening," she said. "But I firmly believe that the NEWRRTH is evolving. This new Thread we've discovered, I think we found it for a reason. It's not a mistake that we're experiencing all this disruption now. And not just disruption in the NEWRRTH. The threat to the Arks. The Settlers rebelling. Why now? It's all connected. And we've been too stupid to see it."

The Seers started talking all at once, and Vennor brought her hands together. "Please," she said over the noise. "I'm doing my best to give you the information so we can all come to the same conclusion."

"Conclusion? About what?" Nilo tilted her cheek to Vennor.

"We've been investigating *what* is happening inside the NEWRRTH, in our Games, in our community. But that's the wrong approach. It's *who*. Who is trying to get our attention. And why."

The Seers were silent.

Enayat clapped his palms to his thighs and leaned back.

Ana's gaze locked onto Vennor's. "Oh, no," she whispered. "I don't think I can—"

"There is a chance, a significant chance, that we are not the only ones accessing the Threads and the NEWRRTH. We need to consider the possibility that there are other entities, other Threads, other factions beyond what we know. The reality we perceive may be only one of many, and finding the Earth Thread is just the tip of the iceberg. We need to prepare for all possibilities, including the possibility that we may not be in control of what we think we are."

"Not in control? How do we even prove that?" Ana's voice was a whisper.

Vennor placed her hand on Ana's, offering a brief squeeze. "We start by acknowledging that we don't know everything. And we affirm our faith in the guidance of the NEWRRTH. We embrace uncertainty and trust in our ability to survive and adapt through the unknown. Like we always have."

Enayat stuffed his cloth into his pocket, a tremble in his hands.

Vennor knew that what she was saying was difficult to accept, but it was a truth that they all needed to confront. "I want to be clear. We will continue to rely on the NEWRRTH and the Thread to protect the Ark and our people. But we must be ready for additional facts to come to light, and to deal with them, no matter how frightening they may be."

Vennor looked around the room, meeting each Seer's gaze with a steely determination.

"I'll do whatever it takes to protect the Arks," Nilo said.

Enayat straightened. "We'll do what needs to be done."

Ana took a deep breath, then met Vennor's gaze. "I'm with you. But we have to go about this the right way. We have to reach out to those Game Designers and restore their Threads.

They weren't committing crimes. They just want what's best for the Ark. Vic has... shown me that in our collaboration."

Vennor raised an eyebrow.

Ana swallowed nervously and put her hands under her thighs.

"My point is that we need to work together," Ana said. "We all do, if what you're saying is true."

"It's true." Vennor stood up, feeling the weight of her responsibilities pressing down on her. "Which is why I must tell you this. We will restore Threads to those who have been punished. And we will make an offer of peace to the Settlers. We will negotiate an alliance with them to the benefit of all our people."

Blank faces stared back at her. She went on.

"The Settlers have also been victims of their own anomaly, in a way," Vennor said. "The new technology they have. The airbirds. The EMP weapon. It's all coming from somewhere."

The Seers rose. Enayat was about to speak when Ana cut him off.

"So who is it?" Ana asked. "Who's trying to get our attention?"

Trueno had been right. Freya's Path wasn't some dusty old myth. They were real, and they were reaching out.

"It's Freya's Path, of course," Vennor said. "They've been trying to get our attention for months. And now, we finally hear them."

The Seers looked at each other, unsure of what to say.

"They're the ones who have been active in our Games, disrupting them, yes, but also trying to tell us something." Vennor's voice held steady, but inside she trembled.

Ana spoke again. "That's what Vic tried to tell me, too. He told me that Freya's Path are the ones who engineered the Thread implantation process, the ones who built the Arks and established the Legacy Settlements. He said that they're the ones who created the NEWRRTH."

Enayat shook his head. "There's no proof of any of that. Even if there were, why would they be trying to get through to us now?"

"I don't know," Vennor said. "But I suspect it's because they're in trouble. Or we are. And before this is all over, we'll have to figure out how to survive what's coming next."

———

VENNOR LET ANA lead her out of the conference room and down the hallway. They reached Vennor's office and stepped inside. The soaring stone ceiling and plush rugs never felt more inviting. A silver tray sat on Vennor's desk, just as she'd left it.

She was home.

Ana's grasp faltered slightly as Vennor eased into her chair. Ana lifted a hand to whisk a tear away from her cheek.

"You're upset?" Vennor summoned her compassion for the young Seer. The Seers' meeting had been revelatory. Ana deserved a moment of grace.

"I'm trying to process everything you said."

Vennor nodded and leaned forward, resting her elbows on the desk. "I understand. It's a lot to take in, even for me."

Ana let out a shaky breath and rubbed her eyes. "Freya's Path. I always thought they were something out of a myth, not an entity that affects our lives. It's just hard to..."

Vennor nodded again. "Yes, it's hard to comprehend. I'd be lying if I said I wasn't afraid."

"Afraid of what?"

"Of losing everything," Vennor said. "Sanity. Reality. Life in the Ark."

Ana puffed her lips out and gestured to the air. "I think we're already losing that."

Vennor locked eyes with Ana's. "You're right, Ana. But remember: we are strong. We will work together. And we have the NEWRRTH. It won't fail us now."

Ana nodded, her expression resolute. "I know. And I'm with you, Vennor. Whatever it takes."

Vennor smiled. "Thank you, Ana. That means a lot to me."

VENNOR PREPARED a cup of lemongrass tea and took it to her desk. The aromatic steam climbed out of the ceramic cup in long, wavering tendrils. She inhaled its sharp scent. Sipping the warm liquid, Vennor's mind drifted back to something Magna had said to her while they were in the Fine, while Vennor fought to stay above the rising tide.

The grand experiment of the Arks is done, Magna said. *All you have to do is join me. We can make the future all we want it to be. Free.*

Vennor chuckled to herself. She had missed it at the time, but now understood Magna's mistake. If Magna truly believed in freedom, then why did she want to destroy the Arks? Magna's rebellion was not about spreading a message of faith, but about destroying what had already been created. It was about power and control. Not freedom.

Magna had wholly misread the situation. The Arks were not perfect, but they were necessary. They were a means to surviving the harsh conditions of the world outside. Vennor knew that firsthand. The Thread was not just an implanted transmission device, but a vessel of hope and conviction. The Thread was a tangible bond between humanity and the infinite intelligence of the NEWRRTH. It was through their Threads that humans would be guided to achieve a higher purpose on this Earth.

Whatever that turned out to be.

She took another sip of tea and set the cup on the tray. Touching her temple, she closed her eyes and focused on her Thread. It pulsed at her wrist beneath her fingertips, a reminder of her purpose.

Vennor knew what she had to do. Her mission was to unite the Settlers and the Arks so they could confront the future together. To embrace what their collective fate held in store.

She had no time to waste.

Jennifer Lewy writes stories about fierce characters, evolving AIs, and the fragile thread that connects us to each other—and to the Earth. Before becoming an author, she worked as a medical assistant, social worker, and voiceover artist, then launched her own healthcare writing business in 2005.

The idea for her young adult science fiction series came to her during the early days of the pandemic. *The One Game*, the first novel in the *Game of Paradise* series, was published in 2022, followed by *The One Exiled* and *The One Reborn*. The prequel, *When the Light Came*, is available free to newsletter subscribers.

Jennifer was born in the Northeast Kingdom of Vermont, grew up just outside New York City, and now lives in New England with her family and two very opinionated cats.

Join her Reader's Club for free extras, behind-the-scenes updates, and early access to new books:

www.JenniferLewy.com

Library of Congress Control Number: 2023913843
ISBN paperback 978-1-959461-03-6
ISBN ebook 978-1-959461-02-9